RACHEL HOMARD

THE GREEN TRIANGLE

Second Edition

Relax. Read. Repeat.

THE GREEN TRIANGLE
By Rachel Homard
Published by TouchPoint Press
Brookland, AR 72417
www.touchpointpress.com

ISBN-13: 978-1-952816-15-4

Connect with Rachel
Facebook @rachelhomardauthor
Twitter @HomardRachel
Instagram @authorrachelhomard

Cover Artist: Wicked Smart Designs, Dar Albert
Second Edition Cover Layout: Colbie Myles

Second Edition

Printed in the United States of America.

There are so many people that have made this journey possible and have turned my dream of being a published author into a reality. I want to thank my wonderful family for always being supportive, especially my son, Asher, who promotes my book like crazy. I want to thank my critique group for reading and rereading until they were probably blue in the face. Thanks to my wonderful agent, Stephanie Hansen, and all my writing sisters for supporting me. Thank you to the publisher at TouchPoint Press. You are all amazing, and I'm blessed to have you in my life. But, when I wrote this book and considered a dedication, I had a very specific group of people in mind: the men and women, like my dad, who served and are serving in the United States Armed Forces. You all sacrifice tremendously to protect our freedom and our way of life. This book was written to honor you.

CHAPTER ONE
Savannah

Savannah Carrington parked her BMW under a streetlight and cut the engine. She leaned against the headrest and groaned, the orange light flooding over her blonde waves and the apron dangling from her purse. It was five o'clock in the morning. Her mother had already sent twelve texts regarding the country club's Charity Week events. It was always something. Her mother had signed her up, without consent, to drive drunk millionaires around the golf course this evening as they "putted for prostates."

She held up the pleated golf skirt packaged and left in the car by her mother. Ridiculous. It'd be comforting to think her parents and their socialite friends had their hearts in the right place, but no. It was all to donate to a member of the club with prostate cancer. The same man whose father invented the microwave and who, just last year, brought his pet peacock yachting with him in Monaco.

Switching her phone over to vibrate, she crammed it in the pocket of her jeans. Each event this week supported a different charity just as ill-deserved as the next. She'd suggested a few, like one that built tiny homes for veterans and one that supplied inner-city kids with meals while they were on summer vacation. Or, better yet, the one closest to her heart: the soup kitchen she poured her life into.

Oh, they all *knew* about it, but discussing her extracurricular activities was frowned upon. The only thing that kept her mother from drinking her weight in martinis during happy hour was Holden Forsyth. One of the thirty-six "eligible bachelors" she'd set her up with over the last few years. The only one Savannah kept around longer than a first date. He was better than the rest: kind, funny, and was coming to the soup kitchen for the first time today to help with the Labor Day crowd.

She bit her lip and wiped a layer of dust from the dash. On paper, and in person, he checked every box. He made her happy, and her mother bounded around with an uncontainable joy. But, after two months of dating, something was missing. Perhaps, when Holden met Allen, she'd have a new perspective.

She looked out the window and smiled. Allen said he'd meet her at five-thirty, and because he was notoriously early, she could just make out his white hair and lanky frame approaching from a distance, between a few early risers headed to work. He was her sounding board, right-hand-man at the soup kitchen and, quite frankly, her best friend.

He was also homeless.

She didn't care, and he didn't mind the streets, even though he'd saved enough money to get his own place. It was a way to connect with other homeless veterans. He always talked about one named Joe, a young guy back from Afghanistan. They'd developed a close bond, and he wouldn't leave him alone on the streets of L.A. Especially since, for some reason, Joe wouldn't come to the soup kitchen.

Allen pulled the door handle. She tossed the skirt on the box before stepping out. "It's gonna be a big crowd this mornin'. You ready, or you need more time starin' at that skirt over there?" He threw a thumb toward the pile of pink wrapping paper in the passenger seat.

Her cheeks brightened. She slammed the door shut so the interior lights would go off, but it was too late. "Don't ask, Allen. It's another one of Dahlia Carrington's stunts." Her hands moved as she talked. "Let's just focus on the menu. We've still got some prepping to do, and I wanted to make strawberry cake."

Allen rubbed his eyes and wrapped a camo-clad arm over her shoulder. "Whatever ya say, boss."

They walked together beneath the shadows cast by the buildings, her leaning in close to him, wrapping her natural-painted nails around his arm. She shook wildly, never able to contain her fear of the dark, and she rarely went to the soup kitchen when the sun wasn't up. Allen never seemed scared of anything. But today, if she wasn't mistaken, she wasn't the only one shaking. They crossed street after street, until she couldn't ignore it anymore. She halted and stared at him under a streetlight two blocks shy of their destination. His eyes were red, and he didn't fill out his jacket as well as he normally did. He'd taken this six-block walk at her side every day for the last five years, but today was different. "What's going on? Your arm is shaking."

"I'm an old man. Don't worry 'bout me. Everythin's fine. Now tell me 'bout that strawberry cake. Sounds awful good." He tugged on her arm and picked up his stride again, this time with a less noticeable shake.

The sidewalks were bustling around the soup kitchen. The sun wouldn't make an appearance for another twenty minutes or so, but people were ready to get inside. Dirty faces smiled at her. Despite all the people she helped each day, she never walked through Skid Row without Allen at her side; when the sun went down, all bets were off. That's why she served lunch. That, and her fear of the dark. The only reason she'd come before sunup today was because of the holiday.

A dozen people filed through the glass doors after she unlocked them, the bell at the top chiming with each new entrant as she washed off a few cartons of strawberries. This morning, instead of her normal background music, she enjoyed the click of shoes across the tile and laughter over a win at cards. She wasn't trading in her comfortable apartment for a tent any time soon, but the soup kitchen wasn't just a haven for the homeless; it was her escape from social obligations.

Maybe that's why, even with Holden's charming personality and supermodel looks, she couldn't give herself over to the idea of forever. He would always be connected to the part of herself she'd tried so hard to break free from.

"Savannah." Allen stood inches away. "I made the tater salad." He stuck a finger in the mixing bowl she'd just emptied between four baking pans and licked the batter. "The strawberry cakes are comin' along. It's six-thirty now. What time's this Holden guy showin' up?"

"He should be here any minute. And Allen?" She rinsed the bowl in the sink as he dried and stacked it back on the shelf behind them. "I do want your honest opinion."

"You got it, boss." He flicked water on her arm and laughed.

"I'm serious, and don't think I've forgotten that something is going on with you. When everybody leaves this evening, let's talk." She squeezed his hand and pulled him over to the giant pile of hamburger meat. "For now, though, I need help forming about one hundred hamburger patties. I'll get some of the guys over here to help you while I wait at the door for Holden. He's as punctual as you. Something to bond over." She passed the sink and flicked water his way this time, laughing as he dodged it.

"Sure thing. Just need to put somethin' in your safe first."

Savannah passed through the tables and mismatched rugs of the dining room, sending a couple guys to the back to help Allen. One of them turned on the stereo, the smooth sounds of Simon and Garfunkel filtering through the room. She wasn't planning on the music, but it calmed her nerves over Allen and Holden's first meeting. She wrapped a few patrons in hugs on her way to the door and straightened a tablecloth.

Holden was on the sidewalk, hands in his pockets, approaching. She bit her lip. She'd told him to dress down so her patrons would be more comfortable. Maybe that wasn't clear enough. He was in jeans and a plain white shirt, but you could practically see where the gold-plated price tags once hung off them. That's what she got for dating someone whose family owned the largest fashion house in L.A. Lucky for him, once he opened his mouth, people tended to like him.

4

"Hey. Come on in."

"Savannah, good morning. You look as stunning, as usual." He leaned down and kissed her cheek. "But I see a card game going over there I just *have* to be a part of." Holden moved away and pulled up a chair between four men. He said something, and they all broke into laughter.

He'd be fine.

She stepped away and found Allen padding over the tile in his tennis shoes and wiping a red stain from the strawberries onto his tee shirt. She came around the counter, with her head down, and nearly ran into him. He held his arms out. "Woah, there!"

She laughed. Hopefully he would like Holden as much as everyone else did. His approval was important. "Hey. It's the moment you've been waiting for. Holden is here."

Allen clapped his hands together. "Great. Can't wait to meet 'im. Had to put an envelope in the safe. Ya mind if I keep it there a couple days until I sort some things out?"

Holden excused himself from the table and approached as they chatted. "It's more than okay. Use the safe as long as you please. Oh, and this is Holden." She extended an arm. "Holden, this is Allen."

They made eye contact, but Allen didn't smile. He just stared at Holden with tight lips. The air around the three of them filled with tension. Allen was protective, but Holden seemed uncomfortable by the icy welcome. His back straightened, and his eyes grew wide. She nudged Allen. He needed to loosen up.

"Um. Sorry. It's nice to meet ya, Holden. Savannah is special. Don't ya ever let any danger or anything come 'er way. Ya hear?" Allen reached his hand forward slowly, and Holden shook it.

"Nice to meet you too, Allen. And don't worry. I will do everything in my power to always keep her safe." Holden wrapped her in a hug and smiled broadly. PDA was something that usually made her wiggle free. She and Holden had taken things slow so far anyway, but he seemed to need the closeness with Allen's intensity. "I'll see you in a bit, Allen. I'm going to have Savannah join in our card game. I need a lucky charm."

Holden dragged her across the room to a wobbly oval table and gave her his seat. He knelt behind her on one knee and put his hands over her shoulders. Most of the cooking was done, so she had a few minutes to spare. She had just picked up her cards, when a wrinkly hand rested on top of hers.

It was Allen. "Savannah, I've got somethin' to do. I'll be back for ya tonight, and we'll talk. I promise."

"Okay." She leaned back, with the cards in her hand, that familiar wrinkle of worry crossing her forehead. She couldn't force Allen to share his troubles, even if her eyes were begging for it. "I'm here for you. If you need anything, tell me."

He opened the front door and stepped through. "You got it, boss."

Holden leaned down to her ear, brushing a strand of blonde hair away. "Is he okay? I can run out and check on him if you'd like."

"No. Allen is private. It's his way of protecting people. After everyone leaves, he'll be back. I can talk to him then." She laid down a three of hearts and spun around in the chair, her face an inch from Holden's, which made her pulse race. Most girls would lean in for a kiss. For that matter, most men would too. He was stunning. Instead, she caught her breath and said, "I will need someone to man the grill today, since Allen left."

Holden straightened with a smile. "Yes, ma'am. Just let me make a call first."

CHAPTER TWO

Joe

The beans were cold, the sun was hot, and the plastic crate beneath him imprinted tiny squares all over his fourth point of contact. It had been three hours, after all. Sitting there, watching, waiting. He scraped the inside of the can for the last bite of beans, but his eyes remained focused on the road.

Joe was hoping for trouble. It didn't matter what kind. He needed something to do, someone to help, a bad guy to test his aim on. He was bored out of his mind with the mundane. Having a friend in Allen was the only thing that kept him sane, but it wasn't enough. He'd been trained to act by the Army and, before that, by his dad. But if it was between this and allowing himself to be found, he'd choose this every time. There was no way he was ever stepping foot in D.C.

So, he waited, sweat rolling in beads down his back and through his thick beard. His foot tapped impatiently. The street was barren. Everyone was at the soup kitchen. He could always go. It would make Allen happy, but there was a high chance he'd try and play matchmaker between him and Savannah. Joe shook his head. Nope. He'd leave that as plan Z. What would he do there, anyway? Play cards and talk to people about their feelings? Pass. He wanted to make a difference, but more than that, he wanted to make up for his failure in Afghanistan. Not that he ever could. He'd bled to earn that Green Beret, just like his dad, and then he disgraced it.

Now he was alone on a street that reeked of piss and cigarette smoke. He ran his hands through his hair, grown out and wavy, and tossed the empty can of beans in a trash bin a few yards away. It clattered to the bottom. Allen would be by at eleven-thirty with good food. Food like his mom used to cook in their rusty, old 1960s kitchen. That woman was talented. Just like Savannah.

He rose from the crate and stretched, adjusting a faded ball cap over his eyes when a woman ran by in hot pink tights and jewel-studded sneakers, shrieking into her phone about taking a wrong turn on her jog. How many clues did she need to sense she'd left high society? Tents, drug needles, dilapidated buildings? Maybe a flashing sign would have helped. It did give him something to do. He'd follow her and make sure she made it safely back to her millennial friends and their venti soy, triple-shot lattes.

He listened for her voice as he shimmied a brick loose in the wall of a run-down chicken factory and retrieved his Glock, catching a reflection of a man he barely recognized in a broken window. He replaced the brick and brushed the mortar crumbs off his hand. He had slicks all over the city. Allen said he was like a squirrel hiding nuts. Instead of nuts though, he stashed pistols, cash, and C4. Any day could be his last in L.A., and he had to be ready in case someone found him. It made good tactical sense, and it kept his hands busy.

He slipped the Glock into a holster at his back and kept a safe distance. She didn't notice, just continued her tirade, waving her free hand all around to signal her distress over the situation. With her boobs bouncing around in a low-cut top that was even tighter than her painted-on pants, she was lucky she'd made it this far without a threatening situation. Savannah's holiday feast probably saved her life. He'd follow her the last block until she was safe.

Just as the thought of safety hit him, a man emerged from a side street behind her, lurking into the available shadows on the side of the street. She missed that, too. Was it possible for someone to lack all basic survival skills? He shook his head.

The man, who was wearing a black hoodie, closed in fast, with a knife reflecting the morning sun in his right hand. Joe sped up, breathing steady. He reached out and jerked the man backward just as he'd brushed the woman with the tip of his blade. She turned and screamed. The man—he appeared to be in his mid-forties—was completely off balance as he threw a lame punch. Joe dodged it and frowned. This wasn't the rush he needed. It could barely be considered a rush at all. With a huff, he smashed his fist against the man's cheek, knocking his head into a brick wall. The man fell to the ground, unconscious.

He looked up. The woman still screamed. It was high pitched, shrill, and drawing a lot of attention. "Oh my gosh! What did you do to that man? Is he alive?" She moved away a step at a time, eyes never leaving his. "Stay back. I'll call the cops. I mean it, mister. Don't touch me!"

She turned and ran. Fast. He'd just saved her from whatever that loser had planned, but all she saw was a scruffy Middle Eastern man with tattoos. Why did skin color dictate threat level? Screw it. She was alive. Job done.

He dragged the guy away and propped his limp body against a decaying dumpster with the rest of the trash. The dude would probably miss the irony when he woke, but whatever. He deserved worse, maybe to lose a finger or a hand, but it wasn't his job to dole out justice. He did take the knife, stowing it in his boot before turning the opposite direction the girl ran. He needed to breathe some fresh air and stretch his legs. Yeah, it was the same air on Skid Row, but it never felt fresh. Each breeze that blew through was sour and stale.

It was fresh here, on this busy street full of banks, office buildings, and chain coffee restaurants. Men and women in suits slipped past him on the sidewalk, careful not to let their bodies brush. They chatted importantly on their cell phones and carried briefcases, missing the bright-blue sky.

He slowed his pace to blend in, but a homeless man garnered looks. There was whispering. Not that it—or those people—mattered. He had bigger problems; ones Allen spent the last six months trying to help him overcome. The flashbacks hadn't improved, but he told Allen they had so Allen could rest easier at night in their shared tent.

A green metal bench was vacant to his left, so he had a seat. After this, he'd go. He leaned against the slats used for backing and allowed the sun to beat down on his upturned face. His eyes pulled closed, and he let out a sigh. Cars raced along the street, their engines and horns muffling the voices around him to hums. The only sound that stood out was a banner flapping on a storefront behind him. The breeze was light, so it flapped slow, popping against the window every ten seconds.

The backs of his eyelids were red from the shining sun, but his brain worked hard to convince him he was seeing red, white, and blue. The cars still drove six yards in front of his feet. He was awake, but he couldn't pull himself away from the flapping sound. It was a banner, but eight months ago it had been a flag. Eleven flags, all draped over wooden caskets, the breeze catching under their folds as they were carried off the C141.

The breeze ceased, and he opened his eyes before he was tugged completely in. He straightened his back and cracked his neck. In a pharmacy window across the street was a large digital clock indicating it was now twelve fifteen. He missed seeing Allen, who was back at the soup kitchen by now. With the holiday festivities, things would carry on until evening. He could catch up with Allen then, over his plate of cold food and five or six stories about Savannah. Allen was relentless once he decided something, and Allen decided months ago that Joe and Savannah were meant to be.

He rose from the bench and caught a flash of white hair across the street in his peripheral vision. His head twisted to the side. A man around seventy, with a camo jacket, yelled something at the police officer beside him before rushing down the street. Then he stopped, looked around, and kept going. It was Allen, and he could tell from across five lanes of traffic something was wrong.

He jogged to the street corner and hit the crosswalk button. It clicked for a few seconds before a green man appeared, and he sped across the street. Keeping Allen in his vision, he weaved through the crowd. Allen was still a block ahead. He moved quicker, steadying his breathing as he jogged. Everyone watched him with expressions ranging from curiosity to fear. One even appeared to be calling the police. He was already to Allen though. He reached out a hand and grabbed Allen's narrow shoulder, pulling him under the awning of an ATM vestibule. Allen jumped and spun around. "Joe, what're you doin' here?"

"I saw you pass by, saw you yelling at a cop. What's going on? I thought you were at the soup kitchen. Where are you going?" He scanned the area. At least twenty skyscrapers were visible, plus restaurants, a pawn shop, a police station, and a theater. It was a valid question.

"Just out for a walk, that's all. Needed to clear my head. And the cop thing, man, it was just a misunderstandin'. Ya know how they are. But the soup kitchen. Busy day, ya know?" Allen crammed his hands into his pockets and jerked his head around.

"If it's busy, then why did you leave Savannah there without any help? And what are you looking for? We've been standing here two minutes and your eyes haven't stopped moving. What's really going on?" His hand rested on the gun at his waist. Allen's nervousness was rubbing off, and now he looked to his left and right for signs of danger.

"I can't tell ya that. Just somethin' I gotta do. I'm fine, so move your hand offa that gun and go back the way ya came."

He set his jaw and glared at Allen as two twenty-somethings with big hair and high heels walked by. cackling at something on their phones. "If things were reversed, you'd never let me shut you out. Stop trying to protect me. Tell me what you're running from. Is it the cops? Maybe I can help."

"Nothin'. That's the honest truth. No one's after me, and don't ya go talkin' to the cops. Now, there's somewhere I gotta be, and trust me, you can't follow. I'll be back tonight. You got my word. Nothin' more important to me than walkin' Savannah to her car. Now make good on your promise and get a bite to eat at the kitchen today." Joe pursed his lips as a breeze blew up the back of his tee shirt. "Fine. I'll give you space, but if whatever you're involved in gets hairy, you better come find me. You have an unlimited supply of IOU's to cash in on, and I could use a distraction."

Allen clapped him on the shoulder and turned, but Joe kept his grip. It didn't feel right to let him go, even if he'd verbally agreed to it. He squeezed harder. He could demand an explanation or drag him back to their tent at gunpoint until he talked.

"I know the wheels are spinnin'. You just gotta trust me. Let go, Joe. I'll see you by sundown."

He relinquished his grip, more so his control, and watched Allen disappear into the crowd. There was no going back. He'd never track Allen down in that mob. He'd have to trust things would be okay, which didn't come easy. If something happened to Allen, it'd be his fault. He shook his head. That was nothing new.

CHAPTER THREE
Savannah

The can of pepper spray was heavy in Savannah's trembling hand as she flipped off the soup kitchen lights. It'd been rolling around the bottom of her purse for the last three years, but tonight she needed it. She'd sent Holden away hours ago so she and Allen would have time to get to the bottom of whatever was bothering him, but he never showed up. She dialed Holden again, her fingers unsteady from her trembling hand, but it went to voicemail, just like the last five calls had. Holden never kept his phone on him at work, and Allen didn't have one. She shifted on her feet. It was just one walk alone. One walk. One. Walk.

She burst through the glass front door, the bell at the top chiming sharply behind her. She jumped, even though she'd heard it a hundred times, and jumped again as the door slammed closed. The humid air stifled her breaths and weighed on her shoulders. She counted each footstep over the uneven sidewalk, praying her good deeds in the neighborhood granted her invisibility from the cussing and drug deals a few feet to the right. Just two more blocks, and she'd be in a safer area. Her heart raced, and her stride picked up to a jog. The traffic light to her left turned red, but three cars accelerated through it. No one lingered.

She kept moving, her breaths rhythmic, when a muffled scream for help escaped an alley to her right. She spun that direction and froze. A lone streetlight buzzed and flickered above her head. Three figures moved in and out of the shadows behind a dumpster, but the screaming came from a form beneath them. She didn't have to see his wrinkly face to recognize his voice. It was Allen. She should have known something was very wrong.

He screamed again. Her insides churned with guilt, but her sneakers wouldn't lift off the ground. They were rooted to the spot. It wasn't the fear of death that left her knees banging together, but the moon tucked away behind the clouds, forcing blackness to drape the alley like a blanket.

Allen was still screaming, maybe even fighting back, but Savannah only heard his laugh as they shared a bowl of soup, his stories from Vietnam, and the Purple Heart medal he still treasured after losing everything else in a fire.

She couldn't leave her friend. Living with that kind of guilt would be impossible. She needed a plan, but her feet were already pounding against the pavement without her consent as she bellowed, "Get out of here! The police are on their way!"

But she hadn't called, and now she couldn't hold back. The wind screeched through the broken windows of the alley and escaped into the sky. Savannah fixed her eyes on the three attackers and gulped, her tongue sticking to the roof of her mouth. What had she been thinking? She didn't know how to fight anything besides a crowd at the annual Burberry sale. One man punched Allen hard across the face and dropped his limp body before turning in her direction. It only took a moment to realize she'd brought pepper spray to a knife fight.

They inched closer like wolves, hungry and impatient, closing the distance to just a few feet. She forced herself to look directly at them. The other option would be pondering what lay waiting in the darkness to her left and right. Her whole body shook, and vomit clung to the inside of her throat.

The one with the crooked teeth licked his lips, salivating, but her eyes fixed on the snake tattoo wrapping around his neck. The man with the ponytail stepped forward and pushed him aside. He was in charge. His forehead dripped with sweat from the fight and the heat. His stringy hair caked across it like a spider web. "Lookin' for some action, princess?"

Her heart pounded furiously in her ears. His rancid breath burned the space between them. Without thinking, she raised the pepper spray and pressed the button. A stream shot wildly at first, but she steadied her hand enough to sear his eyes. He howled, his friends surging forward with eerie sneers. She shrieked, shaking the can hard and trying to spray again, but it was empty. Her heart dropped into her shoes. She froze, eyes wide in horror.

The third man, twice her size, sent her swaying with a blow to the chest. The air ripped from her body and smashed back into her lungs again. He kicked her to the ground while she rocked, pulling her by the ankle deeper into the alley. His broad back was all she could see; that and the knife stuck in his belt. Allen's blood oozed down the blade and dripped slowly from the tip. She tried scooting backward, frantic, eyes wide, the pavement tearing at her palms as he dragged her over cardboard boxes and shattered bottles of booze. She wasn't strong enough to take on even one of these men, and there were three.

The ponytail guy, standing again, wiped his eyes with his dingy shirt sleeve and ordered the other two to back off. She willed her feet to take her away, but they didn't budge. He climbed on top of her rigid body, breath on fire, knife tracing the curve of her waist. Ponytail's tears trickled onto her cheeks and between her lips. "So, you like to play rough, princess? I can do that." Snake Tattoo kicked the can out of her hand as he and Bloody Knife hovered by her head, waiting for their chance to—she wasn't going to finish that thought.

Her lips trembled. Each breath came out ragged. She couldn't answer Ponytail, but she had to do something. They were going to kill her.

Move. Move. Move! Why won't my body move? Please!

His knife dug in, ripping apart the threads on the side of her blouse, each tiny snip bringing her closer to her death. She bit her lip as his blade drew the first drop of blood.

She pictured her body lying lifeless on the concrete, hidden from the world, as the darkness ate away at anything that remained. She couldn't leave the world that way, not when her parents used all their breath to explain why no one with her breeding should be wasting her life helping people that were too lazy to help themselves. It was easy to imagine her mother tossing back martinis at her wake and bawling. *"She was too beautiful to work with homeless people. I warned her. And now she's gone before she even had a chance to marry a respectable man."*

The knife plunged further, grazing muscle and ripping her skin apart. Blood oozed out. She groaned and screamed, but Snake Tattoo slapped his sweaty hand over her mouth. Ponytail leaned down, pressing crusty lips against her forehead before whispering in her ear, "Rough enough, princess, or should we have some more fun first?"

It has to be now. Move, Savannah! There's no other way. Fight back, or you'll die a coward. You have to MOVE!

She exploded with fear and fury: kicking, punching, her whole body an untrained weapon. Savannah jerked the man's ponytail, shocking them both as his head crunched against the pavement. Her heart raced. She pushed his barely conscious body away, scrambling to her knees and holding her wobbling arms in front of her chest. The other two men lurched forward, ready to finish the job, when three gunshots rang through the air, and her heart stopped. The two attackers crumbled to the ground in an instant. Her head jerked back and forth. They were dead, and she was alive. She was alive! Her hands touched all over her body in disbelief. Ponytail stumbled back up with a bloody forehead and began running. He escaped through the metal door of a decrepit building shouting, "Don't worry, princess. You'll see me soon. This ain't over yet."

At the other end of the alley, someone moved closer in the darkness, aiming a gun where Ponytail had just escaped. She leapt to her feet, hands pressing against her bloody side. This mysterious man had just rescued her, but it didn't mean she was safe. She inched backward as the shadows played games with her vision. She was nearly to Allen's unmoving body and the dumpster, but she couldn't outrun anyone right now. The man moved faster, becoming less of a shadowy outline and more human.

Savannah held her breath and dialed 9-1-1 before stuffing her phone back in her pocket.

Just as the man reached her, he dropped to his knees, yelling, and checking Allen for a pulse at his wrist and neck. "Medic! Medic! We need an evac!" His head jerked around, looking into every dark corner of the alley as he stepped from Allen.

His eyes locked onto hers for the first time: intense but distant.

This man wasn't living the same moment she was.

He grabbed her arms and pulled her roughly to her knees. She wobbled and threw a ragged hand onto the pavement for support. "Soldier! Soldier! Stay down! Are you hit?" His head continued moving back and forth, gun poised to shoot anything that came at them again.

Savannah's eyebrows furrowed. She carefully removed her arms from the man and rested her bloody palms against his dirty face. He startled, and then his chest fell. His green eyes focused on hers.

"I just called 9-1-1. They're coming. Do you...know where we are?"

"Afghani—Los Angeles?"

"Yes. Los Angeles."

Streaks of dirt and sweat mixed, streaming through his wooly beard as he breathed slowly and gazed into her eyes with a new confidence. He reeked of body odor. He was the type of person her parents would stick their noses up at. They weren't the only ones. She didn't feel disgust though. His eyes were strangely gentle, and she ached to know his story.

And she just ached.

The sirens were getting closer. She'd forgotten about putting pressure on her wound, and her head swirled as she fell into his arms, vision fading.

He held her, brushed blonde hair away from her face. "You're going to be okay, Savannah."

And everything faded into blackness.

CHAPTER FOUR

Joe

The police were moving in on the alley. They'd be on him in moments, and the last thing Joe needed was the cops to bring him to the station and discover his identity. L.A. was the safest place he'd found to disappear. No one would think to look for him here, and there was no way he'd leave Allen before ensuring he was safe. He was barely breathing, a foot away. He'd seen all the signs and still let him go earlier. Why hadn't he trusted his instincts?

And then there was Savannah. He was having one heck of a time convincing his arms to let her go. She was going to be fine. He was certain of that, but the reason he'd stayed away from the soup kitchen all this time was so he wouldn't get close enough to care.

She was one of a kind, and he'd learned that even without Allen's stories. Now he was close enough to appreciate the freckles on her cheeks and the laugh lines around her mouth. He'd missed those details from a distance, but he didn't need them, not really. He'd lost a good woman once before, and after everything he'd done, he sure didn't deserve Savannah now.

His chest tightened as a vision of his wife filled his head. His mind tried to force him back to her abandonment while he was weak. And he didn't do weak. He breathed deeply and listened. The cops were only fifty yards away, lifting their guns in the darkness, and he wasn't in the mood to dodge bullets. He tenderly eased Savannah's head onto the concrete before slipping through the same exit her attacker took. The police were yelling something, but all his ears could register were their footsteps exploding against the concrete like mortar rounds.

Mortar rounds.

He ran faster.

That narrow Afghani mountain trail crashed into his mind.

Faster.

His men hiked silently behind him to the mountain village as he treaded through a pile of goat dung and turned up his nose. His eyes focused on the hands of his Afghani contact, two feet ahead. Why were they shaking? Why was it so quiet on the outskirts of the village? Something was wrong.

Faster.

Joe tripped. His feet stumbled over the littered L.A. sidewalk, bringing him back to the present. His heart beat like a drum. Why couldn't he keep those memories at bay after all these months? He tucked away behind a dumpster and dropped to the ground. Three homeless men sat whispering near a makeshift tent, five yards to his left, graffiti sprayed onto the brick wall behind them. His hands gripped the back of his head. He forced each breath in through his nose and out through his mouth slowly. The men watched him, likely chalking his erratic behavior up to drugs.

"You alright, man?"

He rose, brushed himself off and nodded. "Yeah, I'm alright." He pulled out his wallet, handed each guy a five, and got moving. "Y'all go get a bite to eat." Their faces scrunched in confusion, but they smiled gratefully.

Joe's head was on a swivel, making sure he wasn't followed for the next ten blocks. It was more than coincidence that Allen was attacked on the same day he'd been arguing with a cop. Why didn't he pry it out of him? Joe sighed and kept moving down the sidewalk, pushing through the crowds. L.A. wasn't the location he envisioned when he left home but avoiding cameras here for the last six months still kept him sharp, even if it was a far cry from hunting and camping in the Smokies. He kept watch and continued on, using reflective surfaces to keep him from having to completely turn around. With all his training, he was good at spotting a tail, and beat cops were obvious anyway.

But all his detailed precautions over the last six months were ending tonight.

That scumbag would be back. He'd promised Savannah that. And with her and Allen both headed to the hospital, it'd be the perfect place to finish the job. It's what he'd do.

Their accosters might've been filthy, not that he could judge, but they clearly had a rich boss, because each of them was wearing a six-hundred-dollar watch. That was curious. He shook his head. Whatever their issue, they wouldn't dare let it fester for more than a few hours, and he had to focus.

He was the only one that could help. And he had to. Besides the draw of being near Savannah again, he had to keep Allen safe. Allen had been there on his first day to town; he'd found him screaming and thrashing in an alley, poisoned by the venom of past mistakes. Allen had lived like that after Vietnam and recognized a soldier in need. But it was more than that. He'd taken him under his wing, been a confidant and a true friend. His duty to his brother in arms wasn't finished. He would protect Allen and Savannah, even if it meant entering a facility full of cameras that he hadn't done any reconnaissance on.

The general layout of cameras would be simple to predict and avoid, but his biggest fear was someone recognizing him. The body odor and long beard were a way of ensuring people moved along quickly, but it'd have the opposite effect in the hospital. He'd have to clean up. Because if anyone there really looked in his eyes, they'd recognize him.

The ambulance sirens ringing out in the distance stole his attention as they sped further away. His ears perked up. They were heading north to

L.A. Med Center. It would take at least forty minutes if he rushed, and he still needed to hit his train locker for weapons and supplies. There wasn't time to second guess his choice, even if it alerted others to his whereabouts. And there was no doubt they were still looking.

CHAPTER FIVE
Savannah

Savannah woke in the hospital to something much more horrifying than the attack: her parents. "Oh, Savannah dear, we were so worried. But now you're awake, thank goodness. Do you need an extra pillow or anything at all?"

She shook her head and rolled her eyes as her mom looked to the door and back in her direction. What she needed was privacy and not an ulcer to go with the pain in her stomach, but there was no way to ask them to leave, was there?

Her mom straightened the bedding and laid her cardigan over the sheet before sitting on top of it. "That's fine. Just let me know if you change your mind. I'm here to help, and I truly want to. So, if I can't help you physically, then I've got something to help you take your mind off things." She rose and lifted her cardigan, brushing it off. "You missed the golf event at the club this evening, which was unfortunate, because we raised a great deal of money, and it was such fun. However, the doctor assures me you'll be up and walking for the last event of the week: the gala and silent auction. Your father has his eye on a new yacht. I've got mine on a vintage Chanel pantsuit. And Holden will have his eye on you. A date like this could be all he needs to understand you're the one for him. He's at your apartment now, prepping everything for your arrival."

Painful. And mildly impressive, the way her mother diverted the conversation to social matters in the twelve steps it took to cross the room and rearrange one of the bouquets from Holden.

She groaned, running her hands over her face and through her hair. She tugged the white sheet up to her chest and stared at a picture of the beach on the wall, wishing that magic was real and her toes could be in the sand. "Mom, I'm not going to that gala. Is the gravity of this situation—*my* situation—lost on you? This isn't a joke. Someone tried to kill me tonight! I'm lucky to be alive, and Holden fluffing my pillows isn't the reassurance I need to feel safe."

Her mother tucked in close, combing Savannah's hair between her French tips. "Darling, there is no one in the world more important to your father and me than you. But how many years have I warned you about the dangers of operating that soup kitchen? We spend more time than you'll ever know worrying about your safety. And though you find the idea of this gala beneath you, understand where I'm coming from. This is a wake-up call for you, darling. Marrying an eligible bachelor like Holden will give you stability, financial security, and the opportunity to do your charity work closer to home."

Savannah pushed away her mother's hand. What was wrong with her? She breathed deeply before responding through her teeth, "Mom, unless you think Jennifer Aniston needs a handout, I doubt a soup kitchen would fit in well in Trousdale. Do you understand anything about what I do? I don't need marriage; I need parents who care."

"Darling, we do care. That's what I've been trying to explain. Just go to the gala with Holden. He's already been fitted for his tux." She nudged her father, who was avoiding the conversation by staring at his cell.

"Do this for your mother, Savannah, and I'll continue funding your little...do-gooder thing." He waved his hand as if to dismiss the entire conversation. Then her father's cell phone rang. His fuzzy eyebrows pulled together like two caterpillars kissing as he chirped, "Hello, Quinton...Yes, she is...Really...That would be perfect...I'll speak with

Dahlia." He hung up, smiling at his wife, a sense of dread filling every inch of Savannah's five-foot-three frame.

"That was Quinton Forsyth. He called with well-wishes for Savannah. He also mentioned that Caroline would like to plan a lunch with you sometime this week. Perhaps she'd like to discuss the possibility of our families joining together in the future?"

Her mother fell into the blue leather of a nearby chair as if hit by a stroke, her shocked face framed by another table full of roses Holden sent, sitting behind her. "Oh, Savannah! This is the miracle I've been praying for! We can't miss out on this opportunity. I'll pick out your dress. I'm thinking something emerald. You heal up. The gala is in five days."

And with that they were gone, practically skipping along the corridor, with no concern for her physical or mental health. Their only focus was the lavish wedding they'd be planning in the near future.

Savannah's head throbbed. They were cardboard cut-outs of actual humans, but unfortunately, she'd grown used to it. Now that they were gone though, she could think, breathe a full breath. The blinds on the window to her left were cracked enough to see it was still dark outside. How much time had passed from her brief conversation with two police officers when she arrived and then fell asleep to when she woke up? A couple of hours?

A nurse—Ebony, according to her nametag—trailed in, black hair wrapped tightly on top of her head. She set down a tray of jiggling food, and Savannah gagged. "How you feelin' honey?"

That was a good question. Savannah reached down and pulled the flimsy blanket and sheet away. A bandage covered her left side. Her fingers trembled as she peeled it back and exposed a stitched-up incision about two inches long. The man with the knife slithered back into her mind, and her whole body broke out in a sweat. A rumbling of nausea tore through her stomach as she stuck the bandage back to her skin.

Somehow, her fingers had already moved across her stomach, eight inches to the right, where they rested on another scar. The man's face disappeared, and Cole's took his place. The day had been so horrifying she hadn't thought of her twin like she usually did. His mischievous smile all the girls had been crazy over, and the way they'd been able to read each other's minds. They loved talking, but it wasn't necessary. Most days, they'd sit together in the tree swing as he strummed an acoustic guitar. Even at seventeen, they still found a way to squeeze in together. Right now, she missed him more than ever before. Her pinky traced the thin white line from the kidney she'd shared, healed cleanly after thirteen years, but the pain wasn't gone. And it would never go away. Neither would the memory of three hours ago. Unless she located the world's largest bottle of bleach.

The nurse patted her shoulder. "No need for a response dear. But I *am* here. Do you need anything?"

She shook away the imagery and fixed her eyes on Ebony. "Yes. A man was brought in with me. His name is Allen. He's homeless. What room is he in? I need to see him."

Ebony's hands shot to her hips, and her head tilted. It didn't take much effort to understand just what that purse in her lips meant: *What's this prissy girl whose mother just walked out in Chanel doing wondering about a homeless man?* It was fine. She was used to the judgement, but she had to know if Allen was okay and if he knew anything about the man who saved their lives.

"Well…" Ebony hesitated but finally said, "He's in 103, down the hall. He's gonna make it, but he's weak. You want me to wheel you over there, or you wanna try walkin'?"

"I'll walk." Savannah shifted her legs off the side of the bed, but vertigo weighed down her head the instant her toes brushed the cool tile. "Actually, I'll take the wheelchair."

Ebony wheeled it over, and she fell in with a sigh, clutching her stomach. "Okay, I'm ready." Ebony shook her head but didn't ask any further questions. She rolled Savannah out the door, lips still pursed.

The hall was quiet except for doctors and nurses shuffling in and out of rooms, the beeping of medical equipment, and a soda machine rumbling. Most patients were asleep. Allen's room was eleven doors down on her right, with closed blinds over the door and wall of windows. She tapped on the door and wheeled inside. He lay quietly in bed, eyes glued to the door and an IV plugged into his arm. She turned her head to Ebony. "You can leave me here."

Allen's eyes darted in her direction, wild with fear. His voice was low and ominous to the point that tears welled up in the corners of her eyes. "I'm going to tell you something, and then you need to go. Don't come back lookin' for me again. Those men who attacked me will be back. Get your discharge papers and leave immediately."

She took his hand in hers and stroked his arm with a shaky hand. His pulse raced beneath her palm. "Allen, the nurses won't let anything bad happen to us. It's over. I know you're worried. I could ask a police officer to sit with you, if it would help. My dad has friends on the force. But if it would calm your mind to have me out of the hospital, I'll go home as soon as possible."

Allen balled his fists together. "Doctors and cops won't do me any good now, especially cops. I just need you to listen, Savannah!" The machines started beeping loudly. Allen's blood pressure was through the roof, and his head was breaking out in a sweat. As two nurses raced over, Allen squeezed her hand tightly. "I stumbled upon something. It was…an accident…but now I'm wrapped up in this, and they're cleaning house. Joe'll keep you safe."

His body rocked violently. Ebony came back in and took the handles of Savannah's wheelchair as one of the other nurses yelled, "Get her out of here! He's going into shock!" Ebony spun her around and started out the door, but she couldn't leave him like this. Allen didn't have anyone else.

"Just a minute. Please."

She tried rising from the wheelchair, but Ebony pulled her back down. "No."

Allen yelled after her, his voice frantic and unclear, "They'll be...back for y-you. R-run. The gr-green triangle. Don't...forget the green tr-triangle! And don't tr...."

Ebony slammed the door shut before she could hear the last of Allen's pleas. She whispered to herself, "I won't forget, Allen. I promise." She didn't have any clue what he was talking about, but if she was in danger and needed this Joe guy to keep her safe, how would she find him? Allen had told her plenty of stories, but never what Joe looked like. Was she meant to scour Skid Row in hopes of stumbling upon him?

Back in bed, she tapped on her sheets restlessly while staring at a giant vase of lilies her mother brought for some ridiculous reason, though she'd only be here until the attendant readied her discharge papers. She rolled her eyes. There was also a fancy aromatherapy diffuser hidden behind Holden's numerous bouquets. She breathed in the lavender, but it didn't grant any sense of relaxation. Her bed at home with all the doors locked was the only thing that would allow any peace. Savannah rubbed her eyes with shaky hands and turned on the news. The captions were running, so she muted it and watched, hoping it would distract her. According to her dad, it'd been the same local headlines the last few weeks: extreme heat, dead bodies, a missing soldier, a congressman accused of harassment, and an influx of opioids on the streets, laced with other chemicals, that teens were overdosing on. That's why she never watched. Not only was it depressing, it wasn't helping. She snapped the TV off again and focused on the lavender, when multiple alarms rang throughout the floor. Nurses and doctors rushed to a room down the hall.

Could it be Allen's room? She had to know, so she gave getting out of bed one more try when a janitor with a bag over his shoulder slipped silently into her room and began shutting the blinds over the glass door and walls. "Hi. Ummm, do you know what the commotion is out there? I have a friend on this floor and I'm a bit worried." She twirled her hair rapidly and sat straight up.

The man turned and she froze. Golden brown skin and those eyes.

She'd seen them before, beautiful, but tired, with dark bags underneath. His wavy beard was trimmed shorter, revealing sharp cheekbones, and he smelled like soap. It was the man from the alley. "Are you Joe?"

A terse nod. "Savannah, I need to get you out of here. Now." His emerald eyes were hard. She hadn't recognized he was Middle Eastern in the alley, and with a name like Joe and no accent, who could blame her? He was obviously raised in America. "I didn't get here in time to save Allen, but I can protect you if you'll let me. Put this on." Joe shut the blinds and thrust another janitor's uniform into her hands.

Her mouth hung open. She couldn't force it shut. And not because her mother would die seeing her baby dressed like a lower-class citizen, but because she was throwing on that uniform without asking any follow-up questions. The main one she had was about Allen, and she couldn't handle hearing him lay it out any more plainly. Her eyes filled with tears. Allen was gone.

Joe's fingers separated the blinds to the left of the door as he looked for someone. "Did Allen tell you anything about why these men were after him?"

Savannah carefully slipped her arms into the uniform so she didn't pull at her wound. "Not much. He said he saw something. It was an accident, and I should leave town. He said they would come for me, too, and that the men in the alley weren't the only ones. And something about finding a green triangle. Oh, and he said to trust you." Savannah pulled up the zipper, her hand brushing past her pounding heart. Things were spiraling out of control. "Okay. I'm ready."

He whipped around. "It's too late for that. He's already here. Plan B. Get in bed and pretend you're sleeping."

Her feet rooted to the spot. It was Ponytail. It had to be. Her breaths came in sharp and fast. Her hands shook in a way she couldn't control. Savannah's voice was a whisper. "I can't move. He's going to kill me."

Compassion flared in his eyes, but just briefly. "It's not up for debate. Get in that bed *now*. You'll be safe. He's the only one of us leaving the hospital in a body bag." He retrieved a taser from his janitorial cart and positioned himself behind the door.

Joe saved her once before. She would have to trust him, but it didn't mean her fear would disappear with a snap of his fingers. Savannah crawled under the covers and focused on the lavender to slow her breathing.

The door creaked, and two feet padded into the room. He was here. She suffocated a scream in her throat and bit her tongue. His thin hand stroked hair away from her ear. "Wake up, princess."

Joe's taser went off, and her body bolted across the room without permission. She squeezed her eyes shut in the corner, her fists against her temples. Her wound throbbed, and nausea tore her stomach apart. Her head spun wildly. A body dropped to the ground with a thud, and then a snap echoed in the room.

"Savannah, time to go."

It was Joe's voice. Relief crashed through her chest. She looked down but couldn't move. Joe was dragging the man into her bathroom, by the ankles, a white doctor's coat trailing across the floor under him. He deserved every bit of what he got, but her stomach couldn't handle it, and the dizziness was overwhelming. Her head poured out in a cold sweat. Grabbing a nearby trash can, she leaned in and vomited. Joe helped her stand and guided her to the janitor's cart calmly, as if he hadn't just snapped that monster's neck.

He pulled on a blue baseball cap and kept his head down as they entered the hall. She was doing her best to not draw attention, even though her eyes were as wide around as bowling balls.

CHAPTER SIX

Joe

He'd failed. Succeeded at rescuing Savannah but failed to come through for Allen. That was another death on his conscience, but he couldn't let himself be drawn any further back to that moment nine months ago, in Afghanistan, along the Pakistani border. He'd come out of the dark for Savannah, and though he didn't believe any cameras caught his face, there was no way to be sure.

They rode the heavily air-conditioned elevator together, him between Savannah and the door. Four more floors to the parking garage. He clenched his teeth together. It was a little unnerving how trusting Savannah was, not asking a single question over the last ten minutes, but it made his task easier. He couldn't lose sight of things though, couldn't let his mind wonder about her or the countless times Allen said they'd be perfect together. And just in case, he'd tucked his Glock 19 into his hip holster.

Three floors.

I've got this. We should be in the clear.

Two floors.

They lurched to a stop. He pushed Savannah directly behind him, hand against her hip so he didn't touch her wound. The doors slid wide. He retrieved the reloaded taser and pulled the Glock behind his thigh. Savannah gasped but didn't move.

A father stepped aboard with a boy who appeared to be around five years old, smacking on a piece of bubblegum. Joe loosened his stance when Savannah's fingers delicately stroked his gun hand. "It's okay," she whispered. His hand tingled under her touch, fogging up his head in a way he couldn't afford mid-mission. No woman had ever distracted him the way that one touch from her had. He couldn't ever let her know it. As soon as she was safe, he'd have to find a new city to lie low in.

The little boy gazed up in wonder, gum hanging out of the gap in his missing teeth. He stiffened but couldn't look away. Neither did the little boy. He tugged at his father's pant leg. "Daddy, Daddy, that's the man. It's him!" The dad didn't wait for an explanation, just wrapped his arms around the little boy, fingers turning white, and ducked into a corner, watching the lights blink to the parking garage level.

He didn't want to be found, but if he'd been white or black, that kid's comment wouldn't have made the dad go rigid like he had a suicide vest under his janitor's uniform. The doors to the parking garage sprung open, and he turned to the pair, even though they weren't likely to move for the next twenty minutes. "You two stay here until we're gone."

Savannah narrowed her eyes but didn't speak. His heart was racing like a torpedo. He couldn't make eye contact with the little boy as he stepped away. That kid needed to learn CNN never gave the full story.

And there it was. He'd been recognized by a child. The question now would be if the dad believed the kid had seen him on the news and decided to turn him in. But despite the months of worry over the Army and, worse, the White House tracking him down, his frustration was coming from another place entirely. He'd never be good enough for Savannah, but protecting her was a rush, and if people started looking for him in L.A., he'd have to go dark again and leave her safety in the hands of someone less skilled until all the loose ends were tied up.

He pursed his lips and led her out of the garage and into the darkness of the early morning hours. It was muggy and hot. He looked at Savannah, who'd gone a little pale after dropping the janitor's cart in the garage. "Where is your car parked?"

"Six blocks from the soup kitchen. Allen always met me there. I could call someone to pick us up. I don't have my car keys." Her body swayed. She seemed lightheaded.

"I've got them. I snatched your personal effects from the hospital, and I've already got an Uber waiting." He wrapped his arms around her and led the way to a silver SUV.

They climbed in together, and she mumbled the address where she parked her car before resting her head on the seat. "I'm exhausted." Her eyes closed, and she yawned. Savannah would feel back to normal in a couple days, and the mission would likely be over too. She would return to her routine, only occasionally thinking of the stranger who saved her life once. He was as sure of that as he was that he'd never be able to sleep without nightmares again. And why shouldn't he? What happened in Afghanistan was all his fault.

I should've died on that mountain.

He slammed his fist into the back of the leather front seat, teeth grinding together. "Man, you need to calm down in here," the driver muttered without making eye contact. He looked over at Savannah for back-up, but she didn't budge.

Joe's memories were forcing their way in, and Allen would never be back to help. Never. Allen always had him run and beat out the negativity with deliberate footsteps. But the memories were just on the edge of his consciousness, and he had nowhere to go. He was suffocating as the walls of the SUV shrunk around him.

He was home, looking at the note she left on the kitchen table before removing every trace they were ever married.

I can't do this anymore. I'm going back to my parents. It's over, Joe. I've found someone else. I'm sorry.

-Nadine

He kicked the table over, sending the note fluttering to the ground. But he wasn't angry; he was desperate. He launched every piece of furniture across the den. Nadine always needed him, but now, with the blood of countless men caked into the soles of his combat boots, he finally needed her. He backed into the corner with his pistol, the moon through the window casting a faint glow across the disaster.

A light switched on. He squinted into the yellowy brightness. The room was rearranged neatly, with an unfamiliar, purple velvet armchair in the center. Savannah lounged in it regally, wearing a navy gown and dark makeup around her eyes. Her hands draped over the armrests, fingers tapping impatiently like a queen ready to sentence him. Her lip curved up eerily as she watched him. He rubbed his eyes. What was she doing here?

"Why are you upset, Joe?"

Savannah didn't belong in this memory, but he couldn't get rid of her. Something inside of him was forcing out the words he'd never willingly say to anyone. "I need someone to tell me I'm not a monster; to believe in me. Maybe my parents did for a while. But Nadine? No. I think I knew all along it wasn't right. She begged me to stay and start a family, but the Army was the only thing I was committed to."

Savannah twirled her hair and laughed so loudly the windows cracked and then shattered, falling in a slow rain around them. "Oh, Joe. Don't pout. That's the way the world works. Come on now, you know better."

It was all a dream, so why couldn't he control himself and wake up? Instead, the words kept spilling out. "But I want you to see me differently, to be the person to believe in me. I knew that from the first time I felt your kindness radiating all the way down the street from the soup kitchen. Please."

She rose from the chair, light around her as she approached. Dropping to his level, her long, purple fingernails stroked his face, and her blonde hair pooled over her shoulder between them. "Joe, seriously. I'm meant to marry a wealthy man whose only concern is where we'll summer each year. I don't have time for lost causes."

Joe was shaking. No. Someone was shaking him. He'd fallen asleep!

He never slept, and now, when Savannah's life was in jeopardy, he decided to snooze? He jerked his eyes open.

"Joe? Are you okay?" Savannah was holding his face again with short, clean nails. Her hands were warm on his skin, eyes gentle. Her presence had a calming effect on him, much stronger than the running ever did, which was frustrating, because his dream was right: She *was* better off without him. He pulled her hands away and looked out the window. They were stopped beside a white BMW sedan.

"Let's go." The driver snatched his fare as Joe adjusted the baseball cap further down over his face. Reaching out a hand, he helped Savannah from the cab, catching a whiff of rose perfume. She wore the same expression as she had in the elevator—eyes narrowed, making a wrinkle across her forehead. He retrieved her keys from his pocket and turned them in his hands. "I'm taking you to a hotel. You'll be safe until I can find the men hunting for you. It shouldn't take more than a couple days to wrap this up, and then you can go back to your regular life. My friend manages security there and he's got a room for us. We'll go through the back entran—"

Savannah threw her hands out and gasped, cutting him off.

Fingers curled around his Glock, he stepped in front of her, searching the street for danger and holding her back. "Ouch. Sorry, we're not in danger. Well, I am, but not at this moment."

She brushed his hand away gently. "I just remembered something. Yesterday morning, in the craziness of my boyfr—um, Holden showing up and serving meals to seventy-five people, Allen said he was putting something in the safe. He was the only person besides me who knew the combination. It was one of those bubble wrap envelope things. I didn't ask what was inside. Do you think it's important?"

He brushed past the mention of a guy's name. Why did it matter? "Yeah, I do. That's probably why they're trying to kill you. If they think Allen told you something or gave you something, they won't stop till you're dead and any evidence is buried. And if this thing is as bad as Allen suggested, I'm guessing it's going to get a lot worse before it gets better."

Joe cracked his knuckles and avoided looking into Savannah's blue eyes. Instead he kept his eyes on their surroundings. The sun was beginning to rise, and they were only six blocks from the soup kitchen, so he couldn't be too careful. "There's a good chance they are all over the soup kitchen waiting for you. I'll take you to the hotel and then double back there. It's too risky to bring you. Just give me the safe combination."

Savannah's hands shook. The gravity of the situation was probably setting in. She grabbed his arm. "Maybe you're used to death, but I'm not. You can't leave me at some random hotel. Allen said you're the only one I can trust to keep me safe. Let the police go to the soup kitchen, and you stay with me. Or I'll risk going with you, but you're not leaving me behind."

She was feisty, and he liked it. Not to mention she was the sexiest looking janitor he'd ever seen, but there was no way he could live with her death on his conscience too. And that was exactly what would happen if she came, and from Allen's tiff with the cop earlier, there was no way in hell he was going to the cops. He jerked her away from the car and into the shadows of an apartment complex, putting one hand on her shoulder while the other still held the pistol. "You may be willing to risk it, but I'm not. And, yeah, I've seen a lot of death. Caused a good deal of it too. Doesn't mean I'm used to it. Now, get in the car."

Savannah started crying in the passenger seat. Not hysterical or anything, just silent streams of tears down her face. He was too rough, too focused on the battle, but that's how he was wired. Maybe a stray thought about his own desires once in a while, but the battle always took priority. A deep breath filled his lungs as he slid into the driver's seat. The luxury sedan was made for comfort, but between his aversion to small spaces and Savannah crying over him being a jerk, this wasn't going to be a great ride.

He gripped the steering wheel with one hand and squeezed his knee with the other, watching for a tail as he shot through the empty streets. "I'm sorry you got dragged into all of this." They pulled up to a stop light, and he looked in her eyes.

"Thank you, but I just can't stop thinking about Allen, about the attack, about the man's voice. He called me…princess, but in this filthy way. I saw you in the Uber and in the alley, so I assumed you'd understand. Painful memories are hard to forget, but you do make me feel safe, as safe as I can feel, anyway. Allen was right about that." Savannah gently took his hand in hers and looked up at him timidly through her eyelashes. Watching her from a distance for six months hadn't clued him in on how annoyingly perceptive she was. All he wanted to do was jerk her body to his and never come up for air. But he couldn't give in, and he wouldn't. The Army had taught him a great deal of restraint.

But Savannah wasn't a soldier.

She leaned over cautiously, slowly, and pressed her lips against his so gently he wouldn't have known they were there if his eyes hadn't been open. She tasted like peppermint, her breath cool against his increasingly hot body. It was all the incentive he needed to tangle his fingers in her blonde waves and give her the kind of kiss she'd never get from a billionaire, and Holden sounded like a billionaire name. But he didn't get the chance. Savannah straightened, and her cheeks turned red. Pulling his eyes away from her, he sped away. Even with months of denying it to Allen and himself, he wanted her.

She twirled her hair nervously, but he kept his eyes fixed to the pavement and mentally bashed his impulses. That couldn't happen again. Being emotionally compromised would be dangerous for them both. There was no room for Savannah in his future. And even if there was, she'd be running for the hills as soon as she discovered he wasn't a knight in shining armor.

CHAPTER SEVEN
Savannah

The only guy Savannah had ever really been drawn to was Peter Cummings, in the tenth grade, and that was because he was the only kid in her class with a cute face and no trust fund. But there was something about Joe, something intriguing. Maybe that's why she'd kissed him. Maybe it was the adrenaline from the attack or medication from the hospital clouding her mind. Maybe.

She shrugged. Either way, she was already developing guilt over it. Holden was probably at her apartment, pacing the floor, and she hadn't so much as called. She'd never needed a man, especially the snooty ones her parents set her up with. They only talked about expensive wine and sports cars. Holden was different though. Kind. He didn't deserve that.

So why was she still analyzing Joe's confident movements, ruggedly handsome features, and every single story Allen told her about him? The fact that any of that had entered her mind was stupid. Truly. All she really knew about Joe was that he was homeless, with a set of incredibly white teeth. And she needed to think straight because she was still in danger. Even though Joe was protecting her; he was dangerous too. He had killed three people in the hours since they first met. She squeezed her eyes shut and opened them. Her side hurt, and she needed a distraction.

"Um, can I ask you a question?"

The steering wheel was loose in Joe's hands one second and in a death grip the next. Evidently, he wasn't big on questions. The smallest hint of a nod was her answer as the sun washed across their bodies through the window. She shifted over the leather, and it squeaked, making her face burn redder.

"Were you in the military? You have a lot of weapons. Allen said you were, but I...just thought I'd ask."

Joe kept his eyes on the road as he turned right. A swanky hotel came into view in the distance. He adjusted the air conditioning, blasting her skin with goosebumps. "Yes. The Army. Technically, I still am. Is that the only question?"

She twirled her hair around her finger and focused on bringing the color of her face back to a light shade of peach. "No. Is there a limit?"

"I don't like questions."

"That's not really an answer." She giggled even though a vein bulged on his forehead.

"Fine. Two more questions." Joe rolled his shoulders and cracked his neck.

She was about to blurt out her second question, when Joe cupped his hand around his face. She looked up. Was he avoiding traffic cameras? Her mind started replaying the last hour they'd spent together. He did that, or something like that, with every camera they passed. And what did the little boy in the elevator mean? Why on Earth would he recognize Joe? She'd been so amped up on adrenaline she was missing details.

What's going on? He is clearly keeping me away from my attackers, but who is he hiding from?

Blonde strands fell into her lap from the twirling. What had she gotten herself into by blindly trusting someone?

The hotel grew closer in her window, with its manicured lawn and rose gardens. She'd had brunch there with her mother last year. He pulled her car through the parking lot and around to a back entrance, where a dark-brown man with huge muscles waited with a hand on his pistol.

"Are you…really homeless?"

Joe slammed the car into park and pushed open the door with his foot. "Not exactly. Now, let's go."

That answer had been a possibility, but hearing it left her stunned and opened up a whole new series of questions. Joe was back in his protection mode though, eyes scanning the parking lot. They both stepped out into the early morning stickiness and the overwhelming odor of the dumpsters fifty feet away. She held her breath. The nausea was just starting to dissipate.

Another man appeared, short but bulky, with pale, vampire-like skin. Joe tossed him the keys and took Savannah's arm as they moved to the door. His other hand was wrapped around his gun. The only guns in her house growing up were old rifles her father used for decoration in his office. He'd never fired one, and neither had she. The explosion of the bullets through the alley rang back into her mind as she inched closer to Joe.

He took her hand, but in a formal way. His eyes kept moving. "You okay?"

"It'll go away," she whispered.

He grunted, but it wasn't exactly a response. The short guy swerved out of the parking lot and down the street with her car. She'd ask where he was going to park it, but she only had one question left, and Joe's mood swings were slightly jarring.

The security guy rushed them inside and shut the door, leaving her breathless. He grinned at Joe and wrapped him in a hug. "Brother, I'm glad you called." His eyes trailed to her, and he laughed. "Dude, Ace, you still got the smell of the streets on ya. Even livin' homeless, you find the most beautiful girl in the city to take care of. Couldn't wrap this thing up quick, killer?" He dug his elbow into Joe's ribcage. "And you must be the lovely Savannah. Let me know if Joe Mac gives you a tough time, and I'll rough him up. I'm Clark, by the way."

She craned her neck to smile at him. "Thank you. I appreciate you letting us stay. I ate here once with my mother. We had the ahi tuna salad and…umm, it's a beautiful hotel."

Clark paused, suppressing a laugh. "Thanks."

Her cheeks brightened again. *Why did I say all of that? And am I mistaken, or did he call Joe 'killer' and laugh? The scariest nickname I ever got was pumpkin...or princess.*

Savannah's stomach flipped like an Olympic gymnast as she attempted to steady herself on the wobbly ground no one else seemed to have issue with.

He's dead. He can't hurt me. Dead. Dead. Dead.

Joe patted her back awkwardly and jumped on Clark, wrapping an arm around his neck and punching him playfully in the stomach. "I can still take you. And if you've got what I asked for, I'll go wrap this situation up at the soup kitchen, too. Shouldn't take more than a day. My aim's solid, what about yours? You haven't gone soft in this cushy hotel gig, have you?"

"Soft? Me? Never." The boys traveled through the back halls of the hotel, painted white at the top and metal plated along the bottom half. Fliers and printouts of different laws were tacked into the plaster as they entered the kitchen. Four men stood there, preparing breakfast for the guests. Joe grabbed a mini muffin from a tray and stuffed it in his mouth. Her stomach growled, and Clark handed her one, too. She took it and smiled, but at this rate, her face would never return to its normal color.

The kitchen doors swung on their hinges and transported them into the dining room. It was dark, even with the lights on, as the hotel had a very rustic yet romantic vibe. Every table was hand-carved and laden with greenery. Turkish rugs overlapped each other on the tile, and lightbulbs hung from black cords at varying lengths. A few more steps and they crossed a section of the lobby into the elevator bank. Her footsteps were audible on the tile, but Joe's feet didn't make a sound. A man was taking advantage of the early morning hours, mopping the floors and humming. Joe tensed up with suspicion.

"Hey, Carlos," Clark said, waving, and slapped Joe's arm before hitting the button to go up. Savannah tried her best to just sit back and listen as they boarded and rode to the fourth floor. The last thing she needed was to say something else ridiculous.

"Ace, I see you lookin' up at the cameras. I got 'em all off right now. My team here is good. All military guys. Don't worry, man. But you know they're gonna find you one day. It's not any of my business when you decide to go back, but just know, about twenty minutes ago, someone from the White House called me askin' if I'd seen you. Said there was a rumor you might be in L.A. Knew if you were, I'd know about it."

Savannah was more confused than ever. Her heart pounded. She was the only person in the elevator that didn't have a clue what was going on, and it was beyond annoying after the night she'd had. She opened her mouth to ask the third question, when her phone vibrated in her pocket. She jerked it out and looked at the screen. It was her mother. Worst timing ever.

Her chest tightened. The guys both stared at her as if she'd suddenly appeared in their presence. "I'm allowed to answer my phone, right?"

Joe's eyes narrowed on Clark, and he answered. "Go ahead, Savannah."

"Hello."

Her mother's voice was frantic on the other end. There was a rattle of hangers in the background and their maid Anika yelling in a thick Dutch accent. "Darling, where are you? Holden waited at your apartment, and you never showed up. He called me, frantic, because he planned a special date this afternoon to get your mind off things. At this point in your relationship, you know every outing counts. I'll prepare everything you need here at the estate. Just answer one question, what shade of blue fits best with your skin tone and eye color?"

She groaned and stepped out of the elevator behind the guys who were now whispering quietly. It was clear how she appeared to them, and it wasn't what she wanted. She needed those guys—or at least Joe—to believe she wasn't hopeless but instead a woman with a head on her shoulders. So, the thought of answering her mother's question was sending a heat wave up her back. "Mom. I don't know. Maybe navy. But you're missing the big picture. I was attacked, and I don't believe it's over. Joe, one of Allen's friends, is keeping me safe until he can find the people that killed Allen and are still after me. All that to say, I don't have the energy to deal with fashion. Don't you care if I'm safe?"

"Darling, of course. I want you to be safe, but really. Those filthy men will never bother you again. They're too busy prowling for *drugs*." She whispered the last word like it was forbidden and though her tone changed to concern, it didn't fool Savannah. She might truly be concerned, but she didn't understand problems past the wrong place settings at a party. Or hadn't for the last thirteen years. That was her way of dealing. Her dad just worked, stared at his phone, and locked himself in his office at nine every night for a whiskey on the rocks. "Savannah, I can hear you sighing. I love you more than anything in this world, and if you truly feel unsafe, dear, I can set you an appointment with my therapist. The police said it would be wise anyway, after what happened. Just come home to pick out a dress. If this"—she cleared her throat—"Joe, is a friend of Allen's, he's probably homeless. Don't bring your *work* home with you. Let your father and Holden sort this out before your date."

The connection cut off before she could argue. She pinched the bridge of her nose and turned off her phone in a flourish when an alert popped up about a murder near an L.A. soup kitchen. She'd played by her parents' rules for the better part of thirty years, but they didn't always know best. Nothing short of an emergency would get her home for that date.

The guys didn't comment on her conversation, thank the Lord. They seemed more focused on this mysterious call from the White House. Clark stopped in front of room 405 and opened the door with a key card. "Change of clothes for each of you in the bathroom and the medical supplies you asked for. I'll give you a bit to get cleaned up. Then come on out, and we'll plan for the soup kitchen."

"We?"

"Dude, I'm not sending you there alone. I got ten guys here that'll keep Savannah safe. You got a death wish or somethin'? Someone's gotta cover your six."

Joe shook Clark's hand and stepped in first to look around.

She slipped through the door before he let it shut on her. The room was nice: more modern than the first floor of the hotel, with black and white finishes and an overwhelming scent of laundry detergent from the freshly washed sheets. One vase of purple orchids rested on the coffee table in the middle of the room, and another sat on the dresser in the back-left corner of the room. And there was a bed. Just one. While Joe's interest in her seemed to change with the wind's direction, her heart would be racing at warp speed tonight with him sleeping only inches away.

CHAPTER EIGHT
Joe

Joe secured the room as thunder rolled across the sky, announcing a surprise morning shower. His fingers twitched—a nervous habit. Savannah was dying to ask him that third question, which would undoubtedly be more personal than the other two. She was planning her words carefully. It made sense. She wanted answers but opening up about his past was a negative. His mission was to keep her out of harm's way, secure the soup kitchen, and disappear without a trace. So, he needed to get her settled and leave as quickly as possible...and try not to look at her lips.

"Clark left you some clothes in the bathroom, so change and I'll clean your stitches. Hurry up, because I need to get to the soup kitchen and find the best vantage point for Clark to set up."

"Okay." Savannah nodded and walked toward the bathroom quietly. He plopped onto the wooden bench at the end of the bed and ran his hands over his face and through his hair. It sucked to treat her like this: emotionless, focused only on the mission. But he'd already slipped up by kissing her and couldn't mess up again. Mistakes led to danger, death, and regret. Now was the time to keep his head on straight and avoid any tangents. There was a possible battle coming.

Breathe, Joe, and pull it together. You're a Green Beret, man. A soup sandwich of one, but still.

44

His head turned as Savannah opened the bathroom door five minutes later. The clothes Clark picked out fit her perfectly: a tank top accentuating just how small her waist was before curving out into hip-hugging blue jean shorts. He smiled. She was hot, and now he was too.

Focus.

"Let me shower off and clean up. I'll be right back." He slipped into the bathroom, with a concerted effort not to look back, and tossed off the janitor's uniform. He turned the shower knob as far cold as it would go.

Four minutes and one heck of a cold shower later, he was cutting his hair. He trimmed the beard up too but still needed to keep it. Ten minutes and he'd slipped on the tee, tactical belt, and pants Clark laid out before stuffing a combat knife in his boot and his Glock on his hip. He was starting to look more like himself, so he couldn't forget the ball cap when they left.

Savannah sat on the couch, with her legs crossed at the ankle, thumbing through a travel magazine from the coffee table when he marched back in the room, the exhaust fan blowing. He snatched up the bag of medical supplies and dropped beside her on the stiff, black couch. "Alright, let's see what we're working with here."

"I'll show you on one condition: I want five questions, not three. Deal?" Savannah was making it hard to stay disconnected. She twirled her hair and blushed, her eyes trailing down his chest and over his arms. When their eyes connected, she looked down.

He chalked the kiss in the car up to nerves and fear on her part. But he wasn't reading this moment wrong. She liked his new look. But what made her special was that she didn't care that he'd been filthy when she'd touched his face for the first time.

After escaping small town USA, he'd had girls thirsting for him like he was water on a hot day. That's how he'd met Nadine, at a bar off base, where the lights were low, and the floor was sticky with stale beer. The music rocked the walls all night, and the women, hell, they all wanted a soldier. Just a flash of dog tags, and they would hop into any available bed.

And it was fun, especially because, for the first time in his life, no one was judging his skin color, whispering in line at the grocery store about how his white parents were so good for adopting a brown boy or how his so-called friends had cut him from their lives after 9-11. It didn't matter that he was Lebanese. They didn't know shit about geography, just called him raghead behind his back.

Savannah stared at him, with her head tilted. He'd forgotten to answer. "Fine," he muttered through tight lips. "Five questions. Now, let me see your side." She lifted her shirt obediently, and Joe blinked his eyes, trying to focus as his fingers grazed her soft skin and removed the bandage.

She breathed slowly and looked everywhere but his face as he finished cleaning her wound and applied a new bandage. "All done."

She pulled her shirt down and grabbed his forearm before he could stand. "First, can I say sorry for throwing myself on you in the car? It's just not like me at all. I'm…dating someone, so I should have behaved differently, but you were so…heroic and—" Savannah covered her face with her hands momentarily then continued. "I promise I'm not a horrible person. Also, thanks for saving my life. Twice. And thank you for killing that…monster." She squeezed her thighs with her fingertips and forced what looked like a well of tears to stay in her eyes.

He was stunned. He took her chin in his hand, so she'd look directly at him. "You have nothing to apologize for. And about the man, pretty soon you'll just think about it once an hour, then once a day, and then once a week. All that fear will go away eventually."

She scrunched her nose. "It doesn't seem like it's worked that way for you, and it's never worked for me, either."

He gritted his teeth.

Don't engage, Joe. Don't get personally involved. Don't fall for her…any harder than you already are.

That's what he repeated in his head as he robotically pulled his Glock out of the hip holster and disassembled it. She might've figured he was crazy. It was his best attempt to draw his attention from Savannah and his past. But it wasn't working. His parents and Nadine had been his family, but they'd known him the way his team had, mostly because he'd never given them the chance. But his guys, they were his brothers. And they were all gone. Except Clark.

"I'm not lying, Savannah," he said, slipping the slide onto the gun again. "I will kill all your monsters, so you never have to wonder what's hiding in the darkness. But me? I'm not dealing with fear, and I don't get scared. My pain isn't going anywhere. Ghosts don't bleed." He slammed the magazine back in, chambered a round, and holstered the Glock again. His throat was thick, and he couldn't swallow. An escape. He needed to escape. He could fall apart after Savannah was gone. Pulling the cap down low over his eyes, he walked to the door, but she jumped up and ran over to him, her hands stroking his tattooed arm. Not really in a sexy way, more comforting, because that's who she was. He just…couldn't.

"I'm a good listener. Talk to me. I won't judge. Trust me." Savannah's voice cracked. "I know about…regret." How could she pinpoint that emotion when he hadn't said anything? Maybe there was a good reason why she left fancy brunches and maid service for the slums. But right now, it didn't matter. He grabbed the doorknob, chest burning. He had to get out quick. Savannah slammed her hand on the door to stop him. "Please."

This was going to hurt. Either her or him. And his mind couldn't afford the airfare to Afghanistan right now. He cringed but jerked open the door as she stumbled backwards on her bare feet. "Back off. Please. One kiss doesn't mean you know me, and I don't want you to. This isn't therapy. Solve your boyfriend's problems instead. Sorry, princess." He slammed the door and grimaced. He wanted her to back off, but never meant to use the word *princess* or throw her boyfriend back in her face. Savannah was going to be hysterical, and he was going to have to live with hurting her. His heart pulled him back toward the hotel room, but his feet were moving the opposite direction.

He'd known all along he wasn't good enough for her, and now he'd proved it. The only positive was she'd be there when he got back. She would hate him, yes, but Clark had given his men explicit instructions: it was too dangerous to let anyone in or out until they returned. So, now he just needed some target practice at the soup kitchen to take the edge off before he came back to say goodbye.

CHAPTER NINE
Savannah

Joe had PTSD. She knew it, even if he didn't, because she traveled down a similar path after Cole left home and disappeared. But that word *princess* sent her hurling into the corner of her hotel room with the TV and all the lights on. She needed to breathe, but it felt like an anchor was slammed on her chest, weighing her down and collapsing her lungs. She rocked back and forth on her butt as pain burned through her arms like lightning. Footsteps from two small children raced up and down the hall just past the wall to her left. She tried to breathe again, but the smell of detergent made her throat close up.

Ponytail was dead. But his words were like clammy fingers against her skin, brushing up her spine and across her neck. How could he have that power over her?

"Breathe. Come on. It'll pass. Pr-princess is just a word. Breathe."

The breaths poured raggedly through her mouth, so she didn't smell the sheets. She crawled over to the coffee table on her hands and knees, fingers digging into the deeply woven carpet. She snapped a bloom off the orchid arrangement and laid on her side in the carpet to calm her heartrate. It didn't have much of a scent, not like a rose, but it gave her an object to focus on. Veins ran through each purple petal, leading to an intricate lip speckled with pink dots. She touched each dot, counting: "One, two, three, four, five..."

Rolling to her back, she held the flower up. It was a thing of beauty, but without the support of the plant, the color would fade and the petals would wither. She dropped it on the carpet and rubbed her face.

Joe wants to stop the bad guys. It's his new mission to distract himself from whatever he left in the past. But why am I still here when I have a wonderful guy waiting for me at home? Mom and Dad's place has top-notch security. I could just as easily stay there until this is over. So why am I with Joe? Am I attracted to him, or do I want to fix him?

The latter had always been true. That's why, in the last minute, she'd filled a cup with water from the bathroom sink and dropped her little bloom inside. It was a temporary fix, but it didn't change her compulsions. After Cole, she'd spent every waking moment trying to repair everything and everyone. Joe was her Everest. But it wasn't a good enough reason to stay.

That settled it. After spending her life in the kiddy pool, she was not diving headfirst into chaos. She *had* to go. She snatched her keys off the coffee table, without a clear plan. How was she going to convince the guards to let her out?

She raced to the door and then paused, turning around and dragging her feet back into the center of the room. The keys jingled in her hand as she turned them over and over. Ugh. She slapped herself in the head. Where was her car parked? Snapping on her cell, she ordered an Uber and tossed the keys on the couch.

She whispered to herself, all alone in the hotel room, hand pressed beside her wound to relieve the dull throb. "I am smart, and this situation isn't. There might not be another guy on the planet that gives me the nerve to spontaneously kiss him, but there are easier men. I've already got one. I can help Joe from a distance, if he'll let me, but I can't do this. I need to go to…Mom and Dad's house."

And as if God himself were needing a good laugh over that revelation, a crash of lightning exploded outside, followed by an enormous clap of thunder, which sent her swaying. She grasped a chair, and her lip curved up.

She left a note for Joe on the coffee table and straightened as another Earth-shattering lightning bolt struck. But, this time, she wasn't smiling. It threw out the hotel's power, and she was in the dark, shaking like a leaf. She fumbled across the room to open the blinds, but the inky black clouds weren't much help. They only cast an eerie light across the bed in streaks from the sliver of moon that had freed itself from their grasp. Savannah bit her lip. She had to get out of the room, fast, for try as she might, her childish fear about someone crawling under her bed, waiting to pounce, outweighed any rational thinking.

One of the guards spoke through her door. "Savannah, the lights should be back on in the next few minutes. I'm going to open the door and check on you if you don't mind."

"Okay." Maybe this was an opportunity: appeal to him, promise him some homemade muffins or something, and see if he'd just let her go. Clark would probably fire him.

He turned the knob and opened the door. With the power out, he didn't have to use the key card. She could make out his form, tell he was white and about six feet tall. That was it.

"I'm by the coffee table," she whispered, biting the inside of her cheek. He moved across the room to where she stood.

"Savannah. Are you okay?"

"Honestly, no. I'm terrified of the dark and of this situation. I know Clark trusts you, but I don't even know him, so how can I? This is too much. I need to go."

"I'm sorry, but I can't let you do that." He reached out to her shoulder. "I can stay with you until the lights are back on if that would ease your nerves. I'm Ted, by the way."

Savannah should've known that answer was coming and needed another approach. She wasn't Joe. Her only special skills were keen observation, baking…and maybe first dates.

Still she shook, even though Ted's form was becoming clearer. She felt for the chair by the coffee table, and her hand brushed against something hard and plastic. The fact she even let her fingers linger on its surface was a problem. But she'd pulled Joe's taser from the table and behind her back before her mind got the command. This was the dumbest thing she'd done to date.

"I'm sorry, Ted. Truly." And, as if it would make the impact of a burst of electricity through his body any more bearable, she delicately placed it on his chest before pulling the trigger.

He screamed, gritting his teeth as he dropped to the ground, shaking. Besides the pain, it was the last thing he expected from her. Savannah dropped the taser and fought the temptation to put a pillow under his head. Time was short, and they certainly wouldn't be friends after this, even if she did bake him that batch of muffins.

Luckily, she'd remembered to put back on her tennis shoes before rushing down the hall. Her heart pounded as she slipped into the darkness of a doorway to avoid the security guard shooting to her room after the scream. As soon as he passed, she started running again, whipped open the stairwell door and darted down, with her footsteps echoing beneath her.

She entered the lobby winded and painfully sore, but the sweat on her forehead wasn't from the run. It was solely from the darkness and her aching side, so she sighed happily when the lights flickered on. There were a few people waiting out the power failure from the couches and three guards waiting for her. The Uber was just through the front doors, but the guards already knew what she was up to. They were closing in calmly, with their hands in the air like she was some unruly criminal. Her head tilted to the side. Fine. They had a point. But forget the last five minutes, and she was a very reasonable person.

The nearest was the pale man that parked her car. "Savannah. I understand you're frightened, but you're safe here. Please allow me to personally escort you back to your room." He was close enough now to rest his hand firmly on her shaking arm.

She'd already chosen her path when, against her better judgement, she'd tasered a man in her hotel room. There was no going back to the scene of the crime. This wasn't how she wanted to live, and if Joe was on a killing spree, she couldn't possibly have anything to fear in the outside world.

So, like an insane person had invaded her body, she threw her knee into his groin and ran as he doubled over, heaving. The other two security guards ran after her, but she was fast, sliding into the pine-scented car, with a hand to her stomach, before they got to the doors.

CHAPTER TEN
Joe

Clark had been a sniper before he got out of the Army. At the time, Joe was mad to see him go. They were close. But now, with everyone else dead, he needed him, and thankfully, Clark wasn't going to force the issue with the White House or his parents.

"I'm almost set." Clark came over the ear mic as Joe approached the soup kitchen from a few blocks away. It was nine forty-five in the morning, and he was soaked. He could make out a couple guys huddled under blankets even though visibility was poor. Some distance separated them, but they didn't look familiar. The street was usually full of activity, but people were probably tucked away inside of tents, waiting things out. His ears twitched with each sound not drowned out by the splattering of rain on the ground or the howl of the wind. Lightning tore through the sky and illuminated everything around them for seconds at a time. The storm raged, but everything else was too quiet.

"Something's up, Clark. Take a look and tell me I'm wrong."

Clark shifted into position and peered through his scope. "Oh shit, man. You can't see any of this, right?" He didn't wait for Joe to answer. "Dude, those tents are splattered with blood from the inside, and there are lines of blood down the alley at the corner of the soup kitchen from draggin' bodies. I got two guys sleepin' on opposite sides of the street, fifty yards up. Since they aren't bloody, I'm assuming they're here for us. These aren't some street guys like the last few. This took manpower and skills. I'm talkin' professionals. Mercenaries."

Joe's pulse raced. He'd been dying for some action, but this was risky. These guys were willing to kill anybody that got in their way, and they pulled out the big guns for him. Awesome. He wasn't afraid to die, if that's what it took—never had been. And that wasn't him trying to be all heroic. It was just what it took sometimes for good to triumph over bad.

"I'm not backing down. You with me? I need to see what's in the safe," Joe said.

"Brother, you know I'm not leaving. Gotta bring you back in one piece to Savannah." He laughed.

"That's irrelevant." Joe had his Glock raised as he inched closer to the action, staying in the shadows of the buildings. He'd lost his chance with her, though he never really had one anyway. And even with the looming gunplay at the forefront of his mind, pain was gnawing away inside him.

Clark groaned. "What did you do to screw it up?"

"I don't want to talk about it. It's better this way. My mind is clearer."

"I met her for five minutes, and it seems like she could be the best thing to ever happen to you. Stop screwing up. You're *choosin'* to hide out. You could have her if you wanted it. On another note, it's time to party. Bogey on your right is reachin' for something."

Boom.

The shot rang through the air and practically knocked the guy's head off. Clark was right about the party. The merc across the street leapt up, and Joe shot. Blood spurted out of his chest as he crumbled to the ground. The men he'd killed the last twenty-four hours deserved to die. He'd always be willing to do the dirty work even if it wasn't easy to take a life.

And just like that, six more baddies emerged from hiding places and joined the fun. His heart pounded in his fingertips. There weren't a lot of hiding places, and he was one block from the soup kitchen. He ducked behind a tent and kept shooting. It was the best he had. The rain really started pouring, but it didn't drown out the sound of Clark's rifle.

Boom. Boom. Boom.

Clark took out three, and he got one with a shot to the head. The thunder came in waves behind the blasts, giving them an extra window before the cops headed over. But another shot was fired, and it didn't come from Clark. In fact, it was aimed *at* Clark. "Joe, give me a minute to find a new position. I'm under fire. They got their own sniper out here. Just clocked him on top of a building one hundred and fifty meters away. Whatever this is, we might be outgunned, man, but I'll ride it out with ya."

"Let's do this." Joe was sopping and cold, aiming at the last guy standing between him and the soup kitchen as the sniper's bullet tore through his slim backpack. Sweat exploded on his face. Even with the rain, its presence was obvious. His heart beat visibly under the shirt plastered to his chest as he leapt behind a nearby dumpster and retrieved two smoke grenades from his vest. He had to get in the building, and his stupid hands were shaking angrily. He was pinned down while they were no doubt emptying the safe and taking his only lead.

From the angle the bullet came, missing the skin by a tenth of an inch, their sniper was planning to take him out before he got inside. If he could just get past the other guy, he'd be set, and Clark could take care of the rest. They would never consider he'd bring his own sniper, but he'd learned years ago to never leave home without one.

He gave his heart a second to slow and was ready to toss out the grenades and run, when his ears twitched again. Boots were approaching. He wasn't scared. Hand to hand combat, tactical awareness, shooting: it was second nature. Had to be, growing up, since his old man had him hunting at four and running homemade Q-courses at eight. *"That Green Beret's in our blood, son,"* his dad said about a million times, and he had just nodded, picked up his rucksack, and followed him through the woods because, God love him, his dad had never taken note of the obvious.

The last baddie rounded the corner. He was shorter than Joe, at almost six feet, muscled up, with a crew cut and a vest full of high-dollar equipment. Best guess was ex-military turned merc, with a swagger that would only annoy him for thirty more seconds, tops.

With his gun in his right hand, he jerked the merc around the corner, plowing his elbow into the man's chin. It crunched, but he kept moving, unfazed as his gun dropped. He punched Joe across the face before Joe could get a shot off. That punch made him see stars, but he managed to fire into the man's foot before they both lost their guns. His senses were focused on the fight. All Joe could hear was the man's scream as he fell to the ground and wrapped his hand around the grip of his Glock. He flipped over and shot twice as the man came down on him with a knife.

The shot was messy from this close up, leaving the guy with no choice but a closed casket funeral. Joe was covered in blood, and his adrenaline shot through the roof. It took a second to realize the bulky mercenary on top of him had gotten a knife into his thigh before he offed him.

He heaved the dead weight off his chest as another pair of boots caught his attention. His ears were still adjusting back to the storm and everything further than a one-foot radius. His gun was up in a flash. But it was Clark. Thank God. He tried standing as Clark talked to him and wrapped his leg.

"Joe!" Clark slapped him in the face. That did the trick.

"Where's the other sniper?"

Clark was tying off the bandage as he stuck the dead guy's Colt 1911 into the waistband of his pants. "You didn't hear the shot? I popped him, so let's get movin'. We're wasting daylight on that papercut." He laughed as Joe rifled through the man's pockets and tucked his wallet and cell into the pack on his back. Clark raised his rifle, and they moved toward the door together, just like the old days.

The rain stopped while they made the thirty second trek, like eerie, snap-of-your-fingers, sunny-day voodoo. He could feel the sudden worry radiating from Clark, though you'd never know just by looking at him. The bell chirped as he pushed the soup kitchen door open. He ripped it down. It gave away their location and reminded him of Savannah. But now it was quiet again. In his experience, quietness meant something was about to go to Hell in a handbasket.

This time, the quiet was just good, old-fashioned quiet. They combed the place, and it was empty. The backdoor was still swinging, and wet footprints made a beeline out the door. If that wasn't enough, Clark had some kind of super-smeller nose and could pick out the scent of cocoa butter and Axe bodywash. It came in handy in Afghanistan, too, though nobody there smelled good.

Pots and pans hung from the kitchen ceiling, and the cabinets overflowed with food. Savannah had pictures on the wall of dozens of homeless people he'd seen on the streets, though Allen was the only one he spent time with. Her arms would be wrapped tightly around them, or they'd be sitting at a table together, enjoying a cup of coffee. She cared.

But for the biggest surprise of the day, Clark was left open-mouthed. These guys, with all their high-tech goodies, hadn't gotten in Savannah's safe. He couldn't be sure why they'd run and not fought them to the bloody end, but he'd take what he could get. His best guess was the sheer magnitude of the thing. They would've been scratching their chins if he hadn't gotten the combo from Savannah. Her rich parents probably picked it out and had it installed: half safe, half safe room. It was a thing of beauty.

It didn't take long to get in and find the envelope. He tore it open, and Clark hovered by the doorway to the safe, rifle drawn. There were only two things inside, and neither of them were the names and locations of the men he was meant to hunt down. One was a box marked for Savannah, but he opened it anyway. It was Allen's Purple Heart. The other was marked for him. A note. He cracked his neck and unfolded it.

Joe,

If you're readin' this, then I'm dead, so I'm not gonna linger on the fact you're here seein' this thing through when you should have snatched up Savannah and run back to DC. You got connections there, and if you really want to end this, you'll need 'em.

Don't go to the police.

Some of the people on the street started going missin' the last few weeks. Heard one say he was makin' money and knew it wasn't anything good. I followed him. Took a video. One of 'em had a business card with a green triangle.

They're makin' drugs and sellin' 'em on a big scale. They've been chasin' me down since they spotted me there. And don't get self-righteous on me about how you could'a helped. Your life is more important than you think, and I didn't want you anywhere near this. These guys have deep pockets and a wide reach. So, I'll say it again: Don't trust the cops. Just don't trust anyone. Get out before it's too late.

And Joe? You do *deserve her.*

-Allen

He folded the note and slid it into his bag. Allen was gone, and that made his chest hurt. He could've helped, but Allen always had a reason. He slipped the box with the medal into his bag too. But where was the video he'd taken?

It was time to get moving, so they both raised their guns and headed for the backdoor. Clark grabbed his arm to stop him a few feet short of the exit and answered his cell. "What? Yeah, I heard you. I'm just surprised. She's one tiny woman!"

Joe froze. Savannah was gone, and apparently in epic fashion. As much as he would've liked to watch her make a run for it, there was a bigger problem. She was out in L.A. without protection. His mind swam with worry as he rushed out the backdoor and into the barrel of a gun.

Five men stood in front of him, dressed in the same expensive gear as the other merc. The guy's team. Duh.

The sun shone high in the sky now, heating the alley and burning it with the stench of fish. The guy whose gun dug into his chest wagged two fingers in the air, and two men broke off and entered the soup kitchen. "Come back with that sniper. And you," he snarled through a gap in his front teeth, "Give us the video and we'll let you out of here alive."

Joe laughed even though the man looked like a modern-day Goliath, with arms so burly they couldn't lie against his sides. "Yeah. Clearly, you're decent guys. I mean, you didn't just massacre a street full of people or anything. So, I should definitely take you at your word, right?"

Goliath drowned Joe's voice out with his own booming baritone. "Look, fellas. We got ourselves a tough guy, but unless you're strapped with a bomb, I'd shut up. Or maybe I could do the world a favor and blow your sorry ass back to Afghanistan and look through your bag myself."

Goliath nodded to the last two guys, and they dumped all of his belongings on the wet concrete, pilfering through them. Any comment could set off Goliath's trigger finger, but his face burned with anger, and he couldn't help himself. "What you lack in brain, you must make up for in muscle. I'm Lebanese, by the way. If anyone qualifies as a terrorist, it's you, killing innocent civilians for your criminal boss."

Goliath growled, his ears magenta. Joe's eyes were on the trigger as Goliath's finger pulled tighter. The gun would go off any second, and he couldn't fight back. One hundred extra pounds on a well-trained opponent would mean failure. A shot to the chest would too, but there were still a few seconds to play with. The other two men were beneath him, frantically searching the sidewalk and coming up short. "Lebanese, Afghani, whatever. You've outrun your usefulness."

And a gun went off. But it wasn't the one pressed against his rapidly beating heart. It came from inside. Instead of squeezing the trigger like he would have done, Goliath's pressure lessened. He took his chance.

He jerked and then snapped the wrist of the hand grasping the gun, and Goliath howled, wrapping a tree-sized arm around Joe's neck, but not before the two shocked men on the ground got matching head shots.

Another blast came from the kitchen. Two shots, three seconds apart, meant Clark was likely alive, but could he get here in time? The sunny day burned his vision into pure white. Joe panted and struggled to shoot the gun, but Goliath knocked the gun across the concrete and continued to squeeze. He kicked, trying to force the heel of his foot into a pressure point on Goliath's leg, but Goliath didn't even react. He was built like a brick wall.

Joe's head felt like it was going to pop off from the pressure, and he was out of tricks. Dying here wasn't an option. It wasn't, but he wasn't strong enough. As everything tunneled into darkness, Goliath's mouth rested against his ear, enveloping him in coffee. "And now for the little blonde girl. Boss has something special planned for her. It'd make your skin crawl if you were gonna live to see it."

Fury poured through every vein in his body, but it wasn't enough. His arms and legs couldn't move anymore. His heart pounded slowly, his head fuzzy, overtaking every other emotion. Joe collapsed on the concrete between the two bloody corpses before a final gunshot rang out.

CHAPTER ELEVEN
Savannah

Savannah's heart beat faster with every one of the ten steps she took from her Uber toward the wrought-iron gate of her parents' estate. Clarence, their head of security, was already waving and pushing the button to let her in as he stood in his hut with the security monitors. He looked the same, with a bit more white in his curly black hair than last time she'd visited. Since childhood, she'd loved him, especially since he was from Savannah, Georgia.

She'd been home twenty-six times in the last thirteen years: Christmas and the Fourth of July. She still saw her parents for brunch every two weeks, where she'd stuff down a plate of eggs benedict between twenty photos of potential dates her mom shoved under her nose. Dating Holden made brunch easier. But home? No. It wasn't worth the heartache.

Yet the series of events over the last twelve hours spurred an action in her she would have never imagined. It wasn't the Fourth or Christmas, and here she was, wrapping the arm of her good side around Clarence, while inhaling his musky aftershave.

"Savannah, your parents'll be thrilled you made it, but take it easy. You've been injured. I can walk you inside."

She smiled. Her eyes drifted into the corner of his little hut and filled with tears.

"I believe you must'a been eight before you figured out this was Cole's spot during hide and seek." Clarence sighed and eyed the ground.

No one ever brought her brother up, but her heart swelled at his name. She squeezed Clarence's veiny hands and made eye contact. "Thank you for remembering. It means more than you know. I'll find him one day. I can…sense him out there."

He brushed a blonde curl from her face. "Yes, ma'am, you will. That feeling's a twin thing, I reckon."

A scream erupted from the driveway, and she dropped Clarence's hands. Her insides froze, and her head jerked around. She wasn't looking for the source of the scream; she was looking for Joe. Not just because she was scared, but because she missed how safe she felt with him, which was pathetic.

Her eyes caught sight of her mother, half happy, half mortified. She was running at warp speed for a woman in stilettos. Her father hadn't come out. It wasn't a surprise. He was undoubtedly locked in his office, closing a business deal.

She reached out to hug her mother, who arrived within the next thirty seconds. Her mother pulled back, Savannah's tank top between her fingers like a slithering snake. "Darling, it's not Halloween. What possessed you to wear this?"

She rolled her eyes. Maybe this was a bad idea.

Her mother turned and began sprinting again as she yelled for Annika. Savannah drifted toward home slower, dragging her feet through the lawn, trying to blink away the dull ache that had taken the place of the throbbing in her stomach. An improvement.

Her gaze shifted to the enormous tire swing hanging from a tree-sized branch of an old Moreton Bay Fig. She and Cole would lie there in the evenings, flat on their backs, watching the sky turn dark through the leaves. Cole told her everything, but like a typical teenage girl, she'd missed the important details and clung to the laughter.

They'd been there the night it happened, Cole's eyes crinkling on the sides the way they always did when he was hurting.

"Something's up. Spill."

"Do you think Dad ever watches the sun set?"

She'd held her arms behind her head as they floated back and forth, shadows dancing over her tanned shoulders. "Yeah, maybe as a clock. Like he peeks out the window of his office and says, 'Oh, dinner time. Maybe I'll stop talking to my clients about work and talk to my family about it." She'd leaned farther back, her fingers brushing the grass as she giggled.

Cole had jerked upright, his fingers tapping restlessly against her knee. He'd always tapped his fingers on whatever was closest. Usually her. "Yeah, I was afraid of that. I...I gotta run upstairs for a bit. Don't be late for dinner."

And she hadn't been, but Cole had missed the steak and mashed potatoes that night and every dinner since. It wasn't just the dinner. It was that he hadn't said anything. He'd run away and cut himself from her life in a way that felt like she'd lost half of her identity.

Her mother left the door open but was nowhere to be seen. Her screeches in the kitchen gave away her location. The house—no, the mansion—Savannah grew up in was charming but on a massive scale. Her mother had an eye for detail, opting for a mid-century modern design years before it made a comeback. She appeared, much less sweaty than she should have been, and swept Savannah through the entryway and up the bamboo steps, past dozens of abstract artworks filling in the places that used to hold family photos. Now the only places you'd find those were the bedrooms.

With the help of Annika, she was prodded and primped within an inch of her life, but at least she got to sit down. Holden would be arriving within the hour. There was no sense in arguing over eye shadow or hairstyle. She was outnumbered. Her mother and Annika were both convinced this was *the* date. The one where Holden would get down on one knee. Two months wasn't long enough to make a decision to last a lifetime. Maybe two years? Or maybe... Maybe he wasn't the one.

Now, dusted head to toe with some shimmering powder, she snuck into her dad's office for a momentary escape. It was heavy with bookshelves, navy velvet curtains, and a desk intricately carved out of mahogany: the only place her mother hadn't touched, at least without the help of a decorator.

Her dad sat at his desk, running two hands over his slicked-down gray hair. The seams of his blue, plaid suit jacket strained over his hunched shoulders. The Chief of Police, a friend of the family, sat in one of the two chairs across from him, pinching the bridge of his oversized nose and turning it red. Her back immediately heated, her head breaking into an all-out sweat. This wasn't an escape after all. It was going to be an inquisition.

"Good, you're here. Sit." Her dad's lips drew tight as he pointed a narrow finger at a leather chair.

She plopped into it obediently, interlacing the fingers of her torn hands. Her head was down, but she looked up nervously through her eyelashes from one man to the other. Her dad wasn't a big man, far from it, but when he spoke up, everyone listened. The muscles in her stomach clenched.

"You know Chief Rollings and why he's here, so I'll let him start. Be honest with him about everything, and don't leave your chair until I say we're done. Holden Forsyth will be here soon, and we have an image to uphold. Your mother would be frantic if the police hauled you away to prison, so be incredibly grateful Rollings is a friend and is willing to hear your side of things."

Her dad only got angry on special occasions, and today was one of them. Her fingers instinctively traced the scar, now scars, on her stomach as she turned her attention his way. She tried looking in Chief Rollings's eyes, but the rifle mounted on the wall behind his head was crooked, about a fifth of an inch off its mark. It was going to be a distraction. The Chief pulled a pen and notebook from his pocket and huffed, his mid-section jiggling. Other than the attempt to cover his age with Botox and tanning, he wasn't bad looking, though his expressionless face was hard to read. He'd spent the majority of his career cultivating relationships with wealthy families and less time actually doing his job. And it was Savannah's lucky day in that regard, but her eyes still cut in his direction, because she'd already be locked up if she was poor.

"Savannah, let's begin with the fact you neglected to sign your discharge papers at the hospital, which wouldn't be a huge concern if a dead man wasn't left in your bathroom. Then there's the mystery of the missing security footage during the time of your departure, the man you were brought in with dying unexpectedly, and thirty-seven people found dead within a block of your soup kitchen. My men are busy with this mess that you seem to be in the middle of."

She couldn't consider how wild she must seem in their eyes, one hand twirling her hair and the other still on her stomach, beads of sweat rolling down her temples in a very unladylike way, and the sound of her rapid breaths filling the room as the men waited for an answer. She stared at the rifle, so she didn't have to look at her dad and Rollings, pulling three distinct thoughts together. One: Allen said she couldn't trust anyone, so did her father and the police count? Two, which of her patrons, her friends, had been killed? And three, if thirty-seven people were dead outside her soup kitchen, was Joe one of them? Tears welled up. She barely knew him, but whether it made any sense or not, she still wanted to.

Chief Rolling's eyebrows were raised, though she guessed he was shooting for impatience. "Savannah, clearly you know more than you're sharing, so I'll just continue." He snatched the remote to her father's small flat screen and clicked it on. The news was running the feed from outside the soup kitchen, but she couldn't focus on the commentary for all the blood. She leapt from the chair and knelt on the floor in front of the TV, searching for Joe's body.

Her father's hand rested on her shoulder, and she slowed her tears and intertwined her fingers so her shaking wouldn't alarm the men. She couldn't form words.

And then the screen changed. A man's picture appeared. Army blues and black hair high and tight. Clean-shaven face revealing full lips and straight teeth. And the eyes. No one in the world had Joe's eyes. She recognized him instantly.

Chief Rollings muted the television, but she couldn't take her eyes off his face and the three pictures circulating in a rotation with him.

"So, I take it you've met Yosef MacArthur?"

Savannah looked down. Her tears stopped, and her hands wrapped around the TV. "Yes…I know Joe. Why?" Her father guided her back to her chair as Chief Rollings continued.

"So, he goes by Joe? That's something, at least, but I'm asking the questions, Savannah. You haven't offered anything, and until you do, I won't either." He pushed the button on the remote, and the screen went black.

"I just need to know—I have to know. Is Joe alive?"

Chief Rollings tapped the pen on his notepad. "This isn't a one-way street, Savannah."

Her jaw clenched. She was going to have to share something if she wanted answers. "Fine. Someone attacked me and Allen in an alley. The cops already know this. Joe saved me. One man got away and came back to the hospital after the attack. I told the cops he'd threatened me, and I guess he meant it. He must've turned off the security cameras when he attacked Allen. Luckily, before he could kill me, Joe saved me again. That's what I know. All I know. He's a hero. Now tell me if he's alive."

Her dad spoke from behind the desk as Rollings cringed. "Give her something, Ted. She's been through an ordeal, and she's told you all she knows. We've got minutes to wrap this up and get Savannah cleaned up again for her date."

Chief Rollings eyed her father and nodded. He wasn't up for a fight with Martin Carrington, which was a prudent choice. "He's not one of the dead. Eight months ago, after a tragic mission in Afghanistan, the White House chose to award Yosef MacArthur the Medal of Honor. But he went missing. His house was ransacked, and traces of blood were found. The White House, Pentagon, and his family have been searching tirelessly for him. Then, today, at L.A. Med Center, of all places, a little boy spotted him...with you. It seemed a miracle, until the bodies began piling up. The rounds fired in the alley match multiple bodies at the soup kitchen. And, as you said, he killed the man in your hospital room. We fear something has snapped in his mind. He was suffering from PTSD after returning home. He's a Green Beret and a trained killer. Yosef is dangerous, and he won't stop killing unless we catch him. If you know where he is, you need to give him up."

She fought tears back because she'd just stopped crying thirty seconds before, and it was embarrassing to be the only emotional one in the room. Her stitches throbbed but held firm, the only part of her that did. She was a good judge of character, wasn't she? Or was she just fooled by a man she wanted to see a certain way? He had been aggressive with her, after all. But a wild man on a rampage? No, it couldn't be... Could it?

Her stomach flopped, but until she knew anything with certainty, she wasn't giving Joe up. He'd be one step ahead anyway. He wouldn't go back to the hotel with them looking.

"Savannah?" Her father asked, and she turned to face him. "Your mother said you were with some man named Joe earlier. Luckily, she isn't familiar with these details. Do you know where he is? You heard Chief Rollings. He's dangerous. You saw his picture. He could be a...terrorist."

She gritted her teeth. Criminal or hero, it didn't matter to her dad, if Joe's skin color and bank account weren't his idea of pristine. She rose and shook the chief's hand, back stiff and invisible steam pouring from her ears. "He's no terrorist. And by the way, Dad, lots of white men are terrorists."

Her father's face flushed. Savannah hadn't talked back to him in her thirty years, but she was building to a point of exploding with all the things she'd never said. And she felt protective of Joe for some reason.

She bit her lip and turned to Rollings, whose face hadn't changed expression at all. "Thank you for coming to us first, Chief. I appreciate your kindness. I have no idea where Joe is. But I do know Holden Forsyth will be here in thirty minutes, and I won't keep him waiting." She forced a society smile and ran upstairs before her mother caught sight of her and beat her down with questions.

Her bedroom changed nearly every season, even though she hadn't lived at home in over a decade. It was in the same location, so she wasn't too confused. She peeked in: pale blue walls and canvas paintings over an upholstered bed. She didn't linger, just grabbed some makeup off the vanity table and drifted one door down.

Cole's room had experienced less change than hers. Maybe because she'd taken most of her things when she moved out at eighteen, and Cole never got the chance. And maybe it was because her mom needed to leave one thing at home that reminded her of her son. His bookshelves were still full, guitars on the wall. Stories and music brought him peace during those years he was sick before the surgery. While she had jumped at the opportunity to save her twin, she'd prepared for losing a kidney differently, spending her summer bikini clad at every pool around town.

She'd been vain and insecure, worried that, after the surgery, her stomach would never be as "pretty" as it was then. Cole's departure gave her the kick in the butt she'd needed to change her ways.

She plopped into the leather chair at Cole's desk by the window and tidied up the knick-knacks her mother stacked there. What was the purpose of four tiny boxes and a plant with no roots? The linen curtains were open, revealing the expansive lawn as she laid out an array of makeup purchased specifically for today to compliment the blue dress her mother picked out.

Beyond their property and across the street were rows of pine and oak trees that backed to the yards of the next estates. She propped her chin into her hands and let her eyes unfocus and wander. How had one kind but reckless act gotten her here? Maybe a date with Holden was just what she needed: mindless chatter and no danger, since Joe killed everyone in a one block radius of the soup kitchen. She shivered and pushed away the image. He couldn't have done that. It had to be the men after them. Either way, she felt sick.

Dating Holden was simple and left no swirling nausea in her stomach. Also, for the sake of her mental health, she needed him. Maybe she could find passion with Holden and, given time, even forget the warmth of Joe's lips against hers.

CHAPTER TWELVE
Joe

J oe woke in a wood-paneled back room of a doctor's office, with a boot to his side. Clark was two feet away, grinning at him from his seat in a rolling chair. "Wake up, Sleepin' Beauty. You haven't lost that much blood, and you're all stitched up now. Let's get going."

He rubbed his eyes and cringed at the pain in his leg. As his vision expanded to the entire room, he clocked a white-haired doctor moving around his left side. "Take these." Dr. Richards, according to the plastic name tag, offered two white pills and leaned against the counter with his arms crossed. "You're lucky this little *kitchen accident* wasn't worse. Quarter inch to the left, and you wouldn't have made it across town to me." He cut his eyes at Clark.

Clark threw his hands up and chuckled. "Poor guy knows he'll never look like me. He was just tryin' to build a talent of some kind, Doc."

Doctor Richards groaned, pulling his white coat tight around his chest before heading out the flimsy door covered in a poster of the human body. He turned back once more before closing it behind him. "Take the back door, Clark. His face is all over the news."

Clark wrapped a hand around something in his pocket and pulled. It was Allen's medal. "So, you gonna give this to Savannah or not? You can jump outta C-130s behind enemy lines, but you can't open your mouth and talk to her? She isn't the first girl you've ever met."

Joe cracked his neck and climbed off the table. That was true, but past the necessary small talk it took to pick up a girl at a bar, he was a crap communicator. He and Nadine had hardly ever spoken about anything important. It was hard to connect with anyone when dangerous situations felt normal and normal situations felt dangerous. Overseas, staying calm and collected in a war zone made others view him as a leader. At home, in everyday scenarios, his behavior seemed distant or erratic. He snatched the medal and stretched his back. "Savannah needs to get back to her life. Stop pushing. I'll keep an eye on her for a couple more days to make sure it's over, and then I'm getting out of town for good. I'm not going to DC, so don't even bring it up."

Clark rolled his eyes. "So, you'll just sit on the long gun, creepily watching her every move in case something happens. That seems healthy."

His fingers twitched. Clark could talk all he wanted to, but it wasn't going to change anything. He didn't deserve Savannah. She'd be better off with rich-boy-billionaire Holden. He limped by Clark and out the back door of the clinic, with his Glock raised.

Clark grabbed his arm and squeezed tight, whispering in his ear. "You're a good soldier, Joe Mac, and a good man. You've just never believed it, and after Afghanistan you found a lot more reasons to blame yourself for everything. I know I joke a lot; that's my way of coping. Yours is bein' hyper-vigilant. But you can't help Savannah if you're dead."

There was no way he'd tell Clark he was right and be forced to endure his ego exploding on the spot. So, he just nudged him like a twelve-year-old girl and walked into the daylight. Everything was calm, not even a breeze rustling the branches of the few trees nearby. They crossed the street to a black Ford Taurus one of Clark's security team guys had dropped off. None of them knew much about the situation, just wanted to be involved somehow, because it kept things more interesting than hotel security and the odd job as a bodyguard for a celebrity. They were proving incredibly helpful at everything except sequestering Savannah.

They shot down the street, with Clark behind the wheel singing an old country tune. Joe wasn't joining in, so there was plenty of time to think about the soup kitchen. Yeah, he'd almost died just an hour ago, and his neck still throbbed from the giant meat hook cutting off his air, but he was a warrior, and those feelings were no more important than someone tapping on your shoulder. However, the black SUV that turned onto the highway two exits back and lingered a car length behind was a very real concern.

"What'd you think? The Pentagon? Too obvious to be more of the mercs we just took out. This car wants us to know they're there."

Clark handed over a pair of binoculars from the glovebox. "Probably. Get a better look at 'em."

Joe turned and focused the binoculars into the tinted window. Four men in black suits stared ahead. There were even briefcases on two of the guys' laps. He laughed. The suits had tracked him down first, which was a huge surprise considering his dad was probably parachuting into L.A after the news went forward with their story of who he was. They turned off the highway and headed into a residential part of town. "When we round this corner, slow down and let me out."

"This is getting ridiculous, Ace. You know they could help."

Eyebrows pinching together, he grasped the handle of the door in his palm. "Yeah, not before I sit around answering questions for the next two days. You're not stupid. We still don't know for sure that we got all the guys looking for Savannah. She could get killed if I go with them."

He launched open the door and fought the pressure of the incoming wind forcing it back toward him like a tank. They hit the curve going about twenty, and he leapt out with his punctured pack and rifle thrust out in front of him. The air hit him like a wall and knocked him a foot from where he planned, but he rolled and ran behind some bushes despite the wetness on his thigh where his stitches tore. Savannah's house was about a mile and a half from where he jumped, which wasn't too bad on most days, considering he'd hauled ninety-pound rucksacks for fifteen miles at a time. But today his leg trickled blood like a broken fountain, and his breath was still strained coming up his throat.

Thirteen minutes later, he was lying in a wooded knoll across the street from Savannah's family estate, with his eye in the scope of Clark's modified M14. From this vantage point, Savannah's face was clear through a window on the second floor. She was at a desk, daydreaming or maybe considering what an idiot he was. She was beautiful.

He took out his cell, even though it was stupid, and typed a message to her. As wrong as it was for them both, he needed an excuse to see her one last time. Meeting to give her Allen's medal would be that chance. His finger hovered over the green button, sweating, though the rest of him was dry. His finger lowered. He kept his eye against the scope.

Savannah got the message. She held her phone up and twirled her hair. The seconds of waiting felt like an eternity. Then his phone vibrated. Before he peeled his eyes off the scope, Savannah wiped away a tear and disappeared.

The rifle balanced on his shoulder as he looked down. He didn't have to. The tear said enough, but he always punished himself rather than fighting for what he wanted. Except freedom. For some reason, he always found courage for Uncle Sam.

I can't meet with you right now. Holden is taking me out this afternoon. I'm sorry.

But I should tell you, the cops know who you are, and they think you've lost it. I disagree, but it's best to keep our distance. Be cautious.

If the engine of a fancy sportscar hadn't turned into Savannah's estate at that minute, he would've crushed the phone against a nearby rock, which would have been stupid. He shot a text to Clark with his thumb while pressing his eye back in the scope and adjusting.

Meet me at the next street over in five.

A guy stepped from the car: about his age but no scars or wrinkles, just a head full of meticulously combed blond hair. Holden. He'd had an easy life and spent a good deal of it in the gym based on the carefully toned muscles. Holden probably even shaved his chest.

Joe got his strength from actual work. He gripped the rifle and his nose scrunched. The guy exuded such a strong vibe of arrogance that Clark's super nose was getting a whiff of it, wherever he was.

Savannah was out the front door moments later, in a blue sundress that was tight around her waist and floated over her hips in the breeze. She pushed her mom back inside as she attempted a clean getaway, walking to the guy and standing on her tiptoes to accept a kiss as he leaned down. He twirled her hair around his finger and laughed before guiding her to the passenger door of his car.

Joe's fingers twitched, and his back was on fire. He could make the shot from here and drop Holden. He shook his head and threw the rifle down. That jumped past jealousy and all the way to crazy, but something about Holden rubbed him the wrong way. And his head was getting heavy.

He rolled over, a thick pool of blood in the grass beneath him. His leg. He'd stayed too long. His fingers deftly packed away the rifle. They didn't need help from his brain for that task. Tossing everything on his back, he started running. Allen's medal beat against his thigh, moving with the mesh lining of his pocket. The trees turned fuzzy in his peripheral vision. Allen's face popped into his head. Where had he stashed the video he mentioned in his note? He couldn't leave until all the loose ends were tied up. It might shine light on something he'd missed. He pumped his arms and forced both eyelids to stay up.

Clark would be waiting at the street only fifty yards away and probably expected Joe would need a repeat visit with Doctor Richards after his impromptu jump. He'd done the right thing. It was that or be forced to go with the suits.

A fence outlining the backyard of an estate lay just feet ahead, and the street was to the left. He fixed his eyes forward when something zipped through the air behind him. Unfortunately, he knew the sound of a silenced round fired from a pistol all too well. The medal thumped quietly as he tucked behind a pine, but besides the whirring, that's all he could hear. The trees weren't as sharp, their leaves and needles forming one giant canopy as two birds darted around above him, cawing silently.

He was down low, leg dripping red into the green grass as he ripped his shirt and tied it around his thigh. A bullet sent bark crumbling onto his head and shoulders. Eyes blinking rapidly, he brought his surroundings into a clarity that could only come with years of training, after this much blood loss.

Seconds later his body relaxed into the comfort of steel under his fingertips. He turned to shoot the fool that came after him alone. Whoever they were, he was going to end them. They knew where Savannah lived, not that the next hopeful assassin couldn't get their hands on the same information.

He scoured the woods with his eyes but couldn't see anyone. Must've run for it. Smart, considering he was ten seconds away from lodging a bullet between their eyes.

CHAPTER THIRTEEN
Savannah

The candlelight from their table flickered across Holden's face, and Savannah sighed, her stomach and mind surprisingly calm. She forced her lips to stay put and not curl up at the thought of the day they'd shared as she fiddled with the black cloth napkin in her lap.

As soon as he wheeled down the drive in his noisy Maserati, she'd inwardly recoiled, envisioning their future, riding over to the club to eat pretentious food and discuss summer homes. It hadn't lasted long though. He'd leaned across the console, eyes bright, and said the day was about her. Anything she wanted to do.

Perfect. What she really wanted was to sleep in her own bed. That was currently her idea of a dream date and was exactly what they had done. Despite the wrinkles that would form in her dress, she'd plopped down on her Memory Foam mattress and slept the afternoon away while Holden worked on his phone and apparently on her apartment as well, since the kitchen was shiny and citrus-smelling when she woke. He'd promised to describe some Dahlia Carrington-worthy afternoon to her parents when he dropped her back at the estate later, since her dad had texted saying Chief Rollings would be back with more questions.

The hour after she woke, they'd just curled on the couch together to talk. Holden loved talking and laughing. She'd just never let herself enjoy it because she wasn't supposed to like him. Right? But after all the chaos with Joe and the horror of the attack emptying her emotional reserve, she granted herself that much…and the delicious food she was gobbling down over the dinner he'd taken her out for. They'd chatted about their favorite vacations, books, and movies. They even talked cookies and cheeseburgers. He probably ran ten miles after eating either, but it was refreshing and kept her in a good headspace.

And now, under the dim lights and checkered tablecloths at a local Italian dive, she was actually relaxed and barely thinking of Joe. Until Holden finally brought it all up.

"I owe you an apology, Savannah. I shouldn't have left you alone at the soup kitchen yesterday. I feel responsible. I'm so sorry and truly impressed with how well you've handled everything. If you want to talk about it, I've been told I'm an excellent listener."

Holden busted out his million-dollar smile, and she couldn't help but laugh. But to talk about everything? Just having him ask sent visions of the alley and the smell of Ponytail's breath on a sprint around her subconscious. A feeling she'd avoided the last six hours.

He was right. It was personal, but the attack wasn't his fault, and there was no time like the present to let down a few walls. He wasn't Joe. This tale wouldn't push the ON button to his hunter switch. He didn't have one anyway.

The waiter removed two empty bowls of spaghetti from their table and began to lay the bill down. Holden took his arm and thrust three crisp one hundred dollars bills into his open palm. "Thanks for the meal. Keep the change, and good luck with college this semester." The boy's mouth hung open as he stuttered out a thank you for his supremely generous tip and stumbled back to the kitchen.

Holden might have done that out of the goodness of his heart or solely to impress her, but either way, he'd done it. And like she'd witnessed throughout their time together, he was a very generous man. That kid hadn't expected a two-hundred-and-fifty-dollar tip for mentioning he was working his way through college because his parents weren't around. It was just a matter-of-fact response to Holden's questions as he dropped off their salads. But the joy in the kid's eyes was one of the reasons she started the soup kitchen. She wanted people to know their value no matter their circumstances. And there was the other reason: the hope that one day Cole would walk through the door.

Without the lingering scent of marinara, Holden's piney cologne pierced the air again. His eyes were fixed on hers, little flecks of gold mixed with the blue. Her gaze wandered from him to the other three tables close enough to hear her musings. She bit her lip.

Holden reached across the table and took her hand, sending a rush of warmth to her cheeks. "Forget I asked. Let's get out of here, yeah?"

Savannah nodded, and Holden guided her to the glass front door of the restaurant, bold red font sprawled across it with the words *Antonio's Italian Eatery*. Holden still had her hand in his as they ventured into the duskiness of eight-thirty, but she didn't pull away. Even with the comfort she felt around him, this nagging voice kept begging for her to text Joe and check on him. And it was ticking her off that he and his emerald eyes were weaseling their way back into her mind when Holden was a great guy. So, when Holden pulled her hand back and turned to kiss her, she let him. Let him brush his lips against hers and wrap his large arms protectively around her shoulders. Then he whispered, "I've got a surprise for you."

She pulled back and laughed. It felt good. Holden's eyes sparkled. "A surprise? As long as it's not anything physical after four pounds of spaghetti, I'm game. But the car's that way." She threw a finger out to the right as they continued their leftward path toward a more industrial part of town with factories and metal buildings. Holden scratched his chin as if he were deep in thought.

"Well some women call it physical, but I'm just praying you call it fun. We don't need the car as long as you're feeling up to walking about six blocks. And please don't hate me, because I know it's not really your thing, but I wanted to treat you to something special because you do so much for other people." Beads of sweat tickled his temples. A medical marvel considering there weren't any pores on his perfectly chiseled Greek god face.

"As long as it's not happy hour with my mom's book club friends, I'll survive."

Holden shivered and contorted his face. "Definitely not that. And please don't ever make me go to one of those. Not tomorrow and not two years from now. It sounds horrifying."

Savannah's lips were pulled up by a magical thread. It had to be. Because she'd had control over her smile all night, and now it was happening freely. Why hadn't she let him in before now? "So, this surprise? Where are we going? You've got me curious."

"Well, besides being the best Italian food in the city, the restaurant happens to be fairly close to one of our warehouses, and I've had my assistant pull some dresses from our fall line for you to choose from for the gala. I also instructed him to bring champagne in case my plan wasn't well received so we could drink to my failure."

They crossed the street, and he turned left down another one that narrowed. "Is it something I said?"

Her eyes met Holden's. She hadn't responded to his joke verbally, but her hands were shaking.

"Um, no. Nothing you said. I'm just a thirty-year-old woman who's scared of the dark, and I never mentioned it before. And last night, nearly dying in an alley while trying to save Allen's life, didn't do anything but compound that fear. I'll be a much better date when we get to the warehouse. I hope."

He frowned, apologizing an upwards of seventy times for his carelessness, just like a good little society boy. It was nice, but she was focused on her footsteps and the tiny blonde hairs standing at attention all over her arms. With such a muscular guy by her side, she shouldn't be worried about the dark. She should only be worried about her eyes scanning every inch of the pavement for Joe to come to her rescue.

Holden still sweated and gripped her hand tighter as they passed three women heading into the last restaurant on the street that now took a dive straight into the industrial buildings. Her fear might be rubbing off on him. "Well," he acknowledged, "clearly it's my fault I've caused our date to take a turn for the worst. And if I'd known about everything, I would have planned differently. But we're just a block away now. After you've tried on a million or so dresses, I'll have my assistant run out for the car so you don't have to make the walk back. Oh, and I'm sorry about Allen. Dahlia told me."

The fingers on her free hand clamped into a fist, and she blinked her eyes. No, she wasn't going to cry, but visions of him on the pavement and in the hospital bed kept brushing any other reasoning to the side. Tears fell down her cheeks, but Holden didn't notice. They passed two guys laughing and messing with their phones, and she tucked a little closer to him. "Thanks for saying that. I know your introduction was less than ideal, but he was a good man and a wonderful friend. I only had a few extra moments at the hospital with him before the men from the alley came back and killed him. And he didn't have anyone else. I always"—she bit her lip— "promised him I'd spread his ashes in the little town in North Carolina where he was born." The tears picked up their speed, falling to the ground.

Blowing out an enormous breath, Holden briefly responded to a text on his phone, which was annoying until he apologized. "Sorry about that. My assistant is wondering where we are, and he'll just keep asking if I don't throw him a bone. I am truly sorry though about last night, about everything. Maybe I could drive you out to North Carolina when you're up for it? It's the least I can do for the friend of the girl I care about. Did he—sorry if this is too personal—did he tell you why those men were after him? The media seems to have their own ideas, but he must've known something. Maybe I can help you piece it together."

It was a sweet gesture, all of it, but the night became darker by the second, and a cold sweat trickled down her neck. This walk was a bad idea. "That's sweet, but let's save that idea for the warehouse. Shouldn't we be able to see it by…agh!"

Savannah's hands clapped against her cheeks and she collapsed onto Holden's chest with a rigid back. His heart raced against her shoulder blade but not as fast as her own at the sight of Joe appearing out of thin air three feet behind them. Holden's breath burned hot on her neck as he gently tugged her shaking arm to pull her behind him, but she ripped free and plowed forward, voice squeaky and nearly incoherent as she sputtered, "What are you *doing?* They asked me if you'd lost it, and I defended you! I said I didn't want to see you! This *is* crazy!"

"They were going to attack you, Savannah! I had to step in! I won't apologize for it!" Joe stood on the sidewalk, his combat boot cutting off the air supply of a man flat on his back, pleading for mercy. Joe's pistol was aimed straight at his head. He was one of the two men they'd passed just a few moments before. The other sputtered beneath the weight of Joe's grip as he pinned him against a dumpster that reeked of burnt rubber. She raced to Joe, more focused on the alarming scene than the darkness, but before she could pull his face to hers, he thrust out an elbow with such force the standing man plummeted to the concrete in half a second. His unconscious body sprawled oddly as she pulled at Joe's gun arm. His eyes were more intense than the first time she saw him, but they weren't distant. She'd wanted him here just moments before, but now that he was, things were getting out of hand fast. Did death and danger follow him, or did he go looking for it?

Holden snapped out of his daze and was at her side again, responding to the situation as only a millionaire could, which wouldn't even sort of work on Joe. "Listen. Whatever is happening here, it's gone far enough. Let this man go. Be reasonable, and we can work this out like gentlemen. Do you want money? I'll drop my wallet here. A new Maserati? I'll leave my keys, but Savannah and I are going. Now."

Joe rolled his eyes, ignoring the pleading under his boot. "No, stupid. I don't want your money. Clearly, Savannah knows me. I'm not some random vigilante out looking for a reward. I'm trying to keep Savannah safe after her attack, and you're walking her through a bunch of warehouses in the dark like a delusional idiot. Wake up. You almost got her killed, and if that happens, you won't have to live with the regret because I'll kill you and bury your body where Daddy Warbucks will never find it."

Holden was a big guy, a couple inches taller than Joe and outweighing him by thirty pounds, but he didn't argue, because he was smart enough to understand that muscles weren't going to cut it. Joe could eliminate Holden before he got his fists up, and they all knew it. Besides, Joe made a compelling argument. Why weren't they there yet? Shouldn't it be visible from where they were standing?

A sharp pain started at the base of Savannah's skull and raced over her head to the back of her eye every five seconds. She slammed her palm over her eye and groaned. Maybe she should leave Holden for the evening and go with Joe. Whether or not he was losing it, she was the last person he wanted to hurt. And it'd be a quick way to get out of the dark so her knees wouldn't wobble like a baby deer walking for the first time.

Holden shivered off the fear that accompanied Joe's very honest threat and bent down to the man on the ground defiantly. "It's okay. We'll get you out of here, sir. I've already texted a cop friend of mine. They're on the way. I'll end this peacefully." The man whispered something, but she was dialed into Joe even though Holden rose again, pulling her arm and begging her to come with him. Every inch of her was shaking—hard. Not only was she horrified, but confrontation usually warranted the same bodily response. Her head was fuzzy from the absurdity of the situation. Her eyes couldn't focus on anything but the gun. Joe wasn't going to shoot someone on a hunch. It was just a fear tactic to get the guy talking. But what if he was innocent?

"Please. Give this man a chance to explain where he was going. If it's not good enough, the cops can take him in and imprison him. Or, I don't know, I'll go with you if you're still wanting to give me what Allen left for me. Just don't knock anyone else out and please lower your gun. He's practically convulsing and I just…I can't take it!" One hand was still over her eye.

Holden didn't pull anymore. He'd dropped her arm like it was a snake. Maybe he'd suddenly given up or hoped she could talk them all out of this catastrophe. She didn't have time to think too hard on it though, because Joe growled and lowered his gun but didn't remove his boot from the man's thick neck. Instead he dug it in farther. "Savannah. These guys were inching in, hunting you like prey. I know what it looks like; I've hunted men before. Doesn't something seem off about this whole situation? This thing with Allen isn't over, and I won't stop protecting you, whether you appreciate it or not!"

The man on the ground waved his arms frantically. "She said...I...could tell...you where...I was...going." He gasped, spit shooting out on Joe's boot as he bargained for freedom. Even in the dark, it was easy to see his face turning white. He didn't have long before he passed out. The faintest hint of police sirens wailed in the distance. The cavalry was coming in hot.

Joe eyed the man and shook his gun at him. Savannah stepped back to listen. It was true, the do-gooder thing was deeply ingrained in her core, but she couldn't be stupid. Yeah, Joe was quite literally following her like a shadow, but was that a good thing? Even after the soup kitchen, people could still be after her. But if these weren't attackers, this was crazy with a capital *C*, and Joe needed help.

Her eyes were much more adjusted to the blackness than her racing mind, but the man on the ground was horrified, black hair wet with sweat and eyes the size of watermelons. "Ok. Thank you...First, just know...I have a...family. Please...please...I have to go...home to them...We are just old friends...He was coming to my apartment...I live four blocks away on Patterson."

Savannah breathed out the air trapped in her throat, and the fuzziness in her head began to dissolve with each wail of the police sirens. Even the headache vanished with the man's simple response. "See. It's okay. The police are coming. Just go, and we will too."

"No."

Joe raised the gun and fired a bullet into the man's skull, pulled the gun across his chest and fired two more into his friend's chest. "There aren't any apartments on Patterson."

She was no athlete: couldn't even leap a hurdle in junior high, but when blood splattered across her face, she ran like never before, and Holden kept pace...and vomited. He wasn't as tough as he looked, but then again, two murders at close range was enough for anyone to lose their spaghetti.

Joe yelled something as she left, hand over her stomach to protect her stitches, but it didn't matter if he was right or wrong about those guys. The police could have sorted it out, and he shot anyway. Why? Why? Why? That was as far as her inner dialogue could get.

Brashly rubbing their blood off her arms, she dove into the brown leather seats of Holden's Maserati. It'd have to be reupholstered, but who cared. She sunk in and shivered, ears ringing from the shots at close proximity. Her head throbbed wildly, expanding with each pulse to the point of exploding. She squeezed her ears and gazed at Holden.

His hands clung to the steering wheel. He stared straight ahead. His hair hadn't moved an inch out of place, but he'd slipped as they started running and his knees and hands were stained dark red.

He didn't look at her but whispered, "I'd love to put together one concise thought, but it's not going to happen. I'm sorry for bringing you out there tonight after everything you experienced with your friend. We should have driven, and I didn't use good judgement. I'll bring you back to my apartment and get you cleaned up before I take you back to your parent's house. I can get us bodyguards for the gala so you are safe with me, if you still feel like going. I understand if you don't, but my parents have demanded my presence. Also, if you're open to suggestions, I don't believe Joe will stop until you accept whatever he's trying to give you from Allen. Set him up to leave it somewhere, and I'll get my cop friend and his partner to pick Joe up and arrest him. It might be his only chance to get the help he needs. You'd be doing him, and all of Los Angeles, a favor."

Savannah slid up into a seated position. The conversation gave her some reprieve from the throbbing in her head. "Maybe you're right. He's gone too far this time. I'll text him when I get home and call you with the details."

CHAPTER FOURTEEN
Joe

Joe cracked his knuckles. He couldn't explain to Savannah how training can overtake reason in a dangerous situation. At that moment, they were a threat, and now they weren't. If they were dead, they'd never have the opportunity to hurt an innocent civilian again.

He set his teeth and dug through the guys' pockets, snatching a wallet and two pistols before running again. A searing pain shot through his left leg as his feet smashed against the pavement, but the second set of stitches, plus body glue, held in place.

As Joe approached their newest car, a silver Camry, Clark raised an eyebrow. He tapped on the black leather console. "My plan would'a been less bloody."

Joe's face flushed as he slipped in and stared at the road ahead. He'd gone off book, and it wasn't like him, but there was something about Savannah. He could live with those deaths, but not hers. And he'd been right. Normal guys didn't carry silenced pistols. But it didn't stop his heart from pounding in his ears. Savannah had been so afraid.

Clark was also right. The White House had found him once, and if he kept killing, they'd track him down again and try to force the Medal of Honor on him. His grandpa had been a recipient. He'd earned it. Joe, not so much.

It was enough to weigh his chest down, have his hand squeezing the door handle as the other clutched the seatbelt. He was suffocating again, the buzz from the air conditioner humming in his ears. His eyes stayed on the road, dry and unwavering, but as the sweat trickled down his neck something happened.

The street ahead, which he knew was pavement, morphed into dirt. The December sun hovered high over their compound, fifty yards away. He was walking, the sweat from his neck soaking his John Wayne rag. It was a blessing for sure to be deployed in the winter, but with all the gear, it was still hot.

A smile spread across his lips. Tonight, he'd be in the mountains. Snow on the ground and icy air was just what he needed after this morning...after talking to his mom. That's why the word blessing so easily popped into his mind. She was always praying, talking to the big man upstairs. Always reminding him to do the same, even though he never did. But she was off today, and he'd nagged her about it until she caved. She didn't want him to lose his focus. It was something she just knew since all the men she ever loved were in the Army.

Eventually, she gave in. Dad's back was worse than ever, and they were trying everything to relieve the pain: heat, massage, acupuncture, oils. And it wasn't just hurting him. Bags were under her eyes, her short hair messy. So was the house behind her. It wasn't normal. They were both neat freaks.

She leaned close to the screen, her narrow lips drawn tight. "Honey, you'd be mad if I didn't tell you, but he's gonna be fine. He just needs rest. Be prayin' for him. That's what you can do. You're doin' important work, and we've got lots of friends here. Don't give it a second thought until you get on that plane next week and go home to Nadine. Okay?"

Hinley clapped him on the shoulder. "Time to get moving, boss. The guys are ready."

They'd gotten a tip early that morning from an informant. Rumors were circulating that Azfaar Mudad snuck back across the Pakistani border for a meeting with his junior leaders in a small village high in the Afghani mountains, about a ten-mile hike from where they were. Most of it was comprised of narrow and hazardous trails. But it was worth it. They'd been waiting for intel on him like kids wait for Christmas morning.

No one had a positive I.D. on Mudad. No one. This could be their chance. And this informant was trustworthy to a fault. He'd tipped them off just two weeks ago about another village stashing opium for Azfaar Mudad's drug business.

Joe considered the mission a success. So had his superiors back home in the so-called Puzzle Palace, snacking on pretentious little salads as they analyzed every detail of the work his team had done, before sending a congratulations their way. Success in his terms was much simpler: he'd lit the match that burned the opium, and his team got out alive. He got out alive.

The intel had been good, the opium was there, but there was much more than they'd anticipated. Each of the huts was lined on the inside with blocks to the ceiling. Men patrolled with rifles while children played with a woven ball in the dirt, every kick sending a brown cloud into the air.

They'd put up a fight when the team showed up. Children ran toward their mothers or their guns as the men fought from behind them like sick cowards, knowing American soldiers would avoid hurting kids and women. The ball sat in the dirt, a symbol of imagined innocence as chaos ensued. His team, along with a small contingent of Afghan Special Forces, worked their way through the village, clearing huts and small buildings, when the sound of a creaking board under his boot gave him pause. He bent down on one knee for a closer look, pulling a faded red rug to the side.

Hidden under it was a wooden door, leading into a small tunnel in the ground. Morrison covered him while he flipped it over onto the dirt floor. The dirt flew in their eyes. He wiped them, getting lower to look inside. It was going to be a tight squeeze, and he wasn't a fan of small spaces. Who was? But feelings didn't matter. There was a job to do. With his own gear, it'd be tough to get through, so bringing Morrison along was off the table. He crawled in and looked back at Morrison. "Take two guys and find the exit in the tree line, while the rest of the team collects the drugs and rounds up any remaining Taliban."

Morrison nodded and left, probably pumped he wasn't the one diving in. His men needed him to be brave, to run toward the enemy, but Joe's stomach churned as he crawled into and down that dark tunnel, his shoulders two inches from each side. It didn't help having the top only four inches above his hunched back. Morrison and the others would be searching four feet above him, stomping over the ground thick enough to collapse and bury him alive. He cracked his neck and inhaled the dirt. If someone was going to risk everything, he'd always been the guy. First to volunteer. But this job made his skin crawl.

Short, hand-hewn wooden beams with scavenged boards held the tunnel together as he crawled, dirt trickling down into his helmet. The tunnel was dark—very dark. His headlight couldn't find the other end or a few feet ahead, for that matter. The Beretta in his hand held a steady aim, his fingers so tightly wound around the grip they lost all sensation. His head light searched for movement, light, or an odd shape. His ears strained for a voice or any sound of company.

Nothing. The tunnel wove to the left about twenty yards away. He laid on his belly in the Earth, listening again over the echo of his own heartbeat. His hands were heavy. The voices were still silent, but he sensed they were still in the tunnel.

Focus. Focus. You don't get scared. You can't get scared. You can't.

Before rounding a curve, the familiar reek of Taliban drifted his direction, with whispers in Pashtun. He must be getting close. He could sense their presence, hear their knees dragging lengthy lines through dirt as they moved deeper into the tunnel. Turning the corner, his vision set on two men as the tunnel widened by a few inches at the exit, ten meters away. Electricity raced through his veins as their eyes connected, all of them crammed together with one way out. That thought made the tunnel even tighter. The smell of goat radiating off their bodies tore through his nose and down his throat. The first man flipped a panel and scurried up a broken ladder and out of the tunnel, looking back once more at the second man, the brightness of the outside enveloping his face. His eyes were round and brown, with a thick scar jaggedly running across his cheek above his wooly beard. He pleaded with the second man to hurry, dropping an arm in to pull him out, but Joe fired his Beretta and surged forward on his knees, grabbing the second man by his ankle. Their sweaty hands slipped apart, and the second man yelled for the other to run. Crashing to the ground, the Taliban soldier's leg bled from the first shot. Joe fired twice more and ended him.

He gasped loudly and dropped his head to the ground. First thought: he was alive. Second thought: he was trapped. The dead man's body blocked the exit, and there was no way around him and definitely not enough room to turn around. The walls crept in, hugging his sides, pushing the breath from his lungs. Joe's chest rattled. He'd always kept calm, breathing in through his nose and out through his mouth. He couldn't even identify where his nose and mouth were on his body now. Every beat of his heart exploded through his ringing ears, and he shook.

I'm going to…die. I'm…going to die…in this hole. I'm…

Thrashing around, he tried to turn, banging into the wall this way and that until clumps of dirt started dropping onto his back and across his neck. He laid flat on his stomach and quaked as worms wriggled by to greet their visitor. His throat closed little by little, dirt on his tongue, between his teeth, down his throat. Why couldn't he stop the pain tightening his chest with every heartbeat? Why couldn't he yell? Why couldn't he brea—

"Joe! Joe! Hey! Come on back, brother. You're havin' a nightmare. Come on."

Joe opened his eyes, looking around as Clark took a seat to his left. Clark had jerked him out of the car and thrown him into the open space of an empty soccer field like a rag doll. His head hurt, but the grass was soft under his back and the stars shone above him. "Thanks for waking me up before my mind took me too far down that path. It isn't the night to relive all our brothers dying."

Clark wrapped an arm over his shoulder. "You did everything you could. You did. And you deserve that medal. But my absolution doesn't change a thing. You gotta make peace with it. The guys are up in the stars, lookin' down on you and wishin' the same thing. 'Cept maybe Carson. That fool might be lookin' up." He nudged Joe and laughed. Carson was a pain, though he probably wasn't going to Hell for that. But Clark's quick wit always left him with a smile. Clark leaned over, "Can I hug ya, or is it weird?"

Joe belly laughed and pushed him away. "It's weird. Always weird, just so you know. Instead, let's decide our next step, if you're still with me."

"Dude." He smacked Joe across his already hurting head. "I just threw you out of a car to watch the stars with me. I think it's safe to say I'm with ya till the end. But we gotta get Savannah, too. She's still in danger. You've studied the security detail at her parent's estate for a few minutes; think about how much time their guys have had. If you can get in, so can they. You've got to get her out of there, and there's no time like the present to make it happen. I'll wait down the road with the car while you sweet talk her into joinin' us. Oh, and do me a solid and don't say anything stupid." Clark clapped his hands together and pulled him to his feet. "Oh, and one more thing. I, uh, opened that wallet while you were in your head. There was only one thing inside: a gray business card with a green triangle."

CHAPTER FIFTEEN
Savannah

Savannah couldn't say how long it took her to fall asleep after the horrific evening they'd had, but it was 2:14 a.m. when she woke with a hand over her mouth.

"Don't scream. I need to talk to you."

Her chest burned like fire, eyes wide in alarm. She flailed, arms smacking at anything within reach, but his hand stayed strong because, evidently, he knew she'd scream. Who wouldn't? *It's Joe. It's Joe.* Her mind tried to convince her she was safe between muffled wailing, but it still felt like a nightmare. Maybe she wasn't in danger, but her heart sped just like it had in the alley.

At 2:17 she stopped fighting, and Joe lifted his hand warily. Savannah leapt up on her bottom, shaking all over, and pushed his lingering hand away, jerking her head back and forth to take in her room. She stroked her mouth, her stomach. It was okay. She breathed slower. It was okay.

Then she looked down. It wasn't okay. She was in a silky pink nightgown. A breeze rolled through the open window Joe had slithered through moments before. She shivered and wrapped her arms across her braless chest. Joe grabbed a blanket from a nearby chair, draping it over her bare shoulders. It was gentle and kind, but his approach to waking her wasn't. Creeping in someone's window wasn't proper and didn't leave many suitable options for waking, but maybe it was the best he could do if he wasn't willing to ring the front doorbell. Shifting in her spot on the bed, she considered that as he watched her.

Holden was adamant that she share every kernel of knowledge about Joe when he'd dropped her off earlier. If Joe had come to the door, her parents' faces would have paled to pure white as they ran for the saferoom and dialed the police.

Maybe he made the right choice after all, though there was no way to know how he'd evaded the security cameras and ten-foot wall around the estate. She shook the thought away and looked into his eyes, glowing like jewels by the bathroom and closet lights. Looking at them was like opening Pandora's box, so why was she willing to risk it? What exactly was it about Joe that made her ignore every reasonable thought and consider leaping across the bed to hug him—or kiss him? She had a boyfriend. Not only was it crazy, but he also wasn't into her. It was just business. He was a soldier. He'd saved her life twice and didn't want her to die. That was all there was to it on his end.

"Thank you for the blanket, but honestly, you could have called if you had something to say. You have a phone, and so do I. Our estate has four security guards. My room is on the second floor, and yet you're in my bedroom in the middle of the night after murdering two men in front of me." She held up a finger before he could interject. "Not to mention, half of my soup kitchen patrons are dead. Then you hand me a blanket to protect my modesty? This is...I don't even have the right word for it. And yet there's this part of me that doesn't want to lose my connection to you, even though I know there's nothing but duty connecting you to me. And there's my annoyingly strong desire to help people, even though you made it clear at the hotel you didn't want my help. Where does it leave us? Holden wants me to turn you in. I agreed to it, but I don't want to unless there's no other way. So, answer me. Tell me who you are. Tell me if you're still in control. Tell me why you keep protecting me when you could just go home?" She sighed and took his hands, sitting him on the bed in front of her and ignoring the tingling of her palms against his. "Please. Look in my eyes and explain, because I need to understand."

Joe shifted his weight in the low light, and the wrinkles between his eyebrows smoothed. But he didn't let go of Savannah's hands. Instead, he gripped them harder. "I know it's time to give you answers, Savannah. But opening up goes against every fiber in my body. I don't let people in. I want you to be different, but I don't think you can be. You deserve better."

His sincerity pulled at her heartstrings, but his smile vanished. He was so guarded. "Savannah, you're right." He shifted gears. "I haven't lost it. There is something much deeper going on with this...green triangle thing Allen mentioned. The men from earlier had business cards with green triangles and 9mm Glocks. It must be a clue, and right now they believe I'm killing their men before getting any leads. I *have* to keep you safe, even if you don't always understand my methods." He moved a little closer, forcing his mouth to let out a few more words despite how uncomfortable it made him. "About you though, you are one in a million, so yeah, this goes beyond duty for me. I realized how special you were six months ago when I saw you at the soup kitchen with Allen for the first time, and every day after as Allen told me about you. But you deserve someone better. So, I watched from a distance in case you needed me. And maybe it doesn't mean much now, but my heart was invested a long time ago."

The hairs on her arms stood straight up as a wave of butterflies dashed through her stomach. That was unexpected, and she didn't know what to say or why Holden's face was going fuzzy in her mind at this particular moment. Guys had liked her in the past, but she'd never *wanted* any of them. She wanted Joe. Didn't really realize it until that moment, or maybe she hadn't allowed herself to realize it. Her fingers traced the purple blanket. And Joe, this ruggedly handsome soldier, wanted her even though he'd been fighting it. He was leaning in, about to kiss her, which made her head dizzy. She was leaning in too, so close the heat from his body warmed her chest.

And then Joe was there, lips pushed against hers, hands tangled in her hair. Still wrapped in the blanket, she pulled him closer, closing the space between their bodies with only a layer of fleecy blanket and her nightgown a barrier. The world froze on that spot on the bed as their lips connected a few more times. She breathed him in: grass and gunpowder. With trembling fingers, she tugged at the bottom of his shirt, pulling it up enough to reveal a set of tanned abs before Joe jerked his shirt back down again.

He kissed her again, and she let him, but what was that emotion she'd felt? Their eyes connected for a moment before he looked away again. It was fear. He'd said he didn't get scared, but everyone was scared of something.

And because of that, she couldn't mask the comfort he needed with passion, even if she wanted to stay like this for the next six months. Her vision cleared slowly, tugging her out of the trance she'd been in. She would never be with him without knowing his past, and he would never be able to stop treading water until he was sure she accepted whatever left such dark rings around his eyes.

She was in her thirties now and had to have answers before she could let him become more than her white knight. Taking Joe's face in her hands, she pulled him away. "Look at me." His eyes lifted to hers warily. "I can't kiss you again until you answer my other questions. I'll still be right here when you've told me everything. I can't get my knowledge of you from the news. This is your chance. You won't scare me off."

Joe pried his body from hers and nodded. They both sat up, and the heat she'd felt disappeared through the crack in the window. His lips formed a straight line. "Then I'll start at the beginning, but it's easier to show than tell. Would you come with me somewhere? I'll have you back before the sun comes up."

She nodded toward the window he'd used as a door. "Not out that thing. I'll take the front door if this is the only way to get you talking. Just make sure those guys, whom I guess we're calling The Green Triangle, aren't lurking around."

"Of course." Joe let go of her hands slowly, seemingly afraid to break his connection to her, and slinked out the window. She was tempted to watch his descent, but just the thought of Joe crawling down her house like Spiderman made her neck sweat. She put the blanket back and remade the bed, imagining what it would feel like if they were wrapped up in the satin sheets together, him stroking her hair, laughing and talking, him happy and not on guard… Could she help him get there?

She stopped and bit her lip. Would things ever be like that if she followed this kiss with Joe to something more? Would he ever laugh or dance with her? Holden would. He'd laugh every day. He already did. What if she gave Holden up for an unrealistic chance with Joe? Had she done that already? Her stomach churned, and she wrapped her arms around it. Was this right? Her toe tapped against the carpet. Joe was outside waiting. Either way, she needed to go.

The lights were already on in the walk-in closet, because sleeping in the dark was horrific, so she rifled through it and retrieved a pair of blue jeans. After shimmying into them, she slipped the nightgown over her head and discovered a Nike pullover, which looked comfortable hanging amid a closet of new designer dresses. Why did her mother restock her closet for the possibility of a few nights at home? That was a mystery for another day.

She pulled her blonde locks into a ponytail and stopped briefly in front of the floor-length mirror, rubbing away the makeup that smudged across her eyes while she slept. People called her pretty, though Savannah was never confident in her looks. There were many beautiful women in the world, and she found herself plain. She wondered what Joe's type was. How silly though; he wasn't the kind of guy to pay too much heed to physical appearance. She did wonder, though, about his past. Allen never told her much, just that he was a hero. But what could have happened to Joe that turned his world upside down? Hopefully, he'd tell her tonight.

She stepped out of the closet and back into her room, her naked toes shifting from the cold bamboo beams to a wooly rug. Her cell lit up on her pillowcase, so she climbed over the covers and grabbed it. Maybe Joe felt like things weren't safe and she shouldn't come down? No. It was Holden. At 2:30 a.m.?

"Hello?" Savannah fluffed the pillow and scooted to the edge of the bed, picking at a loose thread on her jeans.

"Savannah? Hi. I didn't expect you to answer. I know it's late, and I'm sorry, but tonight really shook me up, and I thought it might have done the same for you. I was worried about you and thought I'd leave a message and see if I could swing by and check on you in the morning, maybe take you to breakfast. Or, heck, since you're awake now, I make a mean cup of coffee. We could brainstorm about you bringing Joe in so he can get some help. There's one other thing." She could feel his mood shift from caution to happiness through the void that separated their phones. "If I'm being completely honest, I can't stop thinking about our kiss outside the restaurant, either."

She gulped. How ironic this was all happening tonight, after all they'd been through. But Holden did not need to know what she was about to do. Of that, she was certain.

"Are you there?"

"Yes, I'm sorry. I was just thinking. Tonight was crazy…and great. You're right. I don't think I can turn Joe in like I promised though. I believe I'm still in danger from the attack, and I think Joe is trying to protect me. It probably sounds strange to you. It does to me a little too. But let's do coffee tomorrow morning, okay? I've got something to take care of before then."

He sighed through the phone. "That's fine, but what do you have to take care of in the middle of the night that can't wait until morning?"

Savannah hesitated, rubbing her face. Holden made a little noise, clearly unsure if she was still on the phone. "Savannah, is he there?" His voice raised an octave before he continued. "Don't be insane! He's dangerous! If he wants to give you the item he mentioned, do it with me there. I'm trying to protect you too, and I can do it without guns. I've learned some things about him. Please. You *know* me. He's still a stranger."

She'd pulled until a hole formed in her jeans and now her hands were on the scars. She'd always followed her gut, and it was saying to trust that

Joe wasn't a threat, even though she'd gotten practically nothing as far as answers. But was she too blinded by her affection? "What did you learn about Joe?"

"I'll tell you in person but not over the phone. Just let me come see you. Please?"

She tapped the phone against her ear while she thought. The other hand was busy fixing the little hole in her jeans with a needle and thread from her nightstand drawer. "You're right. I don't know enough about him. Come over tomorrow morning. I'll see you and hear you out, but I'm going down to hear Joe out first. The safest thing I can do for myself is listen to both of you."

Holden groaned out, "Please, just call me after you talk to Joe," before hanging up. He was shaken, so his news about Joe was bad, but she'd already made up her mind. He deserved his chance.

She smoothed the blue-and-yellow comforter and opened her bedroom door, slipping on a pair of socks and tiptoeing through the darkness, ponytail frozen behind her. She was thirty, with a home of her own, but if her parents caught her, the questions would never cease. Although, she and Joe talking outside their first-floor bedroom had a chance of waking them anyway.

Everything was dark as she padded along, with only the light from her cell's flashlight, hand trembling even in a house that was familiar. Landing on the first floor, the air conditioner whizzed to life, and she jumped about a foot in the air, crashing into a vase and steadying it before it shattered.

Her heart pounded as she doubled over with her hands on her knees. *That was close.*

Then her nerves moved to anxious giggling. How absurd to act this way as an adult, and even more absurd was the fact that she was going to continue sneaking around the estate like a burglar. She squeezed the Louis Vuitton sneakers in her hands while her head turned in all directions. The first floor was still empty as far as she could see. But her dad's office light peeked under the bottom of the closed door. Did he forget to turn it off before going to bed?

He'd want the lights off all night to save a nickel, so she'd just flip the switch and dash out to meet Joe. Five feet from the office, she froze. Her father wasn't asleep; he was in there yelling at someone. She'd never heard him really yell before, so she stepped closer and pushed her ear against the solid wood of the door.

"No! I'm in the shipping business, and you had something to ship. I should have done my research before getting into bed with you, but you'll never find those drugs...Sounds like blackmail, and I don't scare easy...The docks? I'll have the police there in ten minutes! No that doesn't mean anything to me. Why should it? My daughter? You leave my family out of this...Then, I'm coming for your heads!"

The phone slammed down with a crack and another bang followed it, something clattering to the floor just after. Shoes clutched to her chest, Savannah ran past all the fancy artwork and expensive furniture. She could've busted in her dad's office, but her mind was telling her to get to Joe. Her ponytail flapped wildly, face tight with fear, visions of the alley and Ponytail scratching into her mind.

After the soup kitchen massacre, she should have known it was just the beginning, not the end. But in her experience, espionage and murder only consumed a two-hour time period until the movie ran out. This was going to linger, and she would need to get back in touch with her taser-wielding self if she wanted to survive.

The antique doorknob was beneath her hand in seconds, its whirly design imprinting on her sweaty palm. She jerked the door open and inhaled the night. Her eyes didn't search long. Joe was there, gun raised in the darkness, about thirty-five yards away. His lips curled up at the sight of her, white teeth shining like miniature stars.

Savannah forced a smile and tried to keep her head. They had a lot to talk about already—even more with what she'd just overheard—so they could share a seat on the front stoop or maybe the tire swing and mull it over for as long as it took. Which couldn't be too long, since Holden would most likely be at the gate at sunrise. Probably Chief Rollings, too, who said he'd be back for another prying session.

Joe's face shifted into a frown as he walked faster toward her, still searching the darkness for signs of danger. He realized she was upset. Her right hand had unconsciously moved to the scars on her stomach again. She shook her hands out and leaned over to slip on her sneakers when Joe broke into a full-fledged sprint.

She straightened, and a hand clamped over her mouth and nose, followed by a prick on the side of her neck like a bug bite. She tried to fight, but her vision swayed. Something in that prick must've had the power to overwhelm her senses. The last thing she saw were the security lights blazing to life over Joe as she collapsed onto the grass by her Louis Vuitton sneakers.

CHAPTER SIXTEEN
Joe

Joe's fists were bloody, and his head was on fire. He'd been trying, unsuccessfully, for the last three minutes to beat the door down in the half-size cargo container he and Savannah were trapped in after being ambushed at her parents' mansion. He could've stopped at any moment and woken Savannah from the shabby mattress to reassure her that he could and *would* rescue her from this.

But his utter fear of tight spaces, coupled with a mix of mortar and machine gun fire being played through a tiny speaker on the ceiling, had him back and forth between the present and Afghanistan, the blood of that night refusing to come clean from his hands though he'd wiped them on his shirt over and over. He'd spun in a dozen circles before leaning against a corner. Out of all the possible torture techniques, why had they chosen this? Waterboarding would be a dream right now. Some bamboo under the fingernails or even a little shock therapy? Hell yes. Something against his physical body, he could manage, but his mind wasn't as strong.

Okay, Joe. Focus now. In through the nose...two, three, four. Hold...two, three, four. Out through the mouth...two, three, four. Hold...two, three, four. Nose...two, three, four. Hold...two, three, four. Out...two, three, four. Hold...two, three, four. One more time. Nose...two, three, four. Hold...two, three, four. Out...two, three, four. Hold...two, three, four.

The lowered heartrate brought clarity to the conex, his Army term for their new prison cell. The air was stale like eggs and death, and a renegade mosquito had squeezed in to suck his blood every chance it got. Four fluorescent panels lined every inch of the ceiling, lighting the room to an irritatingly bright state that made everything appear to be glowing. His teeth grated as he stared ahead at the one wall in the container that was different: a plexiglass type material that was currently dark. It stretched from the floor to the ceiling. What was behind it? Maybe guessing was part of the torture, seeing what horrific things your mind could come up with.

A shuffle in the corner quieted a fraction of his mind. Savannah opened her eyes and screamed, jumping on the mattress and spinning her head around. Her eyes frantically searched for a door. She spotted him instead and rushed over in four steps, grabbing his arms and gasping. The mortar and machine gun fire rose in volume. He clenched his teeth and focused his eyes straight into hers. "What is going on, Joe? I hear guns. So many guns. Where are we? What is this? I can't...breathe."

He pulled her slowly to the cool floor and let her keep squeezing his arms. "I'm not sure where we are yet. I woke up shortly before you. The guns are just sounds coming in through the speaker up there." His thumb jerked toward the ceiling. "Look in my eyes. Do you trust me? If there's a way out, I'll find it."

But she continued panicking, her breaths even more ragged at the suggestion that he was stumped too. He wasn't MacGyver, working his way out of any situation with a paper clip. That wasn't reality. She jolted away from him and beat the wall with her palms. "Let...me...out...of here!" The container rattled under each slap, light dancing with every beat and sending a wave of pain from his neck to the back of his eye.

Joe clasped his arms around Savannah and pulled her uncooperative body to the floor. The pressure of his grasp brought her heartrate down to an even one-ten. He shook his head. This was going to take some time and encouragement: not areas he excelled in. The only hope at this current moment was Clark storming the place with a team. He might've missed the abduction, but he clearly would have known something was up when they didn't come back to the car. Trailing them to their current location was highly unlikely though. Telling Savannah about it would just get her hopes up. The chances were about one hundred to one that Clark found this place.

"I've got you. I've got you. You're in my arms now. Do you feel me against you?"

"Yes." Her voice was weak.

"Now breathe. In through your nose. Breathe in deep. Hold it. Good." He stroked her arms gently, whispering in her ear. "Now let it out, and let's do it again."

Her back rested against his chest, and they breathed in unison ten times before Savannah turned her head and whispered, "Thank you. I'm more like myself now." Her head bobbed back and forth. "Well, more like myself kidnapped in a box, but still, it's something. I'm feeling okay at this moment, but what am I supposed to do to stay calm?"

"Why don't you close your eyes for a few minutes, go to your happy place, and then we'll work together and search every inch of this conex."

Savannah laughed quietly. He got it. It sounded insane to ask her to go to her happy place, but maybe it would help, because in his experience, things were just getting started. "You'll stay with me?"

His eyes went up to the ceiling and back down to hers. Why did he keep doing this to himself? Could he risk being vulnerable with Savannah, only to have her leave him when she knew him better or when she found someone else? That's what Nadine had done. His biological parents left too. It was easy for her to say she wasn't going anywhere after knowing each other for twenty-four hours.

"Yes."

She spun around so they were face to face, and her legs were under his. She squeezed her eyes shut and sighed loudly as he counted the freckles on her cheeks and then mentally slapped himself. He had it bad for her. The skin crinkled on top of her eyebrows, and her bottom lip pursed out as she timidly leaned against his chest. Black smudges from her makeup brushed out under her eyes. She was stunning, even like that.

He grimaced and closed his eyes too, praying for the second time in his life. Dinners growing up—with his dad crushing his toes under the table with a heel so Joe'd volunteer to say grace—didn't count. This was by choice. He'd have laughed if the gunfire wasn't still ringing in his ears, because he was probably sending off some prayer beacon his mom could spot miles away.

God, Jesus...don't know your preferred title. As ironic as it sounds, I've finally found someone that is better than I deserve and more than I've ever known I wanted. She'd make me a better man if you'd just get us out of this place alive. I'll pull my weight without acting like a total jerk, if you could come through on your end. Is the barter system something you do? Just keep her alive. Deal?

He jerked his eyes open. Savannah hovered inches away from his face. "Are you praying? I'm not judging, just wondering if it brings you any peace, because going to my happy place didn't exactly work. This prison isn't much better than the alley Allen and I were attacked in, and thinking about that makes me think about him...about everything. I need an escape. No one in my family ever prayed, except my grandma. She was at church every Sunday. Dad always worked, but every Sunday afternoon, we'd spend a couple hours, the whole family together, watching a movie and eating popcorn. Mom would paint my nails, and we'd laugh. Things were different then, but on Sundays I still always watch a movie and paint my nails."

Joe stared at her. Their faces were just an inch apart, but it wasn't that kind of moment, and he'd promised her answers just hours ago, so it was time to give a little, even though that tug in his chest was saying the opposite. "My mom dragged me to church, kicking and screaming, as a kid, and I spent most of my twenties pushing any thought of God away because I was always angry. My dad never forced it, just had me prepping to be a soldier before I could even walk straight. He thought I needed a good dose of respect and an outlet for my 'energy.' But my mom always stuck with God, kept telling me he'd listen whenever I had something to say. So, does it bring me peace? I don't know. But I think he's listening at the very least, and it makes me feel a connection to my family. That's good enough for me right now."

Savannah smiled and ran her fingers over the stubble on his chin. "Your parents know you love them." His eyebrows raised, and he pulled away. "Did I say something wrong?" She tilted her head, and the light glowed around her like a halo.

"No, it's just that you said exactly what I was thinking to myself while I was talking. I think about it a lot. I never told them, even though I should have hundreds of times, but I never felt deserving of their love. Just something deep inside kept telling me no matter how hard I worked, I'd never give them the happiness they would've had if Mom could've had her own biological child. I see the way you're looking at me. It doesn't make sense, I know." The muscles in his back slowly relaxed. He wiped the sweat off his forehead and gently tugged Savannah to her feet with him, completely ignoring the sounds in the background. "Okay. I'm ready to figure out how to get out of this thing."

His chest puffed out with a new resolve and confidence just as two of the fluorescent panels cut off. The plexiglass wall shone with a view of the warehouse they were stashed in. Savannah dug her fingernails into his arm and gasped. There were clues in the warehouse; things he could and should notice to finetune a plan, but his eyes were frozen in their sockets. The concrete floors were covered in a dusting of sand and eleven men lie dead on the floor in Army fatigues. His heart pounded. His fists rattled the plexiglass over and over again, and that familiar rush of a panic attack in the confined space weighed him down like a ton of bricks.

You can't kill your way out of this. Can't beat your way out or run ten miles, either. Use your mind. Be objective. Breathe.

He shook his head and rolled his shoulders even though Savannah continued to cling to him.

106

Nose…two, three, four. Hold…two, three, four. Out…two, three, four.

Savannah picked up on his cue and breathed too. The running was always Allen's suggestion to relax, and it worked better for his mind, but there was only so far to run in here, and this did the trick for Savannah, too.

Start with the dead dudes.

The bodies probably belonged to the security guards for the warehouse and some other disappointing Green Triangle employees. That was what he and Savannah were calling their company between themselves. Chances were this shadowy organization hadn't gone out and massacred soldiers. If they had though, he'd rip the arms off each man involved.

But the biggest problem was obvious; the Green Triangle knew about him long before Allen died in that alley, and he was going to pay for whatever he'd done. But what was it? He cracked his neck. Mercs were a dime a dozen. They couldn't be mad he'd killed them, and that was just yesterday. This was about Afghanistan, about his team. It had to be. And now his past put Savannah in danger. Couldn't he catch a break? Failure followed him like a lost puppy. So, it was time to get a cat.

Savannah tapped his back, and he jerked around, sending her swaying on impact with his muscular arm. He steadied her, but tears slipped over her freckle-covered cheeks as she stared out. "This is personal."

"I know. And I'm sorry I got you involved. But I'll make it right."

"That's not what I mean." Savannah waved an arm. "The dead bodies and sand are meant to trigger your memories, yes, but take your eyes off them and look around."

She held his hand and grounded him to the present with the heat of her palm against his. No matter what else they threw at him, he had to stay in this headspace, be hyper vigilant, capture very detail. The mini conex they were trapped in had a wide, clear hose attached to a metal screen on the ceiling. But it was impossible to see where the hose went. The warehouse was large and open to the outside, with a few palm trees drooping.

An old street ran nearby, just where the concrete floor ceased. Deep cracks tore through the blacktop, and grass wiggled out of each one, covering seventy percent of it. The street led to a field under a hazy morning sun. They hadn't been there long. Maybe four hours, tops. But there wasn't a single sign of life visible anywhere in the distance.

Inside the warehouse was much the same. Not even a rat scurried around. Streams of water trickled down the walls in three spots, tracing uneven lines before splattering to their deaths. Floodlights dangled unmoving from the twenty-foot ceilings. Even air movement had been sucked from this place, like a disease.

He looked left. The lights revealed twenty large, white cargo containers, all with the doors blasted. They bore the same bold, red logo: *Carrington Cargo, Inc.*

Joe pointed toward the containers. "Your dad's company, right?"

Savannah's finger trailed up and down her stomach. She was nervous. She'd done that before, but he didn't ask. She choked out a whisper. "I heard Dad yelling at them on the phone before I came out to meet you. I think they're mad about some drugs they shipped in a cargo container. My dad must have hidden them or given them to the cops or something. They threatened our family. I should've stayed and asked, but I was scared, and my feet took me to you."

He ignored the warmness expanding in his chest. It wasn't the time to focus on feelings he'd never made time for before. It could wait until he'd ripped the heads off each of these guys. "So, they want their drugs back? We can work with that. But I'm still not sure what they want from me."

The window went dark again, and the room flushed to black in the blink of an eye, stealing away the speaker's volume too. Savannah disappeared from view, leaving only her breathing to know she was there. It'd take a bit for his eyes to adjust to the change, but the shooting pain behind his ear was gone. And that, with the accompanied silence, was a relief. His dad always said, "Darkness is your friend." He shrugged his shoulders. Maybe they weren't friends, but it was like a vacation.

For him.

Savannah shuddered and began whimpering quietly. A bang jolted the wall and then the ceiling. She leapt into his arms as a wave of frigid air shot through the clear tube and into their container. Joe tightened his grip and carried her to the mattress, where he held her and stroked her hair. The rose perfume still lingered as his fingers ran through the strands. She curled into him, rocking back and forth like a ship on a stormy sea. Her ear pressed to his chest, no doubt listening to his racing heart. But what could he do? There was no hiding how he felt for her now, even if he tried to ignore it. He'd already confessed his love in her bedroom even if those exact words hadn't come out, and the way they were together now felt more intimate than when his lips were tracing her jaw. He stiffened at the image, his body on pins and needles. He was only supposed to get in, solve this thing, and get out. This was not supposed to happen.

Savannah lifted her head, and he could almost make out the freckles on her nose if he squinted. "Just so you know, I'm scared of the dark. Pitiful, as far as fears go. But I don't tell many people that, so how would they know to use this against me?"

The speaker above them rattled to life. A voice like velvet slithered through it, dripping with sarcasm and a middle eastern accent. "Good evening, Savannah and Joe. We truly hope you're satisfied with your accommodations, as you could potentially take your last breath right where you're sitting. But don't panic. That causes wrinkles. If you're compliant, we will let you go. And we're expecting Savannah's father to play along as well. Losing one child was probably enough for him, and I've made it clear that your arrangements here are subject to change depending on my…mood." He chuckled softly then started up again. "To be perfectly honest, we have a business to run, and to do that, we need merchandise. Savannah's father stole it and has twelve hours to bring it back to us in exchange for Savannah's life. As for Joe's part in this… Well, that'll have to wait. The boss has…plans for him. I suppose I should leave it at that. While you lounge in our romantic, five-star suite, please do a favor for me.

Your friend, the little old man we offed in the hospital…Oh, I can't remember his name, but he took a video of our operation, and I'd very much like it back. Perhaps you don't even know where it is, but maybe, after bordering on hypothermia for the next few hours, your mind will clear up. Either way, enjoy your time together. Tonight, the real fun begins. See you soon."

"I'm going to pry that guy's teeth out," Joe muttered.

Savannah stared at the wall. Her teeth chattered. "Do you ever consider prison as a viable option?" She used a playful voice, but she most likely meant it. In the last fifty hours, he'd left ten people in the morgue.

"I'm sorry. He's obviously evil. That's all I can say. It's how I deal with black stains on humanity. So, how are you doing with the cold and dark now?" It seemed like the easiest question for her to answer, even with the curiosity about her dad missing another child being right on the tip of his tongue. He tucked it away. Savannah wasn't Nadine, but things could still travel down that road, given time, and he wouldn't share more than necessary. He grimaced. He'd opened up to Nadine a little, but after his first deployment, she pulled away emotionally. After the second deployment, she began using the words he'd confided in her as weapons against him. And after the third deployment, she was gone. It wasn't her fault completely. He'd spent his time fighting for his country instead of his marriage.

He tightened his grip around Savannah. The temperature was hovering around fifty at the moment, but when the air was blowing just a minute before it must've gotten down to thirty-five.

They shivered together in the corner for at least two minutes before she answered in a voice an octave higher than normal. "I guess I'm as fine as I can be. How can I complain about freezing when they're planning something worse for us in just a few hours? I mean, what could that be? You've got to have some guesses, seeing how you're so matter of fact about killing. Sorry. That came out wrong. But I'm scared, and it's bothering me that, out of everything the speaker guy said, all you asked me was if I was okay with the dark and cold. If you want to help me, tell me what you're really thinking."

How did she do that every time? The mosquito buzzed invisibly around his head as he swatted at it. "I'm wondering what he meant about your dad already losing a child. But you don't have to tell me. Actually, don't tell me. It's your life, and the more I know, the harder it will be."

Savannah was on her knees in his face now. He could make out that much and the angry glare meant to burn his skin off. "The harder what will be?"

Joe's head was down, even though his expression was probably lost on her. "When you leave me."

A sharp noise shot through the container. His cheek stung. His eyes were wide with shock. Sweet little Savannah just smacked him across the face.

CHAPTER SEVENTEEN
Savannah

Slapping one of those plastic bracelets on her wrist as a kid probably didn't count as an actual slap. So, Joe was her first, and she'd sure slapped him good. It felt like a hundred tiny snakes biting all over her palm. But where had it come from? A side of her that didn't exist until they met—and kissed. It was the only way she could think to stop him from saying anything else annoying or stupid.

"Oh my lord, Joe. I couldn't leave you if I wanted to. Haven't you seen our current accommodations? It's not the Ritz, and if my dad doesn't come through, we might be killed." She balled her fists and tightened her jaw, forcing out anything but this conversation. "How could I make that any clearer? I told you I cared for you, and you said the same thing. The only difference is you run away from anything that isn't shaped like a bullet. Do I have to shoot you for you to believe me? I can't keep going around on this. Holden wanted me to leave with him tonight. You saw him: blond hair and muscles, looked like a walking Ken doll? If I wanted him, I could have gone, but I didn't. Of course, in hindsight, I might not be stuck in a cargo container, but I picked the right guy. So, start acting like it before I slap you again. I am *not* the person that made you afraid to connect, so don't put that on me. I listen when people talk. I don't make the same mistakes twice. You shouldn't either."

Joe was laughing. *Laughing!* Not exactly the response she'd been shooting for, but it was deep and jolly, like Santa Claus. It made her laugh, too, and for a second the dark seemed lighter, and she didn't feel so cold. "You would have made an excellent drill sergeant. As a peace offering and a distraction, I'll give you this: Back in the hotel room, you still had three questions you could ask me. If it's okay, I'll ask you three questions too. It'll help keep our minds off everything. But you aren't going to die here. I'll get you out."

"Don't make promises you can't keep, Joe."

"I never make a promise I can't keep."

Savannah smiled and adjusted herself tighter against him as he leaned into the corroded metal corner, pretending it was her bed, with candles burning and those soft, gray satin sheets wound around them. Unclenching her fists, she interlaced each of her small fingers between his.

He sighed. "Okay. You start, but don't go easy on me." He laughed again, and a wave of tension spiraled through her fingertips and floated away on the bitterly cold air. She wasn't delusional. Death or torture might come, but she'd be insane before they got to tomorrow if she dwelled on it. All she could do was take this olive branch Joe offered and ignore the thought of the tetanus shot she'd be getting as soon as possible.

"Well, normal Joe would ask what your favorite color was, but because I don't want to get slapped again, I'll ask the obvious. Who was the child your parents lost?" Joe enunciated each word carefully, and not because it was cold. Someone had given him trust issues. Then there was whatever was keeping him from going to DC, his history in Afghanistan, why he killed those two men after her date with Holden instead of waiting for the cops, and that weird moment when he wouldn't let her take his shirt off. Squeezing all that into three questions would be a challenge, but she was resourceful. She made a living feeding sixty people on food donated for twenty.

A spring from the mattress scratched against her blue-jean-covered legs. She scooted an inch to the left as a mosquito buzzed between them.

"His name is Cole. He ran off and disappeared thirteen years ago. We all took it badly, but instead of drawing us closer together, it tore us in different directions. I took it especially hard because I'd thought Cole and I told each other everything. But while I just lived in the moment, he internalized everything. I naively assumed he could brush things off like I had. I didn't get people weren't all the same, and I should have. We shared a womb! He was my twin, and if I hadn't been so worried about popularity, I would've seen that all the signs of discontent had been there for years, with my dad grooming him to take over a business he had no interest in. So, I opened the soup kitchen, against my parent's wishes, because I wasn't going to mess up again. I wanted to show others that someone would listen."

Her eyes were adjusted to the dark enough now, and the creases between Joe's eyebrows had grown deeper. "I'm sorry, Savannah. I know that—" He stopped. He'd wanted to say more, but she couldn't force it, and it was her question anyway.

"What happened in Afghanistan?"

He tensed, his fingers pulling away from hers. But she squeezed, crushing them until they popped. "That's something I don't talk about."

She squeezed harder. "Tell me. I may not know your past, but you're honorable, and I believe that whatever happened, you did everything you could to stop it. Didn't you?"

Joe's voice scratched the chill with a whisper. "Probably, but just saying it is like I'm giving myself an out for what happened or something. My dad and grandpa, they were great soldiers. I always wanted—needed—to prove myself to them. But I let them down, too, even though my gramps is gone now. And my parents are looking for me, along with the White House, and I can't ever face them."

The air kicked on again, the breeze itself absolutely frigid. Each hair stood up on her arms, and her body broke out in a wave of goosebumps. Spending three decades in L.A. gave her a strong aversion to cold. She didn't even use ice in her drinks. Joe roughly alternated between holding her tight and rubbing her arms, but it didn't help her toes. She'd lost control of them, and each finger hurt.

Her teeth chattered. Her lips were frozen, but the words still came out. "Just tell me. I'm literally freezing in here, and I need to consume my mind with something. The only other option would be to take our clothes off and use our body heat to warm up." Although she said it half-heartedly, Joe's reaction was swift; his jaw tightened in a definite no. And the energy in the room shifted like they'd been flipped upside down.

"You're trying to build up to something. You suggest we take off our clothes to warm up because you want me to say why I wouldn't take off my shirt. Right?"

That's exactly what she was getting at, but with the hope he was still the guy laughing five minutes ago. Hitting a nerve had totally backfired and agitated him. He was like the book she'd dropped in her bubble bath last week; the pages were soaked and stuck together. She'd needed a pair of tweezers to separate each one, but even then, the print was running and illegible.

The air cut off abruptly and warmed to a comfortable temperature. Joe dropped her arms and jumped up, likely ready to barrel through the wall and make his own Joe-shaped exit. She fell forward, right hand catching against a loose spring on the mattress and reopening one of her cuts.

"I'm done answering questions now." He ran his fingers over every inch of the wall nearest them and shook his head, those wrinkles between his eyes digging in deep. "This wasn't a good idea. I need to be focused on getting you out of here, and now my mind isn't clear. I'm not ready for you to see me...the way I see myself."

This was the time where her peace, hugs, and love-couldn't-ever-let-a-bonding-moment pass self usually kicked into high gear, and she donned her imaginary glitter cape. She'd kept that soggy old book, so Joe wasn't going anywhere. Her heart ached just thinking about it. But smothering him with her normal approach would end in nothing but trouble. No amount of cupcake baking would get him to confide. She needed to prove his corner wasn't as empty as he thought. She crossed her arms over her bent knees and put her head down so Joe couldn't see the tears rolling over her cheeks. Without his company, she was just stuck with fear and a bunch of unanswered questions.

What happened in Afghanistan? Who gave him those trust issues? And a new question that suddenly popped up out of thin air: what would Holden think when he showed up in the morning after knowing she'd been with Joe, and she was nowhere to be found?

Maybe the answers would never come, but if anyone could get her out of this tiny cargo container, it was Joe. She tugged at a strand of hair and twirled it around a finger on her left hand. Her right hand still trickled blood, but it was time to help, even though she had no idea what to look for. It would keep her mind off the flashbacks of the last day at the very least, as if they were her biggest concern.

Joe was on his knees, on his feet, back on his knees, touching everything. Crawling over, she began doing the same thing. Looking her way, he grunted and kept searching, determined to escape. Savannah watched, hoping for that miracle, when he froze. "What is it?"

With a finger over his lips, he looked toward the speaker. The other things about their lives were okay for their captors to hear, but not this. He must've found something good. Crawling closer, the air vent kicked on again, but it wasn't cold, even though every muscle in her body immediately tensed in anticipation. Instead, she swayed on her hands and knees and collapsed.

CHAPTER EIGHTEEN
Joe

Joe tugged his eyelids open with effort and snarled. They'd gassed them through the panel in the ceiling. And just when he was getting somewhere, too. They knew it. Stopped him before he got too close and sent him into a dark nightmare of death and regret.

The room was still focusing. He jerked at his arms to rub his eyes, but they held fast under the pressure of zip ties. That brought his awareness into overload. He was in the open room by the cargo containers, old fluorescent lights blinking tiredly on the ceiling. But most of the light came from the open end of the building one hundred feet away. A generator or something similar motored away behind the cargo containers. The death-and-eggs odor lived out here too. Not some special perfume their captors had pumped into their prison cell. He'd gotten away from the mosquito though.

It'd be a surprise if there weren't cameras somewhere, but none were visible in the obvious (or less obvious) locations. Everything was cleaned except the sand slithering like snakes between the toes of his bare feet. That was weak for the level of torture they'd implied. More of an agitating afterthought to leave around. Maybe they killed the guy in charge of sweeping because he overcooked dinner.

His wooden chair was bolted to the floor, and his wrists were zip-tied to the arms. He kept his face stoic even though he wanted to smile. Did they want him to escape? All he needed was a bit of leverage to pop the arm rests apart from the bottom of the chair's arm, and he'd be out of it in seconds. But Savannah?

She was four feet to his left, head sagging, blonde hair covering her delicate cheeks and narrow nose, leaving only her full lips in view. Just close enough to boil his blood. They hadn't given her the same set up. She was chained, upright, to a wire frame. It didn't take a genius to understand they were going to torture her to torture him. Or they were *planning* to torture her to torture him. It wouldn't come to that.

He looked over every inch of her face and shook his head. A moan ripped across his dry lips. How did those Green Triangle guys best him at Savannah's house? Green Berets weren't ever supposed to let their guard down, and he hadn't. These guys were good. He cringed as he worked free. Yeah, it was always his fault, but that wasn't the thing eating away at his soul. His cowardice was.

Savannah hadn't woken yet, so staying quiet, he wrapped his hands around the arms of the chair. The zip ties were so tight his skin bubbled with blood blisters before it tore under the pressure. It was insignificant. Both legs were beneath him in the chair now. He positioned himself for the right leverage and pulled. The arms popped free. Not too loud, but in that room, it was like a gunshot. Savannah jerked. He pushed hard to get the zip ties past the rounded end of the chair arm. *Hurry.* Sweat trickled down his forehead. *Faster.* Blood dripped to the floor with rhythmic plops. *Just another second. Come on, Joe. Get her out of here and tell her everything. Don't wuss out again.*

Savannah's eyes fluttered open. Her head tilted toward him, eyes heavy, lips drawn into a frown. It took half a second for her to realize things were worse than before, but she didn't scream, didn't comment. Only stared his way, shaking and groggy, as he popped off the last zip tie and jumped up, smiling. Victory.

But breaking the chair alerted their captors, and what sounded like ten sets of footsteps approached at lightning speed. Savannah forced her head upright, her mouth dropping open. He put a finger to his lips and brushed her hair away from her face, whispering, "I might not be good at sharing, but I never make a promise I can't keep. I told you that in the conex, and it's the truth. Nothing bad is going to happen to you. I'd rather die. Trust me, and I'll tell you about Afghanistan, about everything, when this is over."

She bit her lip, and tears poured down her cheek. "I believe you, but I'm so scared. What if they hurt me? I'm not like you. My head is heavy. I can't think clearly. I want this nightmare over and behind me, if that's even possible. I don't want to have to look over my shoulder. I'll hire someone to reopen the soup kitchen if you'll just promise me we can disappear, get out of town together. Escape. No other stops, no friends, no family. Just the two of us for as long as it takes me to be able to close my eyes without fear again. Can you promise that?"

"Yes."

He dropped back into the chair and wrapped the zip ties over the arms again. His teeth clenched. Thirty-three years, and he'd never said the word *love* to anyone. Anyone. Though he didn't love Savannah, she made him want to be vulnerable, and it felt weak in a time he needed to be tough.

Tough wasn't enough right now though. No doubt their captors would be strapped, and he had nothing but a mind for murder to fall back on. Helpful in general, but not so much against guys that captured him like a ghost squad.

They marched around a cargo container, eleven men total, all armed with frowns and impressive firepower. Except the guy in the back middle. He was smirking, and that level of confidence was way more annoying than the sand. He'd had worse odds than eleven to one before and come out alive, but not without a gun. Even a tightly rolled magazine would get him somewhere. But more importantly, these men did have guns, and it was generally accepted as bad form to fight while the person you were supposed to protect was in the same room. Never a good mission if they got shot accidentally. And this wasn't some diplomat; it was Savannah. She was innocent in this crap situation.

The man in the back middle came forward through the crowd of muscular buzz-cuts clapping. He was no older than Joe, around thirty-four, with a very similar appearance. They were both built like burly runners, with black hair and sharp features, though his skin was darker, and he was most likely Afghani. It was a bit of a surprise, though Joe's face didn't give anything away.

"Yosef MacArthur. So nice to finally meet you face to face. You can call me Leader. I see you've been fighting your restraints." His voice was deep and unnervingly jolly, but his accent was strong. He ceased the clapping and wiped a finger across the blood on the floor from Joe's wrists.

"I got bored, *Leader.* I needed something to do, and I left my crossword puzzles at home. Could we get a television? I love Jeopardy."

Leader, as the arrogant jerk wanted to be called, sneered with two rows of startlingly gray teeth appearing behind his open lips. "Too bad you saved all your conversation for me. Savannah would have liked to hear more from you last night. We would have, too, for that matter. So, to answer your question, a television, no. But my men would be happy to plan some activities for you."

Leader strode around, laughing as he retrieved a blade from a holster at his waist and began spinning it around the tip of his finger. Drops of blood splattered on the concrete as he continued, ignoring them. If it was just him, he would've laughed at the fear Leader was trying to convey, but he wasn't alone. Savannah was here, and based on her audible teeth chattering, the whole knife-on-the-finger thing was working pretty well.

But what was his move? If there were fewer guys in the room or maybe a distraction, it'd lessen the chance of Savannah getting hurt if he went into combat mode, which could give him the chance he needed to get her away from the firefight. How could that be arranged?

Leader turned to his men for a moment, and Savannah glanced at Joe sideways. "*I trust you,*" she mouthed.

Leader spun on his heel and pranced over to Savannah. He stroked her cheek gently. She tensed but didn't utter a sound. Goosebumps splattered over her arms. "And you, my little treasure, my apologies for being caught up in all of this messiness. You've been so brave. What is it about you that has Yosef working such long hours to keep you alive?" He ran his thumb over her bottom lip until it was red and wet with his blood. She crinkled her nose and pursed her lips as he pressed his body against hers. Joe fought every fiber of his being to keep his butt against the wooden chair and not leap over and snap Leader's neck. As easy and enjoyable as that would be, he still had to wait, even if his head caught fire with rage. Leader's men stood five feet behind him in a line, weapons drawn, eyes cut in sharp horizontal lines.

Leader twirled Savannah's hair in his fingers and inhaled deeply, gazing over at Joe as he wrapped his hands under her shirt and around her waist. Savannah was ravished with shudders. She wept. There was no appropriate emotion for what he was having to watch. His mind spun with darkness and violence. All he could picture were his fingers plunging through Leader's eye sockets. Joe clenched the chair tighter. He wasn't going to be able to restrain himself much longer.

Leader laughed. "Oh, Joe, relax. Everything's fine. Maybe I'll take Savannah with me to the back and we'll look for that television you wanted."

Crunch!

Savannah threw her head forward and smashed Leader's nose into an Afghani pancake. Blood spewed out like a fountain and four of his men slipped in stance. Leader grabbed his nose, blood pouring through his finger as he smacked Savannah across the face with his left hand. Her head lolled to the side as he unhooked the metal bracelets on her ankles. If he got away with her now, he'd either kill her or rape her. Or both.

In a smooth motion, Joe slipped free again and bounded from the chair onto Leader, disarming him and slamming his Glock 19 against his skull. Leader's bloody nose made it a cinch. But now ten angry men aimed their sidearms at his head, and Savannah's wrists were still locked behind him. This was grim. Lucky for Leader, he needed a body shield, so snapping his neck was out of the question for now. Dead weight was hard to carry.

So, he rolled the dice and addressed the group while he frisked Leader, handing his keys back to Savannah, who had her head up again. He pocketed two blades and an extra magazine as he talked. "If you're in this scheme for the money, I'll double whatever you're getting paid and you can leave now. You're smart enough to know a good deal. Be smarter than your boss. He's going to eat a bullet soon."

Three men stepped slowly forward, and the energy in the room shifted. Savannah threw off the last lock and jumped to the ground to bury herself in his back, fingers wrapping around the loose fabric of his shirt. The other seven men didn't know where to aim.

Leader didn't fight back; he knew Joe wouldn't hesitate to follow through, but he did chime in with his sickly smooth voice. "Yes, take the deal. Just remember that my boss doesn't cope well with traitors. He'll kill you by tomorrow. Ultimately, the choice is always yours, but whoever kills Joe and Savannah will be rewarded. Oh, and Joe, if you're planning something, do it quickly, because backup will be here in about thirty seconds."

The muscles in his arm reacted, lifting the gun and pistol-whipping Leader across the mouth. A gray tooth rattled onto the floor. More blood consumed his face, so the image was grotesque. Savannah tapped him as he inched back toward the blue sky and empty pavement. "I hear their footsteps, Joe." Each of the men moved forward, keeping his pace and waiting for the right moment to shoot, when a dozen more men barreled around the corner.

Savannah's body rattled against his. What was the move?

No one had fired yet. It was the world's longest and most sweat-inducing standoff. But the fresh air trickled in through his nostrils. They were almost there. A bird tweeted, then her song stopped, and he stumbled back. One of the new men had fired, dropping Leader to the ground with a bullet to the chest and leaving Joe and Savannah exposed.

A humid breeze blew in, swirling around them like a useless barrier. He pushed Savannah behind a metal dumpster and began shooting, vision fixing the scene with a sharpness. Bullets zinged past his head in slow motion. He pointed to a cargo container by the exit. "Go! I've got you!" She shook her head and wrung her hands together. It wasn't going to work. The men inched in closer, and there was no way they could both get to the cargo container for cover.

"I'm not leaving you here! You'll die! And you said you always keep your promises! We can't run away if you're dead. I can't move my feet."

Her knees buckled together, but the men were only a few feet away. "Then, today will be a first. Now get moving. Go!" His heart ached as he launched her to the side and slid into view, shooting, the concrete cold and grainy against his arm and bare feet. There were sixteen men standing, and he had five bullets left in his last magazine and a few rounds in a Beretta he'd picked up off one of the guys. His stomach lurched, and every sound, every movement, amplified times one hundred: Savannah's slapping footsteps leaving the concrete and connecting with the pavement, a bullet grazing the flesh of his left arm, his rapid heartbeat as he ducked behind a dumpster, his last bullet digging through the forehead of his closest attacker and out the other side.

Dropping the guns, he wailed and ran into another man, digging Leader's blade through an eyeball with his right hand while his left launched the last blade into a muscular chest. Another bullet hit his shoulder, as he ripped the knife back out and pressed forward with only that and his fists as weapons.

Bury the pain. Bury the fear. Give her a chance to run, and die knowing this was one promise worth breaking.

His vision reddened along the sides from blood loss, and every sound dimmed to silence as his fist extended. But the intended target was gone. They all were. He blinked. What happened?

Every single man was sprawled on the ground, bleeding out. They were all dead. It was not his imagination. He rubbed his ears and dropped to the concrete. Vision swaying, he blinked and pulled his lids up again with determination as he heard to the sound of footsteps approaching.

His dad was there on a knee, lifting him as a team formed in the background. His voice was all Joe could register. "Joe. Joe. I'm here, son. I love you, and I'm so proud of you. I always have been."

CHAPTER NINETEEN
Savannah

The wind rustled the tall grass around her feet as she dangled them off the back of the ambulance. But her eyes? She kept them on the clouds floating across the setting sun. Palm trees swayed, and birds sang with the crickets as the sky changed from blue to orange to pink.

It was postcard perfect.

Except for the dead bodies, countless soldiers, FBI, and crime scene tape. They'd moved the metal frame, the one she'd been locked onto, the one her imagination said she could still feel, the one she would've died on if Joe hadn't saved her. The half-size cargo container they'd been trapped in still remained. She twirled a blade of grass between her fingers and tapped her head against the door of the ambulance. Why weren't the medics finished yet? It was time to go. Beyond time to go. She couldn't stare at that cargo container much longer.

The paramedics checked her out earlier, and everything was fine, physically. Then there was the chat with a police-sanctioned therapist, followed by a chat with her mother's therapist, followed by a surprisingly short debrief with the FBI, who said they'd finish up later. And even still, Joe's exam was taking longer. All she knew was that his two gunshot wounds were superficial, and he was going to be okay. And that's because his dad had come out to tell her while a medic catalogued her vitals.

Stanley MacArthur was about seventy and in great shape, with thick white hair and a deep crease along his forehead, from either reading or cringing a lot. The way he rubbed his back, she guessed the latter. "Mr. MacArthur? I wanted to tell you that having you show up with the team today and seeing your face... That meant more to Joe that you'll ever know."

His arms were around her before he even responded, and big, fat tears plopped down his cheeks. "Savannah, thank you for saving my son."

Head tilted to the side, she said, "I'm confused. You, Clark, and Delta Force saved Joe. And he saved me. How did I help?"

He squeezed his arm around her shoulder. "Because, honey, his mom and I have been trying for the last thirty-three years to prove to that man how much we love him, how DNA doesn't matter, how..." He burst into tears again. "How proud we are of him. And it wasn't until I saw him today that I knew for certain he believed it. And I know it has everything in the world to do with you. So, thank you." He'd wiped a tear from under her eye and turned on his heel so she could finish her check-up.

But that was hours ago, and waiting was hard. Luckily, her parents had given her a little space after their original frantic arrival to the crime scene.

Clark approached stealthily from the other side of the ambulance and shared a spot on the bumper as she laid the blade of grass she'd been fidgeting with in her lap. "You hangin' in there?" He'd removed most of his gear from their rescue, but the black waves of his buzz cut shimmered with sweat. He propped his hands on his hips uncomfortably, his right one resting on top of a pistol in a holster.

"Is there a right answer? You and all those soldiers, you were life savers showing up when you did, but I'm still reeling. I need to talk to Joe. Can you make that happen?"

Clark flashed his signature smile, but it didn't reach his eyes. "That's why I'm here. I've got some bad news, and since Joe couldn't share it, he thought it'd be more palatable if you heard it from someone who looked like Denzel." He took her hand gently in his and attempted to resurrect his sense of humor. "And please don't slap me or head butt me, Savannah, because I hear you're more lethal than Joe, but he's...already gone."

The blade of grass drifted away on a light breeze, taking with it her optimism. Joe broke his promise, and it was hard to hold back the tears. "Where is he?"

"On an airplane headed back to D.C. for a debriefing and to finally award him the Medal of Honor. Probably didn't tell ya that, did he?"

Savannah shook her head.

"Figures. Still doesn't accept he's earned it, but he has. Even though I'd left the Army before that mission, I spent plenty of 'em with him. Enough to know not another guy out there's bled for it like him." He watched her eyes: confused, proud, sad. "Anyway, he'll be gone about two weeks. But he's comin' back for ya. He said to tell you it might be delayed, but he'd keep his promise to take you away."

Savannah dropped her head against the ambulance door and looked back at the sky. It was pink and navy now. "I don't know what happened in Afghanistan, but I've seen the way Joe takes care of people, the way he took care of me. I'm happy for him that he's being honored. But another part of me, the scared, scarred part...well, I've never been one of those girls that needed a man, so please don't judge me when I say this." She crossed her free hand to the side of her face even though he'd stopped looking. "But I need him, and I can't wait two weeks or even two days."

"First of all, I don't judge you, girl. Far from it. And you're right. Joe hates debriefs and still isn't ready to accept the medal. But compromises had to be made." He tapped his finger over the pistol and shifted on the bumper, letting go of her hand.

If she looked at Clark, she'd cry. It didn't make sense, but she couldn't look at his face. So, he followed suit, and they sat pointing at oddly shaped clouds, identifying them as dragons and cookies and elephants until she calmed down. Sighing loudly, she asked, "What compromises did you guys make?"

"Well, I guess I should start by saying the Pentagon has had men lookin' for Joe for months. His parents have been lookin' too. Anyway, last night, when Joe came to see you, I was there, parked down the street. I was Joe's man on the ground, his extra set of eyes, and I never saw that team enter your parent's compound, only saw them peel down the street like Richard Petty on a bender. Oh, and that rich kid, he's okay, by the way. Showed up around sunrise that mornin'. Been stayin' with your folks until this is over. He's an alright guy, I guess, if you're into the manners and money thing." Clark clicked his tongue rhythmically and paused. He was waiting for her to jump in and confess her undying love for his friend, which was irritating, but somehow Clark could get away with it.

She kept her eyes up but nudged his ribs. "Seriously. Keep talking. We've got a lot of ground to cover. I think the moment for picking the safe choice has come and gone."

"Ouch. Alright, alright. Just checkin'. Gotta take care of my boy, that's all. Anyway, the fact that this team got in without me seeing 'em has been eatin' me up. I should've noticed somethin' was off. But because I was at your parent's estate, I trailed 'em here, to the warehouse." He waved his arms dispassionately since they were still staring at a cloud that resembled a turtle. "Their setup was serious, and I needed precision to get you guys out alive. My security team at the hotel is good, all ex-military guys, but I wasn't gonna risk either of your lives on anything less than the best. So, I made a deal. Contacted Joe's parents, who had a direct line to the White House, since they'd been lookin' for Joe, and the White House got me on the line with the Pentagon. I told 'em I knew where Joe was but needed an extraction team. The Pentagon sent in Delta Force, with the understanding that they'd let Joe's dad and me on the team, since we were both Green Berets, and in exchange I'd give 'em Joe."

The sky was dark now, with a spattering of stars around a crescent moon. Savannah stood up and dusted off her pants. "I guess there's no point in waiting around here. I'll go back to my normal life and pretend none of the last few days happened." Tears welled up and rolled down her cheeks. Her breathing picked up until she was in the middle of a pretty ugly cry. "But I can't go back! I can't! I needed time. Time away. Time with Joe. Time to learn how to deal with what's happened and be alone with the only man I really trust to keep me safe, the man I…care for."

Clark jumped up, his real smile back. "Care for, huh? That dodgin' bullets stuff really works for the ladies, I guess." He looked over to gauge her openness to jokes, but the tears were still falling. "I *am* sorry. But here's the deal: The Pentagon believes this organization's been smothered out and that you don't have anything further to fear. I agree. They pulled out all the stops for this. Anyway, Joe demanded I follow you around like an extravagantly handsome shadow until his return. Take you wherever you wanna go, offer a shoulder to cry on, share a bucket of ice cream. So, where we headed first?"

Clark looked her way and she straightened her back, wiping away the grime and tears from her face. "You sacrificed to keep me alive, so I'll attempt to be less emotional. No promises." She sniffed loudly. "I'd just built things up in my head. Him driving while I slept and camping in a tent under the stars in a state I'd never seen before. Getting to know each other. Falling asleep in his arms, because that's where I'm safe." Savannah shook her head and tried to force her brain to send her blood anywhere but her cheeks. Useless. "It may all sound silly to you. I don't know. But for me, it was an escape. Yes, you said the Green Triangle is gone, but my heart hasn't stopped racing, and I haven't forgotten a millisecond of the last three days. But since that escape isn't going to happen for a while, I'll settle for sleeping in my own bed until my parents and the FBI head back over tomorrow. I'm so tired. And let's revisit your ice cream idea in a few days. For now, all I can ingest is coffee."

Clark rambled the whole way to her apartment about his three sisters, his time in the Army, and then leaving the Army to work hotel security. Maybe it was an attempt to bond with his new roommate or distract her. Either way, it was clear he was very different from Joe. And that was okay. He was comforting and kept her laughing. He did continue scanning their surroundings at each stoplight, and as they pulled into the parking lot of her apartment building, but he'd found a way to do surveillance without a palpable level of tension. "Which one is yours?"

Savannah unbuckled and clutched her hands around Clark's overnight bag like a shield, looking up for the first time in several long minutes. He let her keep it. Before answering, she spied a black Mercedes parked ahead and threw her head against the headrest in defeat. "Just when I thought we could enjoy a sappy romance movie in peace before sleeping for the next twelve hours." Clark raised his eyebrow and she pointed. "My parents are here."

"It's cool. I'm great with parents. And I met 'em already at the crime scene. Safe to assume they love me already."

They stepped out of the car and walked toward the building together. "I appreciate your optimism," she said.

Her parents already knew everything. Obviously. Clark had Delta Force and the feds coordinate with her parents as soon as he learned of the kidnapping, which had proved to be valuable since they learned of the kidnapper's demands that way. Her father agreed to turn over the drugs if they could ensure with one hundred percent certainty this organization would be crushed to nothing and she would be saved. There were apparently multiple threats to ruin the lives of everyone involved if a single hair on her head was out of place. Then, of course, they'd come as soon as Savannah was rescued and fussed over her before her mother pulled her away for a lengthy conversation. One where Holden's name was dropped at least thirty times. They'd probably had some designer fit him for a wedding tux while they waited on her rescue.

But at the end of the day, it felt good. Her dad cared, and so did her mom. But the way they cared was taxing and time-consuming, and it was 3:00 a.m. She'd begged them to give her until tomorrow for a visit and full debrief and had believed her pleas had been received. Every part of her body felt like it'd been run over by a truck, especially her mind. The stress and memories were so fresh she still tasted Leader's coppery blood in her mouth. She gagged and focused her eyes further out.

People popped in and out of the bars across the street, laughing and wobbling around after last call. She scanned the pavement for her mom and dad and looked down self-consciously at the outfit she hadn't had a chance to change out of. Leader's hands had touched her stomach, her back, and higher than that. She shivered. The feeling was still there, but a shower would wash everything away. Hopefully.

They reached two large, glass doors with black handles. Clark whistled quietly as Gene, the doorman, let them in. "Good evening, Ms. Carrington." The floors were black-and-white tile with large, abstract paintings in shades of pink and orange on the walls. Chandeliers full of miniature spherical bulbs hung from the ceiling and sprayed light across the floor. Gene walked them across the lobby and pushed the button on the elevator for the third floor. "Fair warning: Your parents are upstairs waiting. I'm sorry. I couldn't hold your mother down here. I tried but she... Well, she's difficult. And she brought some feds with her. Anyway, good luck, and I'm sorry about what happened. She told me and everyone else she's come across in town."

The elevator chimed, and the door slid to the left like a hoity entrance straight to Hell. Savannah leaned against the wall. Even it felt hot. But Hell would be down, and they were going up. She leaned into Clark's side and grimaced as they rode. One of Joe's prayers would be good right about now.

When the elevator lurched to a stop, her stomach tumbled with it. Her mother waited in the hall under a round sconce, wearing a black Dolce dress and pumps, French tips tapping against her narrow hips. Her dad and four FBI agents stood in her shadow, with creases on their foreheads and tight lips, as if unsure how to ask the first question in case she broke into a crying fit. And, of course, Holden was with them, his face lighting up like a Christmas tree upon seeing her. This, this right here, is why she'd wanted to run away. The energy required for this conversation would leave a chasm too wide to fill with her king-sized bed.

CHAPTER TWENTY
Joe

The private jet was stuffy, and little spots of perspiration popped up all over his neck. The White House sent their brass, the Pentagon sent their brass, and neither wasted any time diving into a series of invasive questioning. Joe groaned and dropped his head against the leather seat of the plane, rubbing his face. He'd prefer a repeat of basic training to these questions, but that hadn't been an option.

His watch peeked out from under his sleeve, reminding him it'd been an hour. The early morning sun poured through the window. Pulling the shade down made his shoulder throb and his left arm tighten. The pain wasn't excruciating, but every time he thought about Savannah, down there beneath the clouds, it bothered him again. She was going to be devastated. He'd broken her trust. A promise was binding; that was something every soldier knew. Operations changed on a dime, war was unpredictable, and sometimes men didn't make it back home. Friends didn't make it back home. Brothers didn't make it back home.

Steve Garring: He'd grown up in the same town as Nadine, best friends since grade school, and clung to Joe during his first deployment. Steve was a good man, a pastor's son. But if he was being honest with himself, Steve wasn't cut out to be a soldier, especially a Green Beret. He wasn't disciplined, was always anxious, and even in combat hadn't learned the basics of tactical awareness. What he lacked in military strategy he made up for in kindness and carpentry. He would've made an excellent humanitarian.

Steve pulled him aside under the heat of the Afghani sun that morning, complaining of a stomachache. The team was going out on a routine recon of the area, and Steve wasn't vomiting or anything. He'd clapped him on the shoulder and told him to gear up and suck it up. And he had. But when Steve thought there was a shimmer of a rifle on a mountain range ahead, he'd stepped off the path, away from the team. The explosion wasn't as clear in Joe's dreams anymore. More of just the moments around it. Dirt dropping onto his shoulders like a fine rain. Ringing ears. Steve's leather pocket Bible landing with a thud in front of his combat boots.

Steve was gone and looking at his face hadn't been an option. Nadine would ask about Steve, and the only way he wanted to picture his face when she asked was as he sat at night, singing under the stars. And she had asked about him. Blamed him for not protecting her best friend.

"Joe. We understand the past few days have been taxing. Do you need a break?" Mr. Smith, one of the White House men, asked. Joe turned his head. The old man had the arm of his glasses between his teeth as he relaxed into his seat and closed a folder. He suspected Joe would say yes. But the sooner it all was over, the better.

"No thank you, sir. I'd like to continue. Any way we could wrap this up before the plane lands?"

The eight men around him laughed. He must be joking, right? "Well, Joe, we're familiar with your mission in Afghanistan. You were a true hero. There are many questions involving The Green Triangle and why you didn't include the local police in your actions, but those questions will still come. For this ride, what we are still trying to ascertain is why you ran and why your house was ransacked. It caused quite a stir."

Joe straightened against the brown leather and tapped his fingers on the conference table in front of him. "*I* ransacked my house because I failed my men and failed at my marriage, too. The short answer is whether you view me as a hero or not, my team died. *My* team. *I* planned the mission. *I* trusted the informant. *I* led my team. *I* failed my team. Every single one of them. Fathers, husbands, sons. Gone. And when I got home to try and repair a marriage on life support, my wife had removed all her things from our house. Left me for someone that jumped at the chance to serve her needs instead of his country's. So, I left because I didn't want you to find me. I didn't want that medal and the honor that comes with it, because I didn't deserve it. I still don't. I grew up knowing two heroes personally: my Dad, Distinguished Service Cross in Vietnam and my Grandfather, Medal of Honor at the Battle of the Bulge. I have known and served with real heroes. Believe me, you've got the wrong guy."

The men weren't laughing anymore. Three of them gazed at their notepads and busied themselves writing. The other four crossed their legs and unbuttoned their blazers, but Mr. Smith folded his glasses on his lap and bridged his hands over his forehead before looking up at Joe again. "I understand, son. I may look like a washed-up old man, but I was a Marine, many moons ago. Serving your country is a calling, and for a few men like yourself, it calls louder than others. You have been blessed by God with the Warrior Spirit. Sometimes it seems like a curse, especially to your family. It tugs on your soul, and you find yourself always volunteering, always willing to sacrifice, so other people can sleep peacefully at night. And while my story and yours are very different, there's something you need to understand: If ninety-nine other men—good men—were put in your position at the warehouse, Savannah would have most likely been severely tortured, molested, and killed. But *you* were there. You acted at the right moment, and you sacrificed yourself to save her. That is the mark of a true hero, and it's exactly what you did in Afghanistan. You are a sheepdog, son, a warrior most others only attempt to emulate. You'll always choose to protect the flock from danger. And though you may never call yourself a hero, you are deserving of it."

Everyone was silent, for a few seconds then a few minutes. The air conditioner whizzed and blew around an American flag mounted to the floor, but everyone was frozen. Who was going to talk first? He should have. Could've at least said thanks or something more eloquent. But it didn't seem good enough, because Mr. Smith was right. Savannah had been too. He would always protect people with everything he had. So, if he couldn't accept the term *hero*, then *sheepdog* would do.

The jet rattled around on rain clouds as they neared Washington D.C., and the pilot came over the speaker. "Gentlemen, we will be landing in D.C. in thirty-one minutes. Buckle your seatbelts, and we will begin our descent."

Mr. Smith nodded to the men around the conference table, and everyone rose, dismissing to their seats on the other side of the make-shift partitions put up for their "private" meeting. He followed the blue diamonds of the carpet over to a seat next to his dad. He'd demanded to ride on the plane with Joe, and since he and his mother would be flown out for the Medal of Honor ceremony in a few days anyway, the White House didn't argue.

Joe buckled and folded his hands in his lap. "I'm glad you rode with us. How much could you hear through the partitions?"

His dad patted his hands and shifted in his seat. "I heard enough, son. Calling yourself a hero is never easy. I wish you could see yourself how your mother an' I see you. How Savannah sees you. And, on that note, let me say this: she's not Nadine. I'm sorry she left ya, but I reckon it was for the best. If you give her a chance, Savannah'll make you as happy as you've always deserved to be. 'Course that's just your old man's two cents."

The men around them carried on conversations over elevator music as the lights of Washington D.C. came into view beneath them. "I wish it was that easy, Dad. I don't think I deserve that kind of happiness, or I'll mess it up if I get it. Do you think she'll look at me differently after I tell her about Afghanistan?"

His dad's voice was husky, with a light southern accent, but at that moment it seemed to catch in his throat. "Yeah, son. I imagine she will.

She'll love you even more than she does right now. Your momma and I tried to show you how brilliant you were, but you always seemed unhappy. Maybe it was our fault. If we'd moved you out of our small town or spent more time talkin' to you or—"

"It wasn't your fault, Dad. You were both great parents. And even though it's taken me a while, I'd like for you to get to see me happy. After the ceremony, I'm going back for Savannah, to take her away like I promised." They sat in silence after that, but his dad was smiling. The landing gear dropped from the bottom of the plane, and they descended rapidly into the rainy D.C. early morning.

The Pentagon had four soldiers waiting on the tarmac with umbrellas. They would transport Joe and his dad to military housing, where they'd settle into a home to call their own for the duration of their stay. The way these things went, it was always best to assume the lengthiest amount of time possible, but you never knew. Most likely it'd be a week or two before he saw Savannah again, because he would talk to loads of people, and they'd all drill him with the same questions. He cracked his fingers and stared out the window of their black SUV as they pulled into the driveway of a detached home of about 1,100 square feet. A winding sidewalk led to a red front door surrounded by blue siding. He pushed open his door and stepped out, stretching his legs. Gray clouds still blanketed the sky, but it was only misting. Skipping over a missing chunk of the sidewalk, Joe flipped his backpack over his shoulder.

Clark found it at the warehouse and had given it back with his usual enthusiasm. And it *was* exciting. Allen's medal was still tucked away inside of it, with the note and all the other things he couldn't part with when he'd gone dark. Clark knew specifically why he'd been so adamant about getting his bag back after the rescue. He had served on Joe's team overseas, before he left the Army, and knew Joe carried the playing card in his ratty backpack. Their Special Forces team had called themselves the Aces, each of them always carrying around a playing card. He had the ace of spades. Clark had the ace of hearts, which made sense, as he was more of a lover. Even when he left for civilian life, he still carried it. Hinley and Morrison had hearts too. And the other guys were a mix of clubs and diamonds. Having the weight of the pack pressing against his back gave him a sense of peace.

Inside, the house was much the same as the outside: outdated and short on TLC. But it did have running water, which was one step up from the streets.

"Sir," Ted, a First Lieutenant spoke up, "we've been instructed to give you the time you need to take a nap or a shower, but we'll need to bring you to the Pentagon for further questioning after that. There are towels, toiletries, and a clean uniform waiting for you in the bathroom down the hall."

A nap sounded better than a shower, so he nodded and turned right down the shag carpet of the hallway. A couple ordinary pictures hung from the walls, of blue flowers in vases and beaches at sunset. It was supposed to convey a sense of hominess, but it didn't. Home would be wherever Savannah was, if she'd still have him. But having both his parents here would help. His mom would be baking in that electrical nightmare of a kitchen as soon as her feet touched the laminate.

He checked the lock on the window and peered out before pulling the frilly curtains to a close. Neighbors lined the street on either side in cookie-cutter houses, but it was quiet. He'd be looking over his shoulder for the rest of his life because it's how his dad trained him, but the immediate threat seemed to be squashed. Slipping off a pair of borrowed boots, he tucked under a quilt and filled his lungs with air, holding it there for a moment. The white metal frame squeaked. Still, it was more comfortable than anything he'd slept on in the last six months.

His eyes were closing involuntarily, when the door creaked, and he leapt up, hand instinctively reaching for the Glock they hadn't allowed him to bring on the plane. "Easy, son. It's just me. Thought you might want to borrow my cell before drifting off, to send Savannah a text. I imagine she's sleeping by now, but maybe ya get lucky and you can hear her voice." He tossed the phone on the bed and snapped the door closed.

Joe was on the phone in seconds, calling Clark. Savannah's phone was destroyed with his. He tapped his grandma-looking quilt restlessly, counting the seconds as each ring resounded in his ears. But his dad was right; they must've been sleeping. So, he texted instead.

Savannah, it's Joe. I'm safe in D.C. and I'll try to wrap all this up as fast as possible. Breaking this promise to you is never what I intended, so I'm sorry. But I'm realizing this is one thing I have to do to move on. The other is telling you everything like I should have in that conex. Don't give up on me.

-Joe

At twelve thirty, Joe bolted upright in bed, wishing again for some sort of weapon. Maybe he would sleep tonight with a steak knife (or three) under the pillow. There had been a clatter in the kitchen. The organization chasing them had been dismantled for good, so everything was fine. On the plane, he'd even given over the business card with the green triangle he discovered in the alley, though no one seemed to be able to make heads or tails of it.

The noise outside his room was undoubtedly his dad trying to make a cup of coffee. He could find his way around a battlefield better than a kitchen, so Joe laid back down and checked the phone. Still no text. The rain splattered against the window, and he sat with his back to the headboard and his eyes closed. Savannah's face filled his mind. What was she doing right now: sleeping or stuck answering questions for the FBI? They would be all over her and her dad after everything, making sure they didn't miss a single detail and to ensure Savannah's family hadn't knowingly committed any crimes. Her dad hiding drugs from the Green Triangle hadn't been his smartest move, and it would bring a lot of heat onto Savannah.

But Savannah didn't mind questions like he did. In fact, she loved to talk, and she was innocent, so there was no way she'd have any blowback. Especially since, after the warehouse, the only surviving guy gave up his boss and died within five minutes. His name was Damon Colter, a thirty-something senator for the state of California and a proud supporter of a gun-free America. Ironic that he ran a drug syndicate hellbent on eliminating anyone that got in their way. Or maybe it was an extraordinary cover. All up until he got caught and hauled to justice by the FBI this morning, claiming it was all a big misunderstanding.

So, Savannah was safe, right?

CHAPTER TWENTY-ONE
Savannah

Savannah yawned, swaying between Clark and Holden on the plush gray sofa of her living room. She wrapped a knitted blanket tightly around her shoulders. The feds had been at it for a while now. Three hours? Four hours? Her six cups of coffee were long gone, only their lingering aroma a reminder that it wasn't enough to keep her functioning for much longer. The clock was in the kitchen, so the sun rising through the glass balcony doors was her only indicator of time. How many questions could four men have? The answer was a lot—sixty-three, to be exact. And despite the comfy couch, they knew she was exhausted and hadn't let up. The only plus in all of this was that they'd finally let her father off the hook for shipping drugs and then hiding them from the organization that everyone, including the feds and the Pentagon, were referring to as the Green Triangle. He hadn't knowingly committed a crime and was attempting to correct his mistake without involving the authorities, even though he probably should have.

She'd been sweating about three hours earlier as they separated her from Clark, Holden, and her parents to make sure their stories matched up. She'd been left with a man whom she mentally referred to as Tall Moustache Guy, also known as Special Agent Dennis. He'd dramatically popped open his leather briefcase and clicked his fountain pen with a huff.

139

He leaned in, glaring at her, twisting his moustache quietly for about a minute as tobacco from his last smoke trailed over the coffee table. She shifted on the couch. Ending up in prison would sure be the icing on the cake. "So, how exactly are you involved in your father's business, Ms. Carrington?"

"Involved?" Her eyebrows scrunched and her neck heated.

"Yes. Involved. Your father hid drugs from The Green Triangle, but you're the one they came after. Your kidnapping wasn't their first attempt. They attacked you in an alley and at a hospital. What did you do that put you at the top of their hit list?"

"Well," she mumbled, squeezing her cup of coffee and inhaling hazelnut, "all I knew about my father's business, growing up, was that he spent more time with it than me. As an adult I haven't learned much more than that. And my attack in the alley had nothing to do with it anyway. I was in the wrong place at the wrong time. Those…monsters were hurting my friend, and I ran to help. You know this already. They thought my friend Allen passed information about their organization on to me before he died. And he left a note to Joe, saying he took a video, which would shed more light on everything, but we never found it. I only found out about my father being blackmailed by them three minutes before I was kidnapped. That's all I know. I promise."

Special Agent Dennis let go of his moustache and smiled. "Good. Thank you, Savannah. I know you've been through an ordeal, but I had to cover my bases. Your testimony aligns perfectly with everyone else's. So, I'll ask you a few more questions, and then we can bring everyone back out to continue together."

And he had. Her mother insisted on Holden sitting with her for the duration of the questioning, and Clark wasn't far behind. Her parents shared the loveseat, and the agents all pulled in kitchen chairs. If her mom hadn't been forcing the relationship with Holden on her every single moment, she would've never offered to sit on the loveseat. It was deep and fluffier than a poodle. Her mother sank into it, with the red soles of her

Louboutin's in the air. She kept her gaze away the best she could because it threatened to send her into a fit of giggles.

And maybe it was better she couldn't see her mother's face clearly, because there were a lot of questions about Joe. A lot. And she was red again, rubbing the scars on her stomach, feeling her mother's grimace. The orchids on the long wooden table behind the couch curved around her head, desperate to catch every whispered answer with their white-and-purple petals. Looking at Holden wasn't an option either. If she gave him an opportunity to talk, he'd say something lovely and so freaking perfect that she'd be forced to use her head in deciding the future instead of her heart. Holden wasn't going to be the one she would live happily ever after with. She needed to make her peace with that.

Special Agent Dennis rose from his white plastic chair and rubbed his hands together. "Thank you all for your patience. I'm sure we've worn out our welcome, but this investigation is coming to a close, and very soon you'll be able to go back to your normal lives. For the next few days though, as we comb every inch of Senator Colter's office to ensure there are no loose ends, we will have agents stationed outside your homes for extra security. If you think of anything else, I'll leave my card." He inched it out of his overflowing wallet with his thumb and dropped it onto the stack of books on her coffee table before motioning to the other agents. In moments, they were out the door, and Savannah let out a sigh. The air in the room wasn't suffocating her anymore.

Holden opened his mouth to speak first, but her mom won, catapulting to her feet with her dad's help, like some fashion ninja. She nonchalantly dusted off the bookshelf by her television and bored her eyes into Savannah's. "Darling, it's time for you to get some rest. Do you mind if I walk you to your room while the boys talk?" Saying no wasn't an option, so a faint nod was the only available response.

Her mom clicked down the hall behind her, past the pictures from work and of her college friends. Savannah spun around tiredly when the clicking halted. Her mother noticed a picture of Cole in the tire swing with

Savannah. They were twelve. It was easy to remember because it was the day before they found out why Cole had been so sick for so long. It represented a time when their family had more fun together. A time before her mom splurged on makeup to cover the dark circles under her eyes so no one asked questions. Fingers covering her open mouth she whispered, "Have you always had this here?"

"Yes. It keeps my memories of him alive. I've got a few others scattered around the apartment. I just…can't…do things the way you and Dad do. I'm sorry." Royal posture was a thing her mother had spent the last fifty-five years perfecting. But her back slumped and then her head. A tear rolled down her cheek and left a smear of black under her eye. Savannah turned back, reaching through the door frame and to the left to flip the light switch on before they entered her room.

"Darling, have a seat please. I planned to speak with you about something, but after seeing that picture, there is a much more pressing conversation to undergo first." She waved her hand toward the bed and dropped onto it beside Savannah, removing her heels and pulling her legs up in a surprisingly casual way. Savannah's heartbeat loudened like it used to when she was a kid in trouble. She picked at the embroidery on a square pillow and tried to not make too much direct eye contact. "Cole had threatened to run off before, join the Peace Corps, Doctors Without Borders, anywhere he could do humanitarian work. He was impetuous and didn't consider what his future would be like, and not just financially. But it was always just a threat. He'd never been healthy enough to follow through, and once he was, once you'd given him your kidney, he seemed more content, so your father and I took a step back and didn't pressure him about running the family business anymore. But obviously you know the rest. He left, and I busied myself with anything and everything to take my mind off my colossal failure as a mother and, ultimately, let it become who I was. It was better than feeling, better than countless hours spent crying. It was what I needed. I never asked what you needed, and as a mother I'm afraid I've failed you too, darling."

Savannah's face flushed, and tears filled her eyes. She opened her mouth to speak, but her mom cut her off. "Please let me finish so I make sure to say this the right way. I believed if I spent my time finding you a man like Holden, you would settle into a life similar to mine, where you could just be...content after such loss. But you aren't me, though it's taken much too long to realize it." Her mother wiped a stray tear from her own eye and squeezed Savannah's arm. "And, for that, I am so grateful. You are much wiser, braver, and more beautiful than I could have ever imagined. And I won't push Holden on you. I see the way you talk about this...Joe. Apparently, your father and I judged him too quickly. Made assumptions that weren't necessarily true. Money isn't everything, and you've shown me that. Let me begin correcting past mistakes by sending you and Clark to Joe's Medal of Honor ceremony. You should be there. But you must promise to find an appropriate moment to let Holden down easy. While you were in that horrid warehouse, he spoke of some party he was going to invite you to when all of this was over. Go with him to that or take him to lunch or something. He kept our household sane when we were running around in despair. He may not be the one for you, but he has a good heart and would make a good friend."

Savannah leapt across the bed, crushing her mother in a hug, and they both cried. How had it taken this long? "Mom, tomorrow is Sunday. I still keep our old tradition alive. Would you like to come over and watch a movie with me? Maybe you could...paint my nails like you used to."

"I'd love nothing more."

Clark came in as her mother, father, and Holden left. If she wasn't absolutely drained, she would've let Holden down right there, but he deserved better. She'd promised her mother something more formal, and that was fair. She'd put him through so much, and he'd still stayed with her parents and aided the investigation until she was home safely. Thinking about him always left a churning in her gut, because they really would be great together.

She was turning off the overhead light and on a number of night lights to quell her fear of the dark as Clark laughed at the doorway. "Girl, I don't think your eyes are even open but somehow you're still functioning. I've checked the perimeter, and everythin's locked down. The FBI's stationed outside, too. Just wanted you to know you could rest easy. And before you do, I thought you might wanna see this. Seems our man Joe sent you a text on my phone. Nothin' for me. Guess he thinks you're prettier."

Her eyes burst open with alertness as she snatched the phone and eyed the message. He was safe and was thinking about her. Only a week or so, and they'd be under the stars together. But for now, this message from her would do:

I'll never give up on you. That's something I thought you knew with certainty after I slapped you. And if you're ready to tell me everything, I'm ready too. I can't wait to have all of this behind us and start fresh...together.

-Savannah

It was late afternoon when she woke, shuffling out of the bed and into the bathroom to look at the clock: 5:32 p.m. Joe hadn't texted back yet. He was knee deep in his own questions and preparing for the Medal of Honor ceremony. It was hard to keep the fact that she was coming a secret, but it was for the best. Coming clean now would only give him time to try and talk her out of it, because he still wasn't comfortable with the attention. Surprising him would show how proud she was of him.

She flipped on the shower and stood in front of the mirror, undressing as hot water poured from the showerhead. She hadn't changed since the warehouse because of the domineering FBI agents. She'd been too tired to even lift the shirt above her head by the time she was alone. But looking at the pullover and jeans now was a filthy reminder of what she went through. She slipped out of the sweater Clark had given her and then the rest. Snatching everything but the sweater off the floor, she padded barefoot over to the trash and stuffed them in, noticing the bruises on her wrists from the handcuffs for the first time. The room was filling with steam now, wrapping around the corners of the large vanity mirror. But she could still see herself, though she didn't usually linger. It felt too exposed, even though the body was hers. Flat stomach beneath the scars, perky boobs, and thick hips with a nagging bit of cellulite that would never go away despite the absurd number of squats she did.

Joe, and the thought of him seeing her naked like this one day, flooded her mind. Her arms and legs broke out in goosebumps, and a tingling sensation ran to her toes as she squeezed her legs together. She had her fun in high school, but things never trailed beyond kissing, even in college. There was this voice in the back of her head telling her to hold out for something special and not a cute co-ed that was too drunk at a party to value that moment. She dropped onto a stool, her head in her hands. Her friends always laughed. Said her chastity belt was locked a little too tight and she was missing out on the fun. Maybe she had, but if Joe was "the one," then waiting for him would be plenty fun. Of course, she'd need to be able to look at herself without that awkwardness first.

She blinked her eyes and rose. Leader's face entered her mind, smiling eerily. Stealing another moment from her. Jerking her eyes open, she darted into the safety of the shower. The water was scalding, but still she let each drop burn over her back and shoulders as she shook. How did he creep in? Somehow he'd found a tear in her subconscious and ripped it wide for other visions to pour in right behind him: Allen bleeding in the alley, Ponytail on top of her calling her princess, the news splaying images of the dead outside her soup kitchen all over the TV. She dropped to the tile floor, the water running in streams down her back. Arms tight around her knees, her nails dug into her flesh. The smells were alive, coppery and rank. Her nostrils burned like fire. The handcuffs restraining her. Leader's fingers under her shirt, a brush against her skin, feeling every inch of him as he pressed against her. Eggs, rotten eggs. And she was cold. Shivering. Shivering against Joe... Shivering against Joe.

The rest of it disappeared.

CHAPTER TWENTY-TWO

Joe

Joe, in stiff dress blues, sat on the uncomfortably springy couch across from his mom and dad. Fatigues would have been his preference, but he was meeting the President today. Someone from the White House would be there any minute to pick the three of them up. His mom smiled from ear to ear. She hadn't stop smiling since she arrived yesterday. She even smiled while she cried and hugged him. His chest had twanged with guilt. He'd put her through the ringer by disappearing. That hadn't been his intention.

But she was forgiving because she loved him so much. She always had. She'd deserved a son the last thirty-three years that took the time to love her back. He'd started by eating an upwards of forty homemade cookies and muffins because it was easier than verbally apologizing. They were sprawled across the coffee table like a buffet to feed the entire Army. She'd made goody bags for everyone up and down the street, all wrapped in cellophane and tied with a ribbon. The whole house had warmed up when she arrived. With the scent of gingerbread and chocolate chips filling the air, it really did change the atmosphere.

He rubbed a hand over his pocket. Allen's medal was in there, along with the ace. Taking the backpack to the White House didn't seem appropriate, and he wasn't leaving without it. His men deserved this medal more than he did. Much more. Having it there would be a way to honor them.

The doorbell rang, and his mom jumped up, her purple dress sparkling and flowing around her ankles. Two soldiers waited at the door, and she waved them in, offering them something from the buffet of desserts. They obliged, each making a baggie of cookies before gazing at Joe with a fierce admiration that made him look away.

"Are you ready, sir? The President is anxious to meet you."

Joe nodded once and rose, following the men, his mother, and his father out the door. Today was much better weather than yesterday. It was so sunny and warm that any trace of rain had long since evaporated.

Two houses across the street had their front doors open. Kids ran in and out, chasing each other as the parents sat in lawn chairs, laughing and chatting. Savannah would make a great mother. But what did you even do with a baby? How old should a kid be when you teach them to create a listening device? He shook his head and climbed into the black SUV behind his dad. Would he ever be cut out for that kind of life?

Why was he even wondering about this stuff? Savannah may never want to get married and have kids. It probably hadn't entered her mind. They'd known each other less than a week. Joe couldn't hold her interest forever. Some other guy could love her better—not more, but better.

He shoved his hands into his pockets, brushing against the medal and card as the sun beat mercilessly into his window. His mom stared at him, with a smile of course, as she leaned against his dad's shoulder. "Joe, honey, I prayed for you this morning, so don't be nervous. Listen to what he has to say, even if your heart doesn't quite beat that same way yet. He's an honorable man, and he will mean every word that comes out of his mouth. It's all gonna be fine."

He rested his head against the window and watched the cars pass by, full of people living with only the care of their nine-to-five jobs and where they'd eat dinner that night. It sounded simple. But he couldn't have done life that way. He was a warrior, and that pull never allowed him to relax when danger was on the horizon.

The White House came into view to his left, bike riders and tourists passing by the fence around the property, taking selfies. The grass was so green, the house so white, and it seemed bigger than it had the last time he was in D.C. The sun beat over it, only adding to the illusion by making it impossible to look directly toward the top. He sat up straight and cracked his back as they pulled around to the private entrance, away from the hustle and bustle, and were waved through a gate. He watched the security detail move with precision, assessing their skills and which was the weakest link. He'd even researched the basic layout of the White House before this morning. It was habit.

Since childhood he'd known the Army was his future. From fighting bullies on the playground in elementary to the archery team in junior high to ROTC in high school, he'd spent a lifetime preparing to make the world a safer place. Not everyone had the stomach for slitting the throat of a tyrant warlord or shooting some backward terrorist who preyed on women and children. He had nightmares, but it wasn't from that; it was from mistakes and losses he'd experienced during those deployments. He did what needed to be done to protect the way of life of all those nine-to-fivers he'd seen moments ago.

As much as the drive for justice always ran front and center, there was a part of him hoping he'd do something during one of his deployments that would make him worthy of a trip to this house, this symbol of freedom and the American people. To have the chance to hear the President say, "Well done." To shake his hand, with no one else watching. But it hadn't ended up that way. He'd made it here, but at what cost?

His mom took his arm as they walked the long corridor together behind the two soldiers, and now a man in a black suit, who'd strapped them all with visitor badges. Joe kept his eyes ahead as they passed portraits of past presidents and American flags galore. Even the floor mimicked the same patriotic theme, with red and white diamonds cut into the blue carpet. The man in the black suit led them all to an elevator and held the door back. "You first, Mr. MacArthur."

His foot lifted slower off the ground than it had since he was in

Afghanistan, avoiding landmines. The elevator was small, and the back of his neck started sweating. They were all meant to cram in here together like a can of sardines. But none of them had spent three hours stuck in an underground tunnel, choking on dirt, with a full-fledged, body-shaking panic attack. They filed in around him, bumping shoulders on both sides as they rode up.

When the door chimed and swung wide again everyone filed out, with Joe exiting last, sweat soaking through the shirt of his dress blues. "Just ahead, Mr. MacArthur. The President is looking forward to making your acquaintance."

Décor was similar on this level too, but it wasn't empty like downstairs had been. People were everywhere, rushing up and down the hall with colleagues, their footsteps, conversation, and clicking ink pens almost reminiscent of a melody. There was a section of offices up the hall to the right where he could make out cubicles, coffee mugs, and televisions all tuned into the news with rapt audiences.

Their group turned the corner and converged upon a corner desk outside the Oval Office. Behind the desk sat a woman, well into her forties, with thick black hair and a black suit. A grocery store salad sat half-eaten beside a stack of files and a ringing phone. Before she could answer, the door to the Oval Office opened, and the President stepped out. His parents were both wide-eyed. He was too, but even the secretary seemed in awe. And the busy melody behind him quieted.

"Mr. MacArthur, I am so honored and humbled to have you and your parents join me today." President Johnson continued forward, putting Joe's right hand between both of his and gripping tightly. His narrow lips were in a wide grin as he looked up at Joe with the same awe everyone else saved for him.

President Johnson wasn't the man anyone pictured running the country when he stepped on the scene a few years ago as a doctor making significant gains in cancer research. Johnson stood at least a head shorter than him, black-rimmed glasses and three barely perceivable holes in his left ear from his years growing up on the southside of Philadelphia. He'd turned his life around and sure seemed to be working his rear off to turn D.C. and the entire country around, too.

"Thank you, sir."

"This way, please." President Johnson turned on his heel and opened the door to the Oval Office, waving him and his parents in.

The room was as powerful as he'd imagined from pictures and movies, but it wasn't as empty as he hoped. The attention was already uncomfortable, but add the President, his speech writer, Commander of the US Army Special Operations, Joint Chief of Staff, Secretary of the Army, Secretary of Defense, Chief of Staff, and a photographer... Yeah, that was overkill, and that sweat from before multiplied tenfold. But he made the rounds, shook hands with everyone, and smiled like his mom had taught him, before having a seat on a blue couch with tiny gold eagles sewn into the fabric. He did his best to keep his hands relaxed while all the eyes in the room rested on him.

President Johnson leaned forward in his wooden chair, elbows on his knees and his fingers interlaced, before sitting back straight again. "I'm going to be honest with you, Joe. Medal of Honor recipients are a small brotherhood. I've never awarded the Medal of Honor to anyone before. Never have learned of a man or woman worthy of such an incredible honor, and I'm a bit flustered to actually see you face to face. I've read the citation from your mission, and I am in such awe of your sacrificing to keep your men alive. I'd like to say I understand what you've been through, but that would be an insult. So, I will say this: Our national security depends on brave men and women coming forward and serving, but you went beyond the call of duty. You answered a call that runs on a frequency only true heroes can hear. You are a warrior, a man of courage and strength. And this I know because those attributes follow you wherever you go. Your heroic actions in Los Angeles were not overlooked; they only served as more reason for me to be blessed and flattered that you accepted the invitation to come to my house. You are always welcome, and while you are here, you are free to say or ask anything, and the same goes for your parents." The President crossed his legs and extended a hand. The words he'd said weren't for show. Johnson meant them. And maybe he was those things—*maybe*—but he'd still failed and on a massive scale.

Unfortunately, answering him was a must, and it needed to be now. The cameraman snapped away in a corner, and all the men in the room waited on bated breath for his reply. He tapped his thighs, his finger running over the edge of the card through his pants. He bit his lip as he pulled the card free from his pocket and slipped it onto the coffee table in front of the group, creased and bloody.

"Thank you, Mr. President. But this card represents the true heroes of that day in Afghanistan. My men. The ones I left on that battlefield. We called ourselves the Aces, and those guys *were* aces. They were the best of the best. Each of us carried a playing card like this one. As the…leader, I carried the sole ace of spades. And I carry the sole responsibility for losing my brothers. I visited each of their homes before I went dark, delivering the aces back to their families, knowing full well it should've been the men themselves, but it was the only piece of them I could offer."

No one touched the card, just stared at it for the most part. Except President Johnson. He watched Joe, with scientific wheels turning behind his eyes, and Joe looked back. There was no intimidation, no argument, only comfort. President Johnson wasn't going to force his opinion or argue about how heroic he was. He was going to listen.

"Joe, I said before that I've never conducted a Medal of Honor ceremony, and I'm sure there is a code, a way it's supposed to progress on that day, which, if you don't mind, will be two days from now. But because this Medal of Honor is yours, I say we do it your way. Bring the card, if you don't mind, and I will speak of your men. I have a list of their names. Despite my feelings, and those of everyone else in America, you still don't view yourself as the hero you are. And that's okay. But maybe it will ease the burden if your brothers are there with you."

"Thank you, sir. That would be an honor."

The men around the room nodded. And it was quiet again. Time enough for everyone to process the conversation before President Johnson spoke up again. "Let me ask a few more questions, if that's okay." He directed his gaze to Joe's parents. "I have a son, and he's connected very quickly to Joe's story. He challenges me daily to be a better man, a better father, a better husband. Frankly, he's going to be all over me tonight, asking about Joe. You changed his diapers, taught him right from wrong, equipped him with the tools to succeed in the world. But you must've known from an early age how incredibly special he was. Is there anything you would like to share?"

Joe's dad motioned to his mother to share, but she was surprisingly quiet as if still in awe of everything happening, so he cleared his throat and spoke up. "After I retired from the military, my wife and I moved out of small-town Georgia and to New York. We'd been tryin' for the better part of five years to have a baby. There was a great clinic there that was willing to take on our case. So, I took a job as a police officer. My partner at the time was a young man named Baqil. He and his wife were third generation Lebanese immigrants and so patient with two small-town folks like Sherry and me as we settled into our new life. They cooked for us weekly and brought us with them to church. They were such special people. But there were reasons Baqil opted to join the force. Most prominent was a strong mob presence in the neighborhood their families had grown up in. Baqil never did anything halfway. He was incredibly brave, as was his wife, and they fought hard to protect those people, to encourage them to speak up. But getting mixed up in that business..." Stanley stopped and tapped his teeth together as if thinking of the way to word a very difficult revelation. "Well, it put a large target on his back. One I couldn't manage to erase. They came to us one night with Yosef, his birth certificate, everything. Asked us to take him back to Georgia and keep him safe until everything died down. We left that night, with him crying in the backseat. He was six months old at the time. About two days later, we got the news they had been killed." He sighed before continuing. "I say all of that to say, Joe had a God-given bravery already ingrained from his birth parents. We just built on that and loved him, showed him how to use his courage positively. We knew goin' to New York was the right move, the one that would end with us having a child. It just happened differently than expected. And there was no kid we could've created that would be anything near as special as Joe. Did I answer your question, sir?"

The President nodded. "My son is adopted too, though it's a struggle for him to accept. But I couldn't have said it any better myself. Thank you."

The conversation continued, as did the flash photography, until all the details of the upcoming ceremony had been brushed out with a fine-tooth comb, and everyone was standing and shaking hands. He listened to each man share throughout their three hours together and accepted their comments. It was a safe place, like they were sequestered just momentarily from the judgement and chaos of the outside world. Even though it still didn't feel right to admit, he'd needed this meeting, and it was a huge relief to have his parents here too. Taking the time to hear not only what they said but the *way* they said it pressed on his heart. There was something else he needed to do.

Everyone exited the room until it was only he and President Johnson standing there. "Mr. President, I know your day is incredibly busy, but would it be alright with you if I said hi to your son on my way out? Maybe I could"—he cleared his throat—"encourage him."

He clapped Joe against the arm and laughed. "See there, Joe? This is what I mean. How many men would offer that? I'll say this as the President of the United States and not a new friend, mainly because I think it gives my words more weight, but you need to start giving yourself more credit."

CHAPTER TWENTY-THREE
Savannah

If Clark didn't think it was a good idea, it was safe to assume Joe wouldn't either. But that wasn't enough of a deterrent for Savannah. Joe brought out a boldness she hadn't possessed since the know-it-all teenager days. And before boarding that plane for Washington D.C.—with an outfit pre-approved by her mother, of course—she was venturing out to the soup kitchen. What was left of it, anyway. It had been days since she'd visited, and though her life had imploded, leaving little room for consideration of much else but immediate safety and sleep, there was this nagging inside her mind to stop by and check on things. At the very least drop off some food to the people she knew on the street. They were probably starving without the warm meal they'd come to expect on a daily basis. Of course, all this was assuming any of her patrons were still alive after the massacre. She squeezed her eyes shut and jerked them back open.

It was still all over the news. So was Joe. But in a positive, less murder-y way. His name had been cleared and so had the bloody streets running by her business. Joe was being praised as instrumental in crushing a drug syndicate into nothingness. And he would be receiving the Medal of Honor for heroic actions overseas. Her mother even texted an article she'd seen about him, which was nothing short of shocking.

Pictures of Joe with the President and all sorts of other important-looking men in sharp suits circulated through the internet. So did his story from Afghanistan, or at least the amount they were willing to share with the public. But she hadn't looked past the pictures. It was his story to tell, so she'd wait, just like she was waiting to have a road trip with him. After thirty-some-odd years of only leaving L.A. for family vacations to Bali and the Amalfi Coast, the prospect was exhilarating—and a little nerve-wracking, if she was being completely honest. They'd been texting like high schoolers, but enjoying him in person without the fear of death was vital. However, his ultimatum of only taking what could fit in a backpack was brutal when she was used to bellhops toting around twelve suitcases for her. Where would she wash her panties when she ran out of the seven pairs that fit? The blow-up mattress had been their biggest compromise. She'd even gotten a text with an old-school smiley face, which was surprising since Joe texted like an eighty-year-old. But it was a necessity. There would be no sleeping bags in her future unless they were being used as blankets. She shook her head. *Crap.* Blankets. Maybe they could squeeze one into Joe's bag. She couldn't lose any more space for undies.

The clock in the car read 8:43 a.m. when they pulled up in front of the soup kitchen. They needed to check in at the airport in an hour and a half, so Clark made sure they wouldn't have time to linger. Whatever. Being here was worth it, even with a tiny allotment of time. Stepping from the car, her foot slipped on a broken chunk of pavement. Clark darted around the car with vampire-like speed, but she nudged him off. "I'm fine. Stop worrying."

She breathed in the stale air and looked to the left and right. It was sunny enough to see the street was about half as full as normal, but everyone noticed them drive up. If a car cut their ignition out here, it was a mistake worth taking note of. Heads raised from sleeping bags and poked out of tents. Reaching into the backseat of Clark's sedan, she pushed aside her outfit for the ceremony and grabbed six grocery bags, only vaguely aware of the wound on her stomach from the weight of the bags. Clark took a few in his left hand, but warily held his right one over his pistol.

Better to be safe than sorry, but the threat was gone. That's what he'd been droning on about like a broken record since he took this babysitting job. So, what was up? Was this the way guys like he and Joe always did things? Ready at a moment's notice to shoot the jaywalking granny or the woman with overdue library books?

"What's got you all tickled?"

She laughed and pulled the last five bags from the car. "Nothing. Oh look, we've got some action down the street. I recognize two people. We can hand out some food and get to the airport. It'll give me some peace to know everyone is full while we're gone."

Clark nodded and unlocked the soup kitchen as she clambered through the door. It smelled like a paint can. And there were new light fixtures hung from the ceiling. Two extra tables rested on the polished tile, and the cabinets stowed more food than ever before. Nice, fancy food. This had Dahlia Carrington written all over it in sparkly gold font.

There wasn't time to cook any of it today, but she ran her fingers over the labels and smiled. Her mom *was* really trying. Clark stood by the door, peering out the windows as she set the premade food bags on the counter and waited. The two people she'd seen on the sidewalk came in quietly, wringing their hands. Catching sight of Clark's gun, they startled, but Savannah ran over. "Hi. It's okay. He's with me. I'm Savannah, by the way. I've only seen you in here once before, on Labor Day. I'll be out a few more days, but please take a bag of food with you." She took the hand of the wiry-haired woman with a scar across her face and led her to the counter. She wore a filthy white shirt with turquoise buttons that made her hair look even redder than the flame color it already was. The man with her tagged along but kept one wild eye fixed on Clark.

"He ain't no cop or nothin', is he? Looks like those guys that was out here the other day. I don't like 'im." He bit his fingernail, spitting it out as his arm twitched repeatedly.

Savannah handed him a bag of food and squeezed the woman's hand as he tucked it under his arm and kept chewing. "No. He's not a cop, just a friend and a soldier who is worried for everyone's safety. His name is Clark. What are your names?"

The woman looked all around the ceiling before making eye contact and whispering, "Claire. And this is Bruce. You sure there aren't any of those listening devices or cameras or somethin'? You should check. Everyone should. They got drones the size of flies buzzin' round our tent every night out here. Someone's always watchin' us. But we got what we were needin', so we better be goin'. We gotta stay outta sight. Never know when those guys'll be back."

What could she say to ease this woman's mind? She was clearly on drugs and paranoid. Both of them were. Strung out right now from what she could tell, but wrong or right, Claire's anxiety sent flames of nausea rolling through Savannah's gut. The confinement, the attack, everything was still so fresh it was hard to ignore this string bean of a woman in front of her.

"Claire, no one is coming back. You have nothing more to fear from those men. I promise."

"I gotta tell you somethin', then." The turquoise buttons on Claire's shirt glistened as she jerked Savannah around the counter, knocking her off balance and into the shadows of a nearby cupboard, where Claire's voice whistled through her missing teeth. Footsteps raced across the floor, and Savannah yelled for Clark to back off for a minute.

Claire hugged her tight and shook all over like a leaf on a tree in the fall. "Those men, the ones that was here. They was cutting peoples' throats and stuff, leavin' 'em for dead. A pretty girl like you don't understand. But I heard some stuff, stuff they said. Ain't nobody safe out here. Next time you come back, I'll show ya what I found okay? Maybe you could bring it to tha cops for me? Bruce won't let me go. Says they'd kill me."

"Thank you, Claire. You be safe out there."

And with that she guided them both out the door and fell into a metal chair. Was Claire right or was Joe? Claire seemed to believe the organization was still at large. Without a TV, she probably hadn't heard about the kidnapping and subsequent squashing of the Green Triangle. But either way, that one percent chance Claire was right made her head spin like a blender.

Get control. She's crazy. She's crazy. She's crazy. Breathe...come on. Just like with Joe.

Clark's hand was warm and comforting against her shoulder. She leaned back and allowed him to wrap her in a giant hug that felt similar to the ones she used to get from Cole. "I heard what she said. Her version of a whisper is practically a scream. It's okay. Joe and I will have someone here with you every time you come. The Green Triangle is gone, Savannah. But your soup kitchen is important, and you deserve to do it without an anxiety attack every time Claire and Bruce come strolling through the door."

"I sure hope you're right, Clark."

Sniffing and wiping her eyes, she stood and put on a big smile to welcome the next person coming through the door. There wasn't any more time to consider Claire and Bruce until they locked up and got back in the car. "Thirty-three bags of food handed out in thirty minutes. Not bad. Nearly makes up for the first two."

"You gotta let what Claire said roll off. I can tell you're still thinkin' about it. So, how to take your mind off it? Hmm. Wanna hear about the time I shaved Joe's eyebrows?"

The weight lifted for about fifteen seconds as their laughter filled the space in the car. When it settled again, it weighed a little less. He spent the entire ride describing Joe's appearance without eyebrows. But try as he might, one of Clark's colorfully embellished stories wouldn't wipe Claire's comments away for a good while.

Drivers zoomed around the pull-through in front of the airport, hugging their passengers and throwing out loads of suitcases. They squeezed into any available space, including the sidewalks, as airport security blew whistles and made a valiant effort to control the madness. Finally emerging from the chaos, they entered the parking garage. It was spooky quiet, not another visible soul moving around: the total opposite of the front of the terminal.

She and Clark grabbed their bags and started walking, their own footsteps echoing around them. She clung close to his side. The garage had a heaviness of doom and gloom even though she knew it was safe. Would she always worry like that, after everything she'd been through? Her life experiences weren't exactly normal. As they entered through the doors to the left of check-in, Clark's phone rang. "It's the hotel. I'll take it out here and meet you inside." He held it up for her to see.

"It's fine. I'll get in line and wait." She strode through the doors of the airport and froze as she got blasted with a wave of air conditioning from the overhead vent. There, standing twenty feet away, with a bouquet and rolling back and forth on the balls of his feet, was Holden. Crap. The last couple of days had been so insane that the promise she'd made to let Holden down easy had gone out the window. He rushed over and took her hand.

"Savannah. Your mother told me you'd be here. Please, can we talk?"

Saying no and telling him it was completely over was the right thing to do.

"Okay…sure. Maybe in those chairs right there? I've got to get checked in for my flight." It was stupid, but he was so darn endearing it was impossible to break his heart. If Joe had never entered the picture, she'd be racing off into the sunset with him now. But Joe had, and her mom knew that. What kind of game was she playing?

"Yeah," he said, with his hand on her back as he led her to a metal bench. "Your mother said Joe was being honored today. Of course, every news outlet is saying the same thing." He waved his arm toward the news feed running with subtitles above them. "He's famous now, I suppose. Pretty hard to compete with that."

"I'm sorry, Holden. You are an amazing guy, but…"

"But you've made your decision. I get it. Really. But I have something for you. It's stupid, I guess, since things aren't going to last between us. I still wanted you to have it though. Could you come with me to my car to get it? I left it in there by accident and didn't want to double back and miss seeing you."

She looked at her new cell. It was way beyond time to get checked in, and Clark was off the phone and rushing inside too. "I don't think there's time. Maybe when I get back?"

His eyes cut over to Clark who was inching in. His cheeks flushed, and he rubbed his palms over his pants. "Oh, I see. Sorry. I didn't realize he was here with you. Yeah, um, that would be okay. It was just a set of tickets for this party because I saw things moving forward and wanted to show you off. I understand Joe won you over, after listening to you recount everything to the FBI, but would you mind going to the party with me as friends? I hired a security detail, so you won't have to worry about a single thing. Then I promise I won't bother you again, unless you change your mind, of course." He grinned. "But maybe it's fitting to end things with this party since we missed the gala."

Wow. The gala hadn't entered her thoughts since their date. It was the night of the kidnapping. Her heart picked up pace, but she kept her cool and nodded. It would hurt him if she said no, even though he was going to be hurt either way. He'd have a more enjoyable time taking someone else, but she'd promised her mom she'd be good to him, and it seemed reasonable to accept the invitation as friends. It would likely be the last time they ever saw each other besides functions at the club. And he needed some encouragement, since he was embarrassed and holding a larger-than-life bouquet he'd be returning home with. "Sure. I'll go with you, Holden. But I've got to go now, or I'll miss my flight." She jumped up and skidded to a stop on her heels. "When is it?"

"Tomorrow afternoon. Will you be back by then?"

"Yes, I'll be back by lunch. See you soon."

Holden thanked her but walked away with his shoulders sagging. Clark hadn't gotten close enough to say anything to Holden, but he was clearly irritated for his best friend. "Captain America will land on his feet,

Savannah. Every woman in here's starin' at him. Even the lesbians are rethinkin' men. You don't have to go to a party with him to give his ego a boost."

"I have a hard time saying no. I don't like to hurt people. But don't worry. Joe didn't need a medal for me to know his worthiness. Please stop getting testy. We've commiserated over—what is it now?—four cartons of ice cream. You know where I stand. So, let's get to D.C. As charming as you are, I need to see Joe. Maybe he can pay your babysitting bill."

CHAPTER TWENTY-FOUR
Joe

Except for him, the East Room of the White House was empty. President Johnson gave Joe an hour alone before the doors would open to let everyone in. His feet hung over the side of the stage to the floor. This was almost over. To the left, the Army band had their instruments waiting on stands. A podium rose behind him. Thick gold curtains hung on each window, and the stage held flags and stands with three pictures: one of himself and two with his team. An oil painting of George Washington stood guard over the room behind his shoulder. Red, white, and blue decorations hung around the white walls. Nothing over the top though, unlike the enormous chandeliers.

From what he'd watched of past Medal of Honor ceremonies on the news, there would be a teleprompter running the President's speech. But that wasn't the case today. President Johnson dismissed the stunned speech writer at the end of their meeting two days ago. Said he already knew what he'd say. So, they'd squeezed in another twenty chairs and left the teleprompter out.

It was hard to imagine the rows of chairs in front of him filling up, but they would be, soon. He stood and tugged at his dress blues before walking the perimeter of the room, running his fingers over every nook and cranny. Rounding the corner, the door creaked, and a woman's heels clicked in. It must've been his mom coming to check and see if he was ready. But *she* didn't smell like roses; Savannah did.

His head jerked around, and there she was, golden waves of hair over her shoulders and a smile that wiped away the need for conversation. Text messaged selfies didn't do Savannah justice. She wore a bright red dress that wrapped around her body and tied on the side. His lip curled up, wondering what would happen if he tugged on that string. He grabbed her, shifting in closer, kissing her, feeling her heartbeat race against his chest.

It might've been a life-or-death situation that brought them together, but the emotions were real—very real. There wasn't another woman in the world for him, and he had to have faith it was the same for her. But stuff like love and God, well you couldn't see it as well as the effects of a bullet piercing a target sheet, and that was a fact.

Faith was hard to accept; some feeling, some entity, controlling him? He'd been trained to act, to solve problems, to face his fears, to prove himself when others thought some outcast kid could never be enough. Because of that, tangible things had nothing on him. He'd snagged that Green Beret while other men were collapsing in the woods with chest pains and tears. Intangible things required more work. But he'd prayed on his own, so that meant something.

The door opened again, and President Johnson appeared with a Secret Service agent. Joe pulled away and looked into Savannah's eyes. Too bad the ceremony was starting. He didn't want to stop thinking about that dress on the floor, but President Johnson was moving in with his hand outstretched. "Thanks for coming," he whispered in Savannah's ear. "I didn't expect to see you. It's a great surprise, but I'm going to kill Clark for leaving you."

"If I said I was coming, you would have tried to talk me out of it. As for your best friend, he's waiting outside. You said yourself I'm safe anyway. Let's let today be a day of grace and give Clark the opportunity to live." She squeezed his hand.

She was trying to ease his mind, but he was always on alert, even if bullets weren't flying. Couldn't ever let your guard down, couldn't ever stop watching, because there was always a threat just out of sight you could miss. That's why he'd done a perimeter check here, at the house they were staying in, at Taco Bell last night. And there was the argument he'd tried to make with the Pentagon: the kidnapping was way too personal to be a consequence of Savannah's dad taking the drugs or Savannah getting involved with Allen's attack, all going back to a senator neither of them had ever met before. It was too easy. They were overlooking some detail, and that was almost as infuriating as the fact he didn't have a gun.

His fingers had been twitching like crazy, and though the President seemed to enjoy his company, Johnson was probably getting annoyed that he kept closing all the curtains and checking for bugs. It was this focus that tended to manifest when things were going well, but if he had a feeling, it was usually right. Unfortunately, it made it hard to dial in on other things, like the ceremony, relationships, or eating.

For now, though, there was no hint of danger, so keeping these thoughts from Savannah was the right thing to do. There was no reason to worry her. And as for the Pentagon getting on board with his theory, it wasn't coming along well. A couple people were biting, but they needed something, a guess at who could be the big, bad boss behind it all. He had nothing, and jealousy over Holden's relentless effort to keep Savannah wasn't a good enough reason to put him on the list. He wasn't smart enough to be a mastermind of anything anyway.

"Hello, Savannah. I'm Ezra Johnson. I'm so pleased you came to join Joe on this special occasion. It's been an honor to spend time with him and have him connect with my son Nathaniel. He told me today that talking to Joe was so 'rad' he didn't need anything for Christmas this year. Of course, we still have a few months to go, and he'll probably think of something. But if I can ever repay his kindness, please let me know. It's been a trying week for you, so I promise to have him back to L.A. as soon as possible. Maybe I can cut it to two more days, tops. There are a few other people who would like to interview and meet him."

"Oh, that would be wonderful!" She clapped her hands and lurched forward, smothering the President in a very unexpected hug that made his Secret Service guy tense like a beam. The three of them laughed as she leapt back again and put her hand on her head. "Oops. Guess you're not supposed to hug the President? Sorry. I'm just ready for him to come back so we can escape for a while together and not worry about anything."

"That sounds like a lovely plan, Savannah. Joe, if you'll come with me, we will begin momentarily. Savannah, feel free to go ahead and find a seat for the ceremony. I'll send your friend in on our way out."

Joe started behind the President, but Savannah's grip on his hand tightened, and her eyes held back tears. It made his heart ache. "You have to be brave a little while longer."

"Easier said than done. Give me something to keep me going, like where is the first stop on our trip?"

There was a twinkle in his eye when he looked back at Savannah and continued walking. "It's a secret." There hadn't been a lot of time to be playful since they'd met, and though he wasn't funny like Clark, it was nice to see her smile. But then it hit him, and he jerked to a halt.

Savannah ran over, arms around his waist. "What's going on?"

"I didn't expect you to be here, so I didn't think of it until now. I promised you'd hear everything from me, but they will read the citation from my mission during the ceremony, and President Johnson will say something about it, too."

She bit her top lip and thought before responding. "It's not what I expected, but if you're okay with it, I am too. Maybe if you see me out in the crowd, it will make it easier. If not, I don't mind waiting outside."

He pulled her close, large hands wrapped over her back. "Wherever I am is where I want you to be. There's no way you're waiting outside."

President Johnson stuck his head back through the door and waved. "Come on. It's time."

Savannah rose onto her tiptoes, running her hands over his hair as she whispered, "Good luck. I believe in you."

His head was heavy as he marched out of the room, behind the President. That woman had no idea what she did to him.

The next half hour went by fast: introducing Clark to the President, hugging his parents, and bouncing back and forth between thinking of Savannah's fingers in his hair and of what he would say to the crowd. When the room was overflowing and the doors would no longer close, Secret Service agents led him to the doorway, along with President Johnson. The Secretary of the Army stood at the podium, and the band blasted a quick note before he announced, "Ladies and gentlemen, The President of the United States, accompanied by Medal of Honor recipient Captain Yosef MacArthur, Commander of Operational Detachment Alpha 111, United States Army Special Forces."

"That's our cue." There was a slap on his back from President Johnson, and he straightened, puffed out his chest, and marched forward. All eyes were on him as the band began playing. Soldiers with their medals, men and women from the Pentagon and White House, civilians: they were all here to see a hero, holding their cells up to catch everything on video. And though he kept his body rigid and professional, he wondered if they would feel the same after hearing the entire story. It sounded brave to say he'd run into a hailstorm of bullets, but his team wouldn't have been in the middle of said hailstorm if he hadn't put them there.

His mom was smiling and wiping away tears in the front row, but his dad made eye contact and nodded as if to say, "You can do this." There were only two more steps to the stage, but they took forever, with the room slowing around him as he looked for Savannah. Three rows back, he spotted her next to Clark. When he landed on the stage at attention beside President Johnson, all the sounds of the room came back to life.

People shifted quietly as they stood waiting for the Army chaplain, now standing at the podium with a Bible. "Let us pray." He bowed his head, and the entire room followed suit. "God, we come to you today, men and women of different cultures and backgrounds. But we hold something in common: our love for America, the country that brings strangers together as brothers and sisters, by the power of Your love.

"Today we have the special privilege to honor a man who has devoted himself to this great country, through service and sacrifice. Today we watch our nation's highest honor bestowed by the President himself onto a leader among warriors, whose dedication is unparalleled. A man who asked for nothing but gave everything selflessly.

"May we lift up this man today so that he feels Your love and the love of his country as he accepts this honor, knowing it was not given lightly but with great consideration and appreciation for his service to the Army and our country, The United States of America. We keep him and all military families in our prayers for their daily sacrifices, for the lives lost and the brothers and sisters watching us from above. On this solemn ground, be with us, God. In Your heavenly name, Amen."

Eyes opened, and heads raised as the chaplain stepped from the stage. Everyone sat. Joe's heartbeat picked up. Savannah was about to hear everything.

President Johnson had a short but very quick gait, and he was at the podium in moments. "Thank you, Chaplain, for that beautiful prayer and to all the men and women who worked tirelessly over the last few days to make this ceremony a reality. And a thank you to everyone joining us today, members of the Armed Forces and other distinguished guests. Please, everyone, have a seat. And please help me welcome Captain Yosef MacArthur to the White House, the house of our nation, our people.

"Men and women like him are the reason we can gather like this today. Their sacrifice can't be fully grasped by someone like me, who has never been part of the Armed Forces. What I do understand though"—he held a finger in the air—"is this: It takes more than a strong body to be a warrior, to be a hero. The capacity to fight through injury and pain is something most people possess as a means to save themselves from death. But that isn't what garners the awe of a nation. That goes to the man beside me. He was willing to fight through pain and injury, even if it meant death, to try and save multiple others. Others, not himself.

"Understand me when I say that it is easy to believe you could be that person, but when bullets fly and blood pours, our good intentions are rarely upheld. You are in the presence of one of the select few. A man who will be joining the ranks of the most elite brotherhood in our country. And if you've been watching the news, you understand all the more that bravery isn't something alive only on the battlefield. It lives in his soul and digs its heels in at the first sign of danger or injustice as it does for all the brave soldiers who wear this badge. On that note, we have three past Medal of Honor recipients in our presence. Men, please rise."

Three men stood, two young and one an older man around seventy. They waved, and the room filled with applause as everyone stood back up again to honor them. He clapped too. He watched every Medal of Honor ceremony over the last twenty years and recognized the men by name before the ceremony. Their stories were amazing and honorable. And his was too if you chose to ignore the fact that he trusted the informant when he should've done his research first, should've looked at the informant's hands sooner. If they'd been shaking longer and he'd missed it...

His jaw set, and he pulled his back even straighter. It wasn't the time to be drawn back to Afghanistan. He had to stay strong. Savannah would still be here tonight, and she would listen to any additions he felt compelled to give...and, hopefully, not run after hearing them.

The clapping died back down, and everyone took their seats again. "Thank you, men, for your outstanding service to our country. Now, over the past few days, I have had the opportunity to spend time with Joe and his parents, to learn more about him. And I did. Besides developing a new friend for myself and a mentor for my son, I was graced with a glimpse of his humility and strength: a rare combination. I can give you the details of his childhood and achievements, as is tradition, or I can leave you with this. Joe comes from a long line of warriors. From his biological parents to the ones he calls Mom and Dad and beyond. His dad and grandfather were both honored soldiers, serving in the Army. His father earned the Distinguished Cross in Vietnam, and his grandfather was a fellow Medal of Honor recipient from the Battle of the Bulge. But, ultimately, no matter the influence, everyone is given the choice to achieve greatness. Understand me, please. Greatness is not a right born only to a few, it's a calling *answered* by only a few."

Joe's heart pumped blood in his ears, but the rest of the room remained silent. President Johnson gave them a moment before continuing his speech. "In a few minutes, our military aide, Mr. Callagny, will come forward to read the citation from the mission, but first, I'd like to give Joe a chance to share. He would like to accept this Medal of Honor on behalf of his team and take a few moments to tell you about them. Not just their names, as that isn't how you truly honor someone, but who they were. Thank you."

President Johnson clapped and waved Joe to the podium, where he gripped its wood frame like the edge of a cliff, the faces of his men flashing in and out of his mind like static on an out-of-range radio station. "Thank you, Mr. President." Breathing heavier to control the tremor shooting through the muscle of his left leg and the inclination to shake his head to try to erase the memories flooding back in, his eyes darted Savannah's direction once more. And they settled there. So did his heartrate. Her face, her presence, anchored him to the room before it had a chance to swirl into darkness. "We called ourselves the Aces, and they were my brothers..."

CHAPTER TWENTY-FIVE
Savannah

Fingers beating rhythmically on her thighs, she waited for Joe in the hotel lobby. It was late, around ten o'clock, and Savannah was tired, fidgeting with the strap on her bra. Her heels were in the blue wingback chair beside her. She'd taken them off about thirty minutes ago when the feeling in her toes dissolved to nothingness. Guys didn't know how good they had it.

Clark was three feet away, across a large, fruit-and-magazine-laden coffee table, sipping on a drink he'd picked up at the hotel bar playing jazz music behind them. He'd gotten her one, too and set it to her left, but she just licked the sugar off the rim and pulled the paperback she'd brought on the plane out of her purse. They were both exhausted, not chatting, and so every available woman took that as a cue to try her hand at picking him up. It was somewhat amusing to watch each of them come flouncing by over the top of her pages, three so far, over the course of an hour, but Clark was not himself. After Joe's speech and the rest of the ceremony, he was quietly reflecting on the men he used to know and waiting on Joe to show up and take over so he could do more than sip his drink.

She hadn't known any of them, but the way Joe shared about their interests and families, it felt familiar. And though it was never his intention, this was the digital age, and his speech was going viral. People were intrigued by this man who was strong, lethal, and skilled but also quiet, selfless, and humble. It was a rare combination—very rare.

To her, though, it was clear from their first moments together, when he was homeless, that he was special. The way he protected her and sacrificed himself was all she'd really needed to know. But today was unreal. It had been a chance to *see* Joe express himself. But there were loose ends he needed to tie up before the night was over, so she agreed to wait in the lobby until he could get away.

Joe had been so collected through hundreds of people clambering toward him with a hand outstretched and even tonight, conceding to another interview. He was probably going to want to decompress for a while when he did show up, because it wasn't him. Talking was her thing, not his. It's what she did for a living. Although, tonight hadn't been her finest display of communication. She was always delightfully awkward, but tonight bordered on just plain awkward. Maybe it wasn't as bad as she thought, but nerves had definitely taken over.

The President—yes, the President of the United States—had invited Joe, his parents, herself, and Clark to an early dinner with his family. How many people got to pass mashed potatoes to the President? Even more than that, it was a chance to spend time with Joe's parents. Being a serial first-dater, she hadn't had the opportunity in her thirty years to meet a parent, let alone two…or a dog, for that matter. Not even when she dated Holden for the extreme length of two months. Still, they were only human, but her head had felt as if it would explode from the pressure, and there was this constant throbbing behind her left ear as she rambled incessantly about the soup kitchen and Joe.

All these years, she'd been convinced the problem lay in her mother's snooty dating choices, but to be honest, she never made the effort on her own. Even with perfect Holden, she only responded when he reached out. There had always been this thought, in the back of her mind, that her perfect guy would show up one day and she shouldn't waste time on the others—and he had. Although, it hadn't been necessary to share that story with his parents. It was one of those times when you wanted to throw your hands over your face and disappear. But just about that moment, Joe had reached over and taken her hand in his, kissing it and laying it back in her lap. It was simple and sweet, and thankfully, it shut her up for about fifteen minutes as the President began a story.

She had looked his way and smiled, but her thoughts had immediately drifted to Cole. He'd always wanted to be President; teenage Cole would've given anything to be sitting with them. But where was adult Cole? He was alive, no doubt in her mind, so why hadn't he reached out? A question with no real answer, or no good one at least.

A yawn creeped up her throat in the chair, and she covered her mouth, pulling her feet in beside her and smiling at Clark's newest suitor. All she wanted was time with Joe, although there was a chance she'd fall asleep before he arrived. She swayed to the sounds of a saxophone solo at the bar and closed the book when a pair of black loafers stopped a foot away. Joe was finally here. A smile tore across her face as she tossed the book in her purse. Then it immediately fell. Apparently, Clark wasn't the only one attracting attention.

"Hi. I noticed you over at the bar. My name is Hunter. Would you like to have a drink together or some more sugar for your current one?" He brushed a hand through black, slicked-back hair and hung a thumb in the pocket of his slacks, practically oozing testosterone.

She couldn't control her laugh. Was it some bar game to pick up the two least interested-looking people in the entire hotel? It had to be, though it made sense why the girls were all over Clark. But with no shoes and a book to her nose, it seemed a bit desperate on Hunter's part. "Umm, no. I don't think so."

"Okay. Maybe I could join you *here*, then?"

Finger around a blonde wave, she giggled, "Sorry. Not tonight."

Hunter took a step closer, his purple-striped tie dangling close to her face. "Well, if you change your mind, I'm right over there."

She was still reining in the laughter when a hand wrapped around Hunter's arm. "I don't think she'll be changing her mind. Goodnight."

Her gaze cut over to a pair of combat boots, jeans, and a tee shirt. Now, *that* was Joe, and she was suddenly wide awake. He looked good. She bit her lip and jumped into his arms, knocking him back a step.

"Apparently, I can't trust Clark to keep the guys away from you for an hour. Worst sitter ever." He smiled and wagged a finger jokingly at Clark, who was paying at the bar and saluting him. Hunter quietly slipped back to the bar alone, correctly choosing not to poke the bear any further.

"He knew you'd show up if I needed you. He's had his hands full anyway with half the girls over there, but he's been on his best behavior."

"Well, let's give him some time off the clock. There were a few things I wanted to talk to you about." He grasped her hands between his and took in every inch of the lobby and bar with his eyes, totally unaware of the heat coursing through her veins at his touch.

"Okay. If you want to come up, I can make us some coffee."

"Sure." They strode to the elevator, not talking, and Savannah doing her very best to act normal like Joe. Was she the only one whose body was pulsing with anticipation of a kiss, of any chance to be closer?

Joe's finger tapped against the top of her palm. His arms and legs tensed as they walked, prepared to leap forward at any moment and rip the arms off any possible threat. Apparently, she and Joe had their minds in two very different places. When he focused on something, it was all he saw, and right now it didn't feel like he saw her. "Is something wrong? You're extra vigilant, and I thought our time with the Green Triangle was over. We're safe, right?"

"I'd feel better if I had a gun, but yeah, we're safe. It's just the Medal of Honor ceremony brought that day in Afghanistan back into the front of my mind, and all I can think is that I missed a detail and that's why those guys aren't alive. I won't let anything happen to you. And until I'm as sure as the feds and The Pentagon that the Green Triangle is permanently dismantled, I won't rest. I refuse to let myself miss a single detail, and unfortunately, until we get back to L.A., the closest thing I've got to a weapon is a zip tie in my pocket."

She leaned against the wall next to the elevator and pulled Joe by the shirt in front of her as a maid rolled by with her cart. "I'd say even with bare hands you're still pretty dangerous, and I am all about trusting your gut, but don't you think if they were still in business, they would've made a move against us by now? It seems like you're taking a lot of precautions." She whispered the words, but it was hard, even in her mind, to tell if it was a statement or a question.

"You should never enter a building without knowing where all the exits are."

"Huh?"

He smiled, revealing those white teeth again, but it was always the eyes that pulled her in like gravity. "I mean safety is important. If you're prepared for the worst, nothing ever catches you off guard."

"That's kind of pessimistic, but I do tend to attract bullets. Maybe a different perfume?" She pressed a finger against the button and watched the numbers ding and change until the door slid open to an empty elevator on the first floor.

"We can discuss your options more in depth when we get upstairs." Savannah laughed, but with his focus, it was hard to tell if he was being serious or flirting. Either way, she was still battling her wakening desires. The door slid to a close and trapped them together for the duration of the ride.

She needed a kiss. She hit the button for the fifteenth floor, nervously tapping her toes in the heels she'd wedged back on. *Come on, isn't he going to kiss me?* She couldn't take it. Not only was it Joe, this was no ordinary elevator, playing wordless guitar music; Barry White sang at a low volume, just tempting her to make the first move yet again, and God help her, she wasn't doing it. Her lips puckered in a frown as they reached floor five and then six. What was the deal? She contained a huff and looked down. His feet were tapping too, and not to the music. He was nervous. But about security or closeness?

Seven.

Eight.

Nine.

The mirrors on the wall behind them were fogging up and they hadn't even touched. The tension was palpable, and her chest was heavy, sweat building on the back of her neck. There was no way she was the only one turned on. She squeezed the bar behind her with one hand and fidgeted with the tie on her dress with the other. And in that second, he turned and ran his hand over her cheek, leaning in. Finally.

But he was moving like molasses, and they were up to the tenth floor now. She rose on tiptoes and closed the distance, his lips open against hers, breath hot. He laughed and pulled in closer, hands trailing down her back and across her stomach but carefully avoiding the tie on the side of her dress, even though they kept moving that way. The muscles in her stomach clenched as he tossed her hair to the side and kissed her neck, tongue tracing the curve of her jawbone.

He slid his hands behind her thighs and lifted her onto the metal bar she'd had in her hands. He slid between her legs, pushing them apart and wrapping them around his waist. She uttered a cry that made him laugh again, body hot against Joe's as he ran his rough palms over her thighs. Her legs turned to jelly at the friction between their bodies, the pressure of him against her. Head spinning, she couldn't form words, her only thought was the taste of his lips between hers. This couldn't get any better, could it?

Ding.

The elevator door slid open, and Joe retrieved her limp body from the bar, straightening her dress for her since her mind was mush. A family of four climbed aboard the Scandalous Savannah Express, and her heart dropped to her knees in a wave of embarrassment she'd take to her grave. Joe saluted the father, who donned an old Navy hat and wide eyes. Politeness only went so far when you were caught making out in a hotel elevator, but Joe gave it a good try. She ran off, looking back once to see an imprint of her form in the fogginess of the mirror.

Joe cracked his neck and slapped his hand into hers to slow her down. "Can't ever let me make the first move, huh?"

"Maybe one day." Her voice came out deeply, every part of her still yearning for more of the last few seconds. But it was more than nerves holding him back in the elevator, because his feet were tapping again as they waited outside her door. She pulled the key out and patted it on her palm, leaning against the door and blinking a few times to steady her mind. "Are you going to tell me what's really going on?"

"My mind is running a hundred miles an hour, and it's hard to relax. Except when I let myself focus on you." A wry grin played over his lips. "I guess it's time to do some talking, then. Not my favorite activity, but I still want you to hear everything that happened in Afghanistan, from me. That citation didn't tell the whole story. Whether you think it's necessary or not, I do. Please." His green eyes fixed on hers with a plea.

"Come on in. If I know everything, maybe you won't ever doubt my feelings again, though I assumed the eight hundred plus text messages between us had convinced you." She ran the card over the lock, and Joe pushed the door open for her, immediately flipping the switch so the lights would be bright before she entered. He really didn't miss anything.

The room wasn't big: a couch just longer than a loveseat, a desk, and a chair stuffed in beside a queen-sized bed. Another door across from them adjoined to Clark's identical room. "So, where do you want to sit, the bed or the couch?"

He raised an eyebrow. "Definitely the couch."

She blushed and took a seat, wrapping a blanket over her legs. "I'm ready."

He walked around the room, locking both doors before sitting too. She laid her feet over his lap and leaned against the thick arm of the couch. "I've been prepping to tell you everything for days, but I need a minute. I was trying to avoid kissing you until after I opened up so my mind would be clear. But you and that red dress... Well, I couldn't wait any longer." He squeezed his hands into fists and let them back out. "Okay, I'll start with something they didn't share at the ceremony. It was winter in Afghanistan, and my team and I had been after this drug-lord-slash-terrorist named Azfaar Mudad. A trusted informant had already led us to a mountain village he'd been stashing his opium in. For this part of the story, I'll keep it short; we found the considerable drug stash and burned it. I cornered two men that seemed important in an underground tunnel but got trapped when I killed one man and couldn't wedge past his body to escape through the hatch. Because of that, the other man got away."

Her eyes shot open. Stuck in an underground Afghani tunnel? That had to be torture and trying to picture it made her own breathing speed up. Was that why Joe had such trouble with tight spaces? Asking would give more clarity on Joe and how his mind worked, but he wasn't going to answer that right now.

"Fast forward two weeks. The informant made contact again, said Mudad was meeting with some other Taliban in the mountains, and he'd lead us to him like before. It was an opportunity to bring him down, and I didn't think twice, because our window for catching him was small. We were headed back to the states shortly after. I'd actually talked to my mom that morning. She said my dad's back was in bad shape, and I was upset and wanted to take my mind off things. Target practice usually took care of that."

He shifted on the couch and rested his hands on her blanketed feet. She kept her lips closed so he'd keep talking. Any question from her could potentially end his story. "So, this informant, I'd used him more than once, and his info always panned out. We ran it up the chain of command and got things rolling. The orders were clear. I was to take the team in for recon only, unless we made a positive I.D. If we did, we had orders to assess the situation and snatch or kill him if possible.

"So, we started hiking, planning to get there when it was dusky dark. I knew how to lead a team and keep my mind clear, so I pushed thoughts of my parents to the back of my mind like I'd been taught. They only creeped back a time or two. The mission had to be front and center in my brain. Each of my men had a life to get back to, and it was my job to ensure that happened. Hinley had a baby girl on the way. Thomas was having a late Christmas with his wife in eight days. Morrison's parents were relying on him to get them moved into a retirement community.

"I remember puffing out my chest. I'd always kept them safe, and I believed that night would be no different. Getting Azfaar Mudad out of business would be a huge win in the fight against the Taliban, and the guys would go home feeling like heroes. And I'd go home too. I had a...um, marriage to fix, and my parents needed me, even though they'd never admit it."

A squeak escaped between her lips even though she was desperately trying to remain quiet. He'd dropped a bomb and expected her to ignore it and move right along with him, but she had no emotional filter, so she bit her lip and kept it between her teeth.

"It wasn't an easy walk to the village. The cold air snuck through my fatigues and erased all the sweat I'd accumulated on the ground that morning. The terrain was rocky, and the paths were so narrow you could just as easily fall to your death as anything else. Snowflakes drifted around us, covering everything in a quarter inch of white. I took deliberate footsteps and focused on my breathing as the air thinned."

Joe had been telling the story for the past few minutes, but now he was living it. His eyes drifted away from the hotel room, and his fingers dug roughly into her feet. He didn't know he was hurting her, but there was no way she was going to interrupt and draw his focus away now if she'd avoided the marriage comment. Joe needed to get some of the guilt off his chest, and she could handle the pain. She squeezed her hands together and waited for him to continue.

"We got to the village. It was cloudy from the snowfall, and darkness would be coming on quickly. A fire glowed over the ridge. Wood-and-mud huts formed a circle around a sputtering fire. We needed a closer look, so I signaled to the guys, and they began creeping to their positions. But in that second, I looked at my informant's hands. They were shaking. Shaking!"

He gripped her feet harder, and a toe popped. "Something was wrong. How long had that been going on? Did it just start, or had I missed it five minutes before because I was thinking about my footsteps or my dad's back? It was unsteadying, and the air ripped from my chest, freezing all the snowflakes around me in midair.

"I lurched forward and dug my fingers into his arm, but he pulled away and ran, screaming, to the village. And it didn't matter that Hinley popped him and he dropped like a rock. They'd been waiting on us with a planned attack that they'd recruited for. I like to think the informant wasn't all bad. Maybe they threatened his family or something. Who knows. But he signed our death certificates.

"Taliban were everywhere, rising from behind every tree, every rock. I couldn't breathe, could only shoot. One man down, two men, six men. But there were too many. Rounds pierced the air like a steady rain falling over us. It was an ambush, and no amount of training could defeat better ground and dozens more men.

"Hinley called for air support, his voice raging over an army of at least fifty, but they weren't going to make it in time. The Taliban had a machine gun nest poised right at the head of the trail, and unless it was taken out, it'd all be over in under four minutes. This team of guys—*my* team of guys—was the best of the best, but we were outgunned."

Besides the tears wetting Savannah's cheeks, she remained unmoving.

Joe choked back his own tears and forced them into his throat with his unused breath. He wasn't going to let a single one drop. "Morrison took two rounds to the chest and rose onto his side, never hesitating, still fighting. It's how we were trained, but he didn't fight back for himself. He kept fighting for the chance that the rest of us could live.

"My eyes fixed on that machine gun nest, but I needed to get Morrison out of immediate danger. I yelled for Harvey to lay down cover fire as I rolled and stumbled over a heap of rocks to get to him. My fingers dug into Morrison's gear as I dragged him over boulders and earth.

"That's when the snow unfroze from the sky and poured down with ferocity. Men with AKs kept appearing, and firing. And with the machine gun choking off our movement, firing a steady stream of death, there were only two options: take out the machine gun nest and get to higher ground or run back the way we'd come while being ripped to shreds by the machine gun.

"There was no way the Aces were running. We never ran from anybody or anything. So, we fought. A grenade flew through the air in slow motion and landed between my boots and Hinley's. I didn't have to think about it. If I was getting anyone home, it was him, and all the other guys would have agreed too. I kicked the grenade away and pushed Hinley down, shielding him from the blast with my body."

Joe's eyes burned with something visceral, this fire of rage and regret that made her tremble in fear. "Dirt flew up, turning the sky brown. It erased all hearing in my left ear. Blood poured out, and my left boot was ragged. Harvey and Thomas each threw grenades too, and they landed with accuracy, sending several Taliban flying back. Only a few rose again. But I guess with the machine gun roasting everything in sight, I'd missed the sniper perched in the trees, and Thomas and Harvey suddenly dropped sideways."

Joe's words came out heavy and unclear for a moment before resuming their normal seriousness. "I focused my eyes on the trees until I made out his figure and got into position. My nose only alerted my brain to gunpowder and burning flesh. My stomach churned like crazy because it was my fault. I should've sensed something was wrong. I was their leader, damn it! Me!"

His fist slammed onto the top of the couch, and Savannah brushed it with her fingers until each finger unclenched. "My heart tore my ribs further apart with each beat, and I realized, for the first time, I'd taken a round to the side of my chest. There was no time to waste. I wrapped my finger around the trigger and lit up the tree where he was hiding and shooting. The man dropped, and relief flooded through my fingertips.

"But when my eye left the rifle, that relief was instantly smothered out. For the first time in my life, I was terrified. Not terrified of dying. If death came for me, it would be okay. I would have served my country with honor, but my guys? No. I couldn't let them go out like this.

Adrenaline burned my veins like fire, and my vision went red around the edges, closing in. These men were warriors, brothers, family. Hinley and Parker were the only ones still proactively moving and engaging. Two were on the ground, unable to move but still fighting like true heroes. The others were dead."

Savannah's heart raced like a thoroughbred in the Kentucky Derby. *That's the guilt that tears him apart*, she realized. He thought if he'd noticed a missing detail, his friends would be alive. She was no soldier, but he seemed to notice everything. Everything. Parents having problems or not, it seemed unlikely he missed that guy's hands shaking. But even if he had, it wasn't his fault. It wasn't. And it didn't change her feelings at all. It just made her hurt all over—physically hurt—that he'd never be able to outrun the pain. She cared more with each passing moment.

"Hinley cupped his ear. Air Support was close, but not close enough. And Hinley and Parker couldn't move the other guys without taking on more fire. I ordered Hinley and Parker to pull everyone away while I held back the Taliban's men and fought through the machine gun nest. My chest exploded with pain, but I raised my fingers and started to count. Parker shook his head too, but it was the only way, and it had to be me.

On three, I lunged toward that machine gun nest shooting. Twenty men shot back. My shoulder stung, then my stomach, but I kept moving, dodging left and right and gaining cover for half a second here and there.

"One of the men behind the machine gun was down with a shot to the head, and four others bled out beside him. They might not have been dead, but they didn't have the same resolve as a Green Beret, so they gave up. Cowards. One more grenade blast sent me swerving, but nothing short of a freight train would stop me. I had to save my men from the mess I got them into."

Joe closed his eyes before continuing. "In that moment, bullets tearing me apart, I prayed for the first time without mom forcing me into it. I prayed God would get those men out of that mountain and leave me there to…see the stars fade before I was gone. There were five men left when air support showed up. Their heads jerked up, and I took out two. They got the other three and lit the entire camp and treeline up with rounds, just in case. And then it was quiet. But it might've been because I lost too much blood. I scanned my surroundings, ready to run back to the team and administer CPR, when my heavy eyes fixed on an image, and vomit fought its way up."

His eyes squeezed so tightly together that every wrinkle on his face ran deep. "There, skulking through the trees, with two Taliban soldiers, was the man that had gotten away from me two weeks before in that tunnel…with an RPG. That sick bastard planned all of it as revenge. I was in excruciating pain from the countless bullet holes and my foot resembling something put through a meat grinder. But if God was taking me, the Devil would get some new tenants too. My vision was down to ten percent, and my head felt like a bowling ball, but I ran.

"My rifle pierced the temple of the man with the RPG, and another fought me as the familiar man took over. It had to be Azfaar Mudad. It made sense, and I'd stupidly missed it last time. I flipped the other Taliban soldier on his back and thrust a blade into his throat before ripping it out again and launching forward, covered in his blood, mine, everyone's. My mouth fell slack. It was too late. The RPG sailed toward my men anyway. I lost control.

"Mudad…smiled. He smiled at me and spoke in a voice that scratched against my skin like razorblades as he dug a finger into the wound at my side and leaned in my face. 'So, we meet again. I've been waiting for this moment. Quite the set-up, yes? Your team had it coming. But you, always the resilient little cockroach. You alone burned my drugs, and you alone killed my brother and left him to rot in that tunnel. You, Mr. MacArthur, will die today, and I'll find a nice hole for your body, too.'

"He raised a pistol to my head, but my vision was black, and my consciousness hung on by a thread. I clenched my teeth and propelled my head forward, crunching Mudad's nose and sending him howling. And I yelled or whispered, I don't know, and I don't remember what I said. I grabbed the knife in Mudad's belt and plunged it through his chest before tumbling down the hill, my body smashing against the rocks.

"I administered CPR to the men, but only Hinley and Parker had a chance to live, and it was about as good as mine. The last thing I remember was Rangers suddenly surrounding me. I hadn't heard their Blackhawk approach, but they'd already set up a perimeter and were probing the area for surviving Taliban as the others carried my guys and forced my hands off Morrison. His ace playing card slipped from a pocket with blood soaking it. I clutched it and fell back to say goodbye to the stars."

CHAPTER TWENTY-SIX

Joe

S avannah was quiet, and that woman was never quiet. It was a relief to get everything out there, but at some point in the story, he'd gotten lost in memories and closed his eyes, ending his ability to gauge her responsiveness. Savannah's opinion meant more than everyone in the world combined, so if this was too much for her, he'd have to let her go. Thinking that sucked every ounce of happiness from his chest, but it was true, and partially why he'd shown an ounce of restraint in the elevator.

His watch ticked along as he waited, a constant reminder that the longer she chose not to answer, the less likely it would be a good one. He couldn't imagine spending his future with anyone else, so if she was out, he'd end up that bearded old man living off the land in some shabby cabin, deep in the woods. Well, a cabin in the woods wasn't bad, but without her to spice the place up, it'd only be him and a bunch of stuffed deer heads. So, he just sat there, with his back painfully straight and his feet plastered to the carpet, as they inched toward the five-minute mark. Three seconds shy of it, Savannah crossed her legs and sat up, effectively cutting off all physical contact.

Years of marriage dissolving to nothing but a goodbye note, and that one movement from Savannah hurt worse. Wait, had he mentioned Nadine? Oh man, he had. But Savannah hadn't brought it up, so maybe she didn't notice. He had this reveal of information carefully planned out, and it was supposed to happen when he got back to L.A.

His hands were on the couch, pushing his body up, when she made eye contact. "Don't even think about it." Savannah jerked him back down by his shirt sleeve. "I'm sorry. This all took me a minute to process. I have some questions, because a few things you said shocked me a bit. Really, I need to say this first though: I have seen you in action. I have seen you sacrifice yourself for me. And I believe if it had been anyone else, you would've done the same thing, not because I'm not important to you, but because you are a protector.

"And though my saying so won't change how you feel about Afghanistan, nor will it bring your friends back, I believe you didn't miss a single detail. I wish you'd stop living with shame over never feeling good enough. You are, and no matter what mistakes or problems come our way, I'm not giving up on you.

"But mostly I want you to know that I sat there that entire time thinking, 'Oh my gosh. This guy wants me. He picked *me*. What did I do to get so lucky?' Now kiss me again already, wouldn't you? Wait, does that count as making the first—"

He leapt across the foot of space separating them before Savannah could finish, pulling her legs out from under her so she fell backwards onto the couch with a *poof*. She was startled but smiling, body warm against his as she wrapped her arms and legs around him. Face half an inch above hers, he dove in first for that kiss.

That's when his phone started ringing. He sat up and growled. Fate always had something jumping in the way of a kiss lasting longer than thirty seconds. But fate was another of those intangible things, so he couldn't wring its neck. He would've just let it go to voicemail, but out of the corner of his eye, the screen was flashing with the President's name. Monumentally bad timing, but he was one of the only people on Earth you didn't ignore. "Hello, Mr. President."

"Joe, you can call me Ezra. I just wanted to call with some good news.

There are still a number of people anxious to interview you, but I listened to Savannah tonight, and you two need some time together after everything that happened. If you can be here before dawn, we'll squeeze the interviews in back to back to back, and I'll have you out of here on a flight sometime mid-afternoon. How does that sound?"

"I'll be there at zero four hundred hours. Thank you, Mr. President."

"Ezra. See you in the morning, Joe." He hung up, laughing, since Savannah's squeal of delight was clearly audible at the other end of the line.

Savannah was still on her back under him, smiling from ear to ear, when he tossed the cell over to the coffee table. Now she seemed ready to talk, which was all Ezra's fault, because other things were on his mind. But getting back to the house he'd been using was vital despite the direction his body pulled him. He'd known a lot of women, but Savannah, man, it was different. Every muscle and bone in his body wanted her forever.

He slipped off the couch and opened his hands in an apology. He'd be able to squeeze in maybe an hour-long nap and then change before the interviews, and it severed her chance to dive into the Nadine thing. "I want to stay, but I've got to get moving. Those interviews are just a few hours away, and I've got to pack so I can leave straight after. I know you've been wanting to start our trip. I made that promise, and I intend to keep it. We can leave tomorrow evening."

Savannah sat up on the couch and covered her mouth with her hand. "Tomorrow should work, but I just remembered something. When Clark and I got to the airport this morning, Holden was there, waiting. He apparently got tickets for some party tomorrow afternoon a while ago, assuming our relationship would continue. My mom paid for Clark and me to get out here with the agreement that I'd let Holden down easy after helping my parents so much during the kidnapping, and she hasn't let me forget it…So, I told him I'd go as friends."

Joe was nodding rapidly with his lips pursed. His fingers twitched.

He needed to shoot something—or someone. Holden's face came to mind. He flipped his cell repeatedly in his hand since there was no gun. Why did she have to be so nice? What was it with rich people and their social obligations? Savannah was his. Holden wasn't going to get the luxury of spending the afternoon showing her off to all his rich friends, hand on her back as he led her through the crowds. The heat in his hands spread to his face, his chest, encompassing him in fury. How did this guy keep weaseling his way back to her? And was he supposed to have confidence that Savannah's life was safe in Holden's unskilled hands?

"I won't leave you alone with him. He nearly got you killed in that alley." His feet took him back and forth across the room.

"He's hired a security detail to keep us safe, and I thought we were safe now anyway. Really, it will be a couple hours, and you'll never have to think about him again. It will be over before you even get back to L.A. I can bring Clark if it would make you feel better. I made a promise to my mom, and she was right. He was good to my family. He knows I'm not interested anymore, Joe. I made that very clear." Savannah reached out as he neared her end of the room again, but he turned and kept pacing.

"I get that you're not interested, but seriously, Savannah. Don't you think it's suspicious that he still wants to take you, when all he's going to get out of it is good conversation? There are hundreds of girls that would let him into their beds with minimal effort, and he still wants you? It's either desperate or he's up to something."

"Gosh. You make all guys sound awful. I'm not discounting your concerns, but despite what I've seen and felt the last week, I still believe he's a good person. You haven't tried dating in L.A., especially with the people that run in our circles. Maybe he just wants to take someone on the date that isn't going to talk about liposuction and Kim Kardashian the whole time."

He was making eye contact with Savannah now, but in a piercing way that didn't register her emotions or her attempt at humor. This conversation had done a one-eighty, and he hadn't recovered. He needed to, quickly, because it was now headed in a direction that would only end badly for him, but he couldn't help himself.

He was jealous, which didn't happen ever, but there was no reason not to trust Holden. To believe Holden was stupid, yes, but clearly his love for Savannah was clouding reason. *Love.* Man, there he was, thinking it again. He'd only known her for a matter of days, and they'd been dangerous and messy. If there were loose ends she needed to tie up from her life, then a reasonable man would say yes. So, why couldn't he form those words?

"Sorry, but no. I'm going to make the decision here. You aren't going to that party with Holden. It's not safe. I haven't done any reconnaissance on the location, I don't have a guest list to run background checks, and I know nothing about the party. It sounds like you don't either."

She jumped off the couch and stood in front of him, looking up with a trembling jaw. "What happened in the last thirty seconds? Is this how you're going to respond every time I want to go to the movies or out to dinner? Will that ever be an option again, or are you going to lock the two of us inside some steel castle with laser beams so I'm safe from everything except a severe Vitamin D deficiency? You trusted Clark with me until now, so what changed? Me going on a date with someone I don't have any interest in? I'm safer at a party with Clark and a half dozen bodyguards than at my apartment, downing a half-gallon of ice cream with just Clark. There is danger in life, but there's also good. You have to be able to see both, and you're not willing to. Or you don't trust me. Either way, I'm tired. It's time for you to go. You have interviews to prep for, and I have a plane to catch in the morning." She turned on a heel and slammed the bathroom door, immediately bringing the shower to life.

No one had ever spoken to him in a way that froze his insides before. But he deserved it. That was stupid.

Odds were Savannah was in there crying, even though it wasn't audible over the shower. All his points had been valid, but they mainly stemmed from jealousy, and she could smell it on him. She'd been all over town with Clark since the kidnapping, and nothing bad had happened. This party wasn't any different in that aspect, and his fears about any lingering trace of the Green Triangle seemed less likely every day. If he'd confessed his jealousy, told her that the decision was hers but he didn't feel comfortable with the party even with Clark there, or been truly transparent and confessed his fear of losing her to someone else, maybe things would have gone better. But he'd gone for the straight Army face, talking down to her like she wasn't a smoking-hot grown woman.

Clark would bust down the bathroom door and wrap her in his arms, dramatically begging for forgiveness. But he wasn't Clark, and to be honest, he wasn't sure what to do. Pulling from past experience with Nadine felt dicey. The fact of the matter was that Savannah asked him to leave. Did that mean for tonight or forever? Either way, he had to respect her wishes. He set his jaw, nostrils flared and eyes heavy with tears that he hadn't let out since he was four and broke his arm. It was emotional, and it compromised your vision. Right now, it didn't matter, because all he could focus on was one thought: Had he lost Savannah for good because he claimed not to have run background checks on the guest list?

He picked up his feet with effort and wrapped his hand around a notepad and pen. He left a note and entered the hall, cringing. All that inner monologue, stress, anxiety… Why couldn't he voice what he was thinking? Why couldn't he say, "I care about you, so can we please work this out?" Even writing that, or something else nice on the note, would have been better. His note sucked. His fists balled up against his temples as he scanned the hall. It was clear except for Clark leaning against his open doorframe, with a woman in a short dress. She clung to him with one hand, a martini glass in the other.

"Didn't expect to see you leavin' so quick, man," Clark said.

Joe cut his eyes at the woman, and she slipped inside. "The President called. Seems he can get me out of here tomorrow if I'm at the White House for interviews before sunrise. So, I need to pack up." Joe leaned against the blue wall, tapping his fingers as Clark closed in. "Oh, and did

Savannah mention this party Holden invited her to?"

Clark laughed loudly and sent a text to someone before looking back up and slapping Joe on the arm. "A little jealous there, lovebird?"

"I don't have time to be jealous. I'm worried about her safety, that's all."

"Yeah, okay. My mistake. Clearly, you're handling the whole situation incredibly well."

Joe pushed away from the wall, with a frown. "Just go with her, okay?"

"Sure thing. Just admit you're jealous or in love. I'll settle for either."

"It doesn't matter. Keep her safe until I'm back in town."

Clark grabbed him by the arm and dug his fingers in. "What did you do this time?"

Joe could've pulled away, but he didn't. "I told her she couldn't go. Then she told me to leave."

Clark dropped his arm and threw his hands on his head. "And you actually left? Are you stupid?"

"I'm not going to answer that. She needs space. Just tell me. Is it over?"

Clark was still worked up, but he muttered a laugh. "Dude, she's crazy about you, and 'cause you're an idiot, I'll spell it out for you: She. Will. *Never*. Leave. You. She's not Nadine. I mean, seriously, if she was, she's had all the opportunities in the world to upgrade, and I'm still standin' here." He doubled over, cackling, while Joe turned and walked away, reigning in the floodgate of tears. She just needed time.

Maybe Clark was right. He couldn't project his past with Nadine onto his present with Savannah. There were only a few things he seemed to get right when it came to women, and Savannah probably wouldn't even kiss him right now, so any of that was off the table. He could send a text, but did she want to hear from him? Would the best thing be to wait until they were face-to-face tomorrow? Whatever he chose would be wrong. Add it to the list.

The anxiety weighed on his chest like a ton of bricks for the entire ride back and continued as he approached the house. It was dark except for a small flicker of light shining through the front window: probably his mom. She always stayed up late to read or pray, but tonight was most likely in hopes he'd show up so she could have some time alone with him. Even as a teen, they'd stay up late together, sitting quietly as he cleaned his guns and she worked a puzzle. It took a while to realize she wasn't smothering him to make sure he didn't sneak out or something, and even longer to realize how hard it was for an extrovert like her to give up any hope of engaging conversation. It was her way of being a part of his world.

She pulled open the door before he had a grip on it, but her approaching footsteps had been perceptible, so it wasn't a surprise. "I was wondering when you'd be back tonight. Come on in. I've got some hot cocoa on the stove." She padded through the kitchen, in her fuzzy house slippers, and retrieved two coffee mugs from the cabinet. It was past 1:15 a.m., and she'd been waiting for him, so responding with a *no thanks* wouldn't work. He just found a spot on the couch and yawned as she placed a cup in his hands, which he promptly began tapping with his index finger.

"Honey, while you were gone, I packed up all your things. They're sitting by your door. The President told your dad and me after dinner that he was going to try and get you out of D.C. tomorrow. I thought, with packing off the list, it might give you a chance to rest a bit and maybe for us to talk? I won't keep you up long, I promise. I wanted to tell you something."

Joe stretched his legs out and crossed them over the coffee table, holding back another yawn as he took a swig of chocolate. "What's on your mind?"

"Honey, I can see you're tired. I won't keep you. I'm just not sure when I'll get to see you again, and I want you to know how much these last few days with you have meant to your dad and me. When you disappeared after everything with Nadine, well… Anyway, we were worried sick for our boy. That's why we kept tryin' to find you. The point I'm getting to is this: Your father and I adore that quirky, vivacious, beautiful girl you brought into our lives, and you're different around her—happy, even. It's clear you're in love, though maybe you haven't realized it yet. But you have to *choose* to let her love you, and love shouldn't be hard just because you won't allow yourself to be vulnerable. Don't shut 'er out. You show your love by protecting, by makin' things orderly and routine. She's a talker. You don't have to say those three words today, but you *will* have to say them. There'll be a moment, when your defenses are down, when you're raw. Give her that confirmation, and don't chicken out."

Joe sat the cup down and leaned across the table. "Mom, you know— you and Dad, you know that I...how much I..."

"Honey. We know. Don't worry. But don't make Savannah wait thirty-three years to hear it, okay?"

"Yes, ma'am. But I messed things up."

"What happened?"

"I overreacted to something, and she asked me to leave her hotel room. I wanted to keep her safe, that's all. I just handled it like an idiot."

His mom removed her slippers and pulled her feet onto the couch, smile as wide as Texas because he never asked for advice, never asked for anything his whole life, except more ammo. "First of all, as a woman, you shouldn't've left. But, seein' as you already did, let's work from there. She knows you'd do anything to keep her safe, but she's not a man, so you don't talk to her like you do Clark. However, there's nothing that can't be fixed with a little apology and a lotta prayer." She rested her cup on the coffee table and patted his hand. "While I'm giving advice, let me just add, you know the rule. You shouldn't've opened this door before closing the other one." She reached into her pocket and handed him a piece of paper as his face flushed at the reprimand. "Here's Nadine's new address. I realize you've been runnin', and it slipped your mind because this relationship ended long ago, but it's time to make it official with divorce papers. Let her and her new boyfriend move on, and you can too. If you ask the President, although it'd be awkward, I'll bet he can expedite this thing for you. It may not be as big of a deal to you, but Savannah and God probably don't see it that way."

She was right, although she'd brought God into it to dig the knife a little deeper between his ribs. Old-fashioned Southern justice was alive and thriving with June MacArthur.

CHAPTER TWENTY-SEVEN
Savannah

"Well?"

Clark shifted beside Savannah and tightened his seatbelt as a heavy wave of turbulence shocked the plane's cabin. She'd been slamming questions at him since the wheels went up, with an "intensity," as Clark put it. He'd been evasive, but she was wearing him down.

Last night had been crummy with a capital *C*. The bags under her eyes were proof of that, all puffy from crying, though concealer and large sunglasses had temporarily taken care of the problem. But she developed a question long before the fight erupted and wanted an answer.

She could've texted Joe, hoping to hit all the right keys with her tear-filled eyes, though he wouldn't have opened up over text anyway. And besides that, there was no way on God's green earth she was texting, calling, or reaching out to him first. The fight was bad enough to make her second guess her intense feelings for him, but that note he left boiled her blood: *Just go to the party.*

No smiley face. No "I'm sorry. Please forgive my horrific communication skills." Nothing. Didn't set a good mood for a road trip, but despite feelings of rage and disappointment, her annoying side was still desperate to find out if he had a gooey heart behind that tough exterior. Oh, that tough exterior. Darn. That's all it took to pull her attention to his tight body and tattooed arms. It was a constant distraction, and she didn't want to be distracted; she wanted to be mad. Or maybe mad and distracted?

He cared, even though he couldn't say it and was being protective. Fine, message received. But his protectiveness came across as overbearing and condescending. Mostly, though, it was the stress of his belief that danger lurked around every corner. That couldn't be true and certainly wasn't true of some hoity party with Holden.

Joe should've texted at the very least to say sorry. What was he thinking? She had boundless patience and acceptance for every single person in the world, and yet he worked her up into the kind of lather she hadn't felt since season fourteen of *The Bachelor*. Ugh. Is this what it felt like to be in love? Rock-your-world fabulous one moment and just the opposite in the next? Or was this what it was like to be in love with Joe? And that's what it really boiled down to because she was starting to fall for him, and it was terrifying.

What was the smart decision? This wouldn't be the last fight over similar things, nor would it be the last time he'd respond like the military's answering machine. Could she live with that? Did the good outweigh the bad?

Clark tapped her on the arm. "Earth to Savannah? I get ready to answer, and you drift off with a look on your face that isn't so pretty."

She contorted the muscles in her face until it probably looked better. Probably. "Okay. Yes. I want an answer."

"Okay, but the others are way outta my comfort zone. Joe hasn't said anything to you, because the dude isn't like a regular person. He knows he screwed up, but he's never gonna believe that someone like him deserves you."

"But I—"

Clark threw up a hand to stop what would have been a five-minute monologue. "Suck it up. Either text him when we land or wait. He'll be runnin' to you as soon as his boots touch the ground. So, let's go to this party to make your momma happy, and then you two drama queens can get on the road and never have to argue about pretty boy again."

Pushing his hand away, she spoke fast before he cut her off again. "First, you've spent enough time around Holden to call him by his name. But, bigger picture, will Joe always be like this? Every girl likes to feel like her knight in shining armor has come, but you know, after he saves you, he's supposed to be a little more um..."

"Happy? Romantic? Sure. Joe's an acquired taste. I can't convince you to be with him, and I'm still here for ya either way. Just hear him out when he gets back to L.A., please. He's the smartest guy I've ever met in a lot of ways, but he's always worried someone's gonna leave him. It's how he's wired. When his wife, Na—umm, never mind."

Crossing her legs in the seat, she inched in close. "Give me something, Clark. You're trapped on this plane with me for at least another forty-five minutes, and we both know you said *wife*. So did he. Last night." There was no giving up, because as irritating as the argument with Joe was, something dug even harder at her heart, making her decision that much more gut wrenching. It was the one question that kept her eyes open as she wrapped up in the hotel comforter last night. Joe seemed to blow right past it in his tale, like they were ordering hamburgers at the drive-through and he'd just remembered to add ketchup. No biggie. But this was. He'd said he was married. Savannah was no mathematician, but there seemed to be some logistical issues she couldn't overlook.

"Savannah. Have I told you how beautiful you look today?"

"Noted and appreciated. But let's get to the nitty gritty. Between the time Joe returned home from Afghanistan, ran all over the United States, and found me, eight months passed. If I'm not mistaken, he hasn't been frequenting a lawyer's office, so it would make sense that I've gotten involved with a married man."

"That's a statement, not a question." He was always joking, but his words were strained as tight as his full lips.

Savannah clenched her teeth and feigned reaching over to ring his neck. "You are infuriating. Just tell me if I stepped into a big pile of relationship poo. He told me in the hotel room, maybe inadvertently, that when his deployment was over, he had a marriage to fix. Please give me something, because my stomach is churning, and not just from motion sickness."

Clark met her gaze and laid his arm on the armrest between them, trying to get his large, muscular body situated in his seat. It was funny to see him uncomfortable, because that rarely happened. "Listen. It's not my story to tell. It's Joe's, and I'm more scared'a him than I am of you. What I can say is that Nadine—that's her name—and Joe both made some mistakes, and maybe the situation isn't legally ideal, but there isn't anything to be gettin' in the middle of. That good enough for ya?"

The stomachache was easing a bit, but she still sipped the ginger ale the stewardess dropped off fifteen minutes before. She set it back down and spun it around slowly with her fingers, the light from the window making her pink nail polish shimmer. "Yes. I mean, I'd like to know everything now, but you eased my mind." She let go of the cup, tapped her fingernails, and went back to spinning it. Nadine left Joe, and since he was clearly adopted, he might have those same feelings about his birth parents. She'd promised him she would never leave.

Her stomach tumbled sideways, and she threw her head on the tray in front of her.

Clark slid on headphones and closed his eyes. "You 'n' Joe got it bad for each other, huh? Try and cut him a little slack. Around you his intelligence drops to like a sixteen-year-old's level. Never seen him like this. Kinda fun though."

She couldn't help but giggle from her face-down position, even though Clark had already tuned out. Her laughter died quickly, fading into the rumble of the engine and the two passengers behind her debating politics. The real ones, not the society politics her parents were always droning on about. The stewardess clicked through the aisle to her left with a garbage sack, collecting dirty cups in preparation for landing. She moved slowly, calmly, floating around despite the turbulence. Savannah's ears followed the rhythmic clicking, and she, too, let her eyelids fall.

Joe's face was there in her subconscious. She didn't force it out, considering it was him or Leader. She squeezed her eyes tighter. She always, always, always did what was best for everyone else. She didn't have to grin and bear it, but if she didn't, there wouldn't be a day she didn't long for him. There it was. A sort-of decision in the midst of fury.

If she was determined to stay, all that remained was the relationship he was still in. Nothing was done until everyone signed the dotted line. Even though her parents were still trucking along after forty years, it wasn't the case for ninety-nine percent of their friends. The majority were divorced for various reasons like hiding money, affairs with the gardener or yoga instructor, or expensive bottles of booze being shattered during a fight: rich people problems. It was always petty, and therefore the word *divorce* left a bad taste in her mouth. It would quite literally be the shock of her life if any of those examples related to Joe's marriage. He was too disciplined, but answers were still important…and, of course, divorce papers.

It was another two hours before Savannah turned the key to her soup kitchen doors and crossed the threshold. It always smelled of lemons and cinnamon in here, even now, when her mother had changed so much here. Outside those doors was chaos, but in here, a few steps away, there was peace, hope for those that had none. And this week, she'd been low on both. A couple from a nearby church offered to take over things while she was gone with Joe, assuming the trip was on, which still had her head bobbing back and forth at the thought. Maybe one day, but today she wasn't going. He still hadn't texted or called, and the couple was flexible.

Either way, it was hard to put this place into someone else's hands for the unforeseeable future. They could be gone five days or five weeks. Clark was hesitant to go back to the soup kitchen so soon, but they had twelve bags of food that hadn't been handed out, and she wanted the chance to do it. If Joe returned, apologized, and made a convincing argument in his defense tonight, like his hands had been chopped off, rendering him helpless to pick up a phone, she might reconsider leaving today. Her lips pursed and a chill ran over her thighs. No, he definitely needed to keep his hands.

The party was inching closer, so they needed to hurry. There was something in the back of her closet that was adequately sparkly, and Clark had a guy from the hotel drop off a suit at her apartment.

Clark stationed himself by the door, out of the line of sight, as he had before. This place held only bad memories for him, or at least violent ones. If he hadn't been here, Joe wouldn't have made it out alive. And all that for evidence she was convinced Allen hid here, when it turned out to be only his medal and a letter. Priceless, and of course Allen's letter claimed he did take a video of the bad guys at work and saw business cards with green triangles. Well, claimed sounded like she didn't believe him. She had trusted Allen the same way she trusted Clark and Joe: with her life.

She tugged at her hair and treaded around the counter to the wall under the cabinets where she hung pictures. Pulling the pin out of one, she hopped onto the counter and crossed her legs, holding it in her hands and stroking her and Allen's faces as they wore Santa hats at Christmas. He always helped her serve the meals before he allowed her to serve him. He was selfless, gentle, and a better friend than she'd had in years.

None of this made any sense, and she hadn't had any time to mourn him. With the constant danger, she was only able to recently consider him again. He wanted her and Joe to leave town and be happy, despite his impending fate. Maybe they should have, but they would've just brought the danger to another town. Now at least it was over.

Her lips turned into a frown, and a tear fought its way out of her eye. She shoved the picture into her back pocket. She'd do it all again, the fear and torture, if she could have her friend back.

"Savannah." Clark broke her focus with an agitated growl. "Bruce is on his way in. He doesn't have Claire with him though. Want me to meet him with a bag of food outside?"

"That would lovely. Thanks." She lowered herself from the counter as three other women entered first. She greeted them warmly, keeping one eye on Clark exiting the building and stopping fifteen yards shy of the front door. The three women shared their names, which she immediately forgot when her peripheral vision caught Bruce pushing the bag back against Clark's chest as he shook his fist in the air. It could be rage, frustration, or fear. Clark would handle the situation with nothing short of charm and humor, but she had to know first-hand what was going on.

"Please, help yourselves to a bag of food. I need to attend to an issue outside. We will begin serving our daily lunch again tomorrow. Please pass the word along." She shook hands with the two women. Then Savannah leaned in for a hug with the teenage girl beside them, because she looked like she needed it. "It was nice to meet you," she said, before moving to the door with an extra speed to her steps.

The door blocked a scream much more guttural than expected. It exploded into the kitchen as soon as she tugged on the door handle, sending the teenage girl shivering and ducking between the two older women. He was jerking Clark's shirt. "Where is she? Everythin' was fine, but then she talked to—" He turned to Savannah. "You!"

Her heart skipped a beat as Bruce rushed forward in a frenzy. Clark kept his cool and snagged the back of Bruce's shirt before his ragged fingernails made contact with her face.

She jumped back, tripping on a hole in the sidewalk and falling to her butt. Her heart woke back up and started racing as she looked into Bruce's bloodshot eyes. "You! Where is she! Where's Claire?"

Clark held him back by his arms. Bruce didn't seem to notice that he wasn't going to be able to break free; he just kept struggling. Savannah jumped up, holding her left palm where it had torn open for the third time. "Bruce, I don't understand. Please slow down. Are you saying Claire is missing?"

"That's what I been tellin' you...and him!" He thrust his head back toward Clark. "You ain't listenin'! She talked to ya. I heard her tell you she been seein' things out here! Then she disappears. That ain't her."

Clark turned him around and tried to reason with him, but Bruce was still lost to his emotions. "I think that's enough, dude. She doesn't know where Claire is. You need to go sleep this off. She'll turn up. Or go to the cops. We can't change this situation for you. I'm sorry."

"Course that's what ya say! You don't care 'bout us! I'm the only one who's gonna be missin' her!" Bruce thrust a worn picture of himself and Claire in Clark's face.

It was most likely the only one he had. She moved behind Clark, still rubbing her hand, and asked, "Do you mind if I see it?"

He took a step back and squinted his eyes her way. "Fine."

He didn't hand it over. Clearly Claire was the only thing that kept him going each day besides the thought of the next hit, and he was unraveling. She wore that same blouse in the picture she'd worn the day they met, the white one with turquoise buttons. "She's beautiful, Bruce. But she didn't tell me anything. She wanted to, but she didn't. Would you like me to bring her picture to the police and have them file a missing persons report?"

He was still sizing her up, and the muscles in Clark's back were tightened like a brick wall. "You might be scared 'nough to listen, but that don't mean I trust ya, rich girl. I ain't handin' this picture over for you to go talk to those pigs." He yanked the picture away from them, took a food bag from the ground, and shot off at a run.

"I think I'm done here for today. Would you mind locking up while I go sit in the car?" Clark nodded, and Savannah switched keys with him and climbed in the driver's seat of her Lexus. Digging around in the glovebox, she retrieved a band-aide and some Neosporin for her hand. Working both into her palm, she rested against the headrest, absorbing the silence, as the last of Bruce's shoes disappeared behind a brick building wall.

The passenger door opened, and Clark plopped down with a sigh. "I need a drink the size of my head."

She reached over and squeezed his hand before starting the ignition. "I'm sure there will be a bar at the party, so let's head back to my apartment and get ready. Hey, Clark?"

"Yeah?"

"It feels like I can't catch a break. Danger is becoming routine. It's sexy that Joe can protect me, sure, that's what every woman likes. But I don't want the kind of life I need protection from. Joe seems to think there's never a moment to let your guard down. What do you believe? It won't always be like this, will it?"

Clark rubbed his hands over his face. "I'd sure like to ease your mind, beautiful, but you and Joe...I don't know. Y'all tend to attract bullets. Let's get through this party, okay?"

She didn't respond, just drove. She spent all her time trying to understand people, and she'd taken Clark for granted. Sure, they'd bonded and were true friends at this point. But as a friend, she should've spent more time saying "thank you." He had a life, and he'd put it on the backburner so she and Joe could get out of this horrific mess. He never questioned the sheer volume of bullets and danger that were pumped his way over the last week. She owed him way more than ice cream and delivery pizza. She tapped her fingers on the steering wheel. "Why did the picture go to jail?"

"Huh?"

"Because it was framed."

"Oh, that was terrible. But thanks for tryin'. That joke should probably stay between us." The smile didn't reach his eyes, but he patted her hand as she parked the car.

It was worth a try to cheer him up. Maybe the gated country club party with loads of single women and an open bar would do better to soothe his soul than a knock-knock joke.

She rolled her eyes as she crossed the parking lot to the front door. *Duh.* He wouldn't have a chance to talk to anyone, because he'd still have to watch her. But Joe would be back in a matter of hours, and Clark would be free of them for a little while at least.

"Clark," she whispered, passing through the front door Gene was already holding open and continuing into the elevator, "thank you for putting aside every part of your life to help us. We haven't made things easy on you, and for that I'm sorry. Is there anything I can do for you?"

They exited the elevator, and Savannah turned the key to her apartment in the lock. "I do like tropical vacations." Clark forced a pretty big grin.

"You forget who you're talking to. I'll see what I can do to make that happen."

He really smiled then, but not a smile of expectancy, a smile of friendship. As she pushed open the door, sun rays beat over the den, lighting the couch. She texted her mother about the party that morning, so it shouldn't have been much of a surprise to see a dress for herself and a tuxedo for Clark lying side by side, except that her mother didn't have a key. But honestly, no door—no gate of Hell, for that matter—was any match for Dahlia Carrington.

It wasn't even so much the invasion that had her rubbing her temples, but the clear advantage Holden still held over Joe in her eyes. The dress was more expensive than those plane tickets to D.C.—more expensive than six plane tickets to D.C. Hadn't the two of them made progress? Sometimes it was hard to tell, but she wasn't in the mood for the grand display of couture after everything with Bruce. She waved toward the tux as she snatched her emerald silk gown from the couch and began dragging it to the bedroom behind her in a huff.

"That's yours. Don't worry, it'll fit. My mother probably tracked down the size of your last tuxedo rental from your high school prom or sister's wedding or something. It's her superpower."

Clark stroked the tux and tossed it over his shoulder, leaving the suit his friend brought on the couch. "That's equally frightening and impressive, but I haven't ever worn a tux. I guess we'll see pretty quick how on point her skills are."

Savannah leaned into the doorway and removed the dress from the hanger. "Twenty minutes."

"Well, let's get movin', then. I've never seen a woman get dressed that fast for breakfast, let alone a fancy gala."

She laughed and closed the door, shooting a text to Holden: *We'll be ready and downstairs in twenty minutes.*

A response came almost immediately: *We?*

She was already on the bed, pouring out a few items from her makeup bag with one hand and rubbing on foundation with the other. Even though there was no reason to impress Holden, you couldn't go to a gala without makeup. And, of course, Joe would be here soon, and she needed to look good so he'd really lay on the apology thick.

Her fingers tingled with anticipation even though she was undeniably irate. Why, even at her maddest, did she still want him all over her? When everything was laid out on her comforter, she crossed her legs and responded to Holden's message.

Did I forget to tell you I was bringing Clark? I'm so sorry. I feel most comfortable with him as my extra security at the party. Is that alright?

The little gray dots moved along the screen of her cell, indicating he was responding, for a good minute and a half. But when the message came through, it just said, *"That's fine."*

Maybe he was agitated about her forgetfulness, or maybe he was driving through L.A. traffic. No time to dwell on that or the picture Bruce flashed of Claire. There were only fifteen minutes left, and they still had to walk downstairs. She rolled over the bed and grabbed a pair of heels she'd tossed on the floor two weeks ago; they would work with the dress. The reach made her sleeve come up a bit, revealing the bruises still on her wrists—the ones she'd been purposefully covering so the reminder of the warehouse would fade. Her breath caught momentarily, but Joe would be back soon. He'd keep all her fears at bay if she could just stay strong for another few hours.

Joe's affection might be rough, but can I accept it in the way he shows it? Or will I be angry more often than I'm happy? Happiness is like oxygen to me.

So, she breathed in through her nose and out through her mouth, just like they'd practiced, as she brushed concealer over each wrist, covering any trace of a blemish on her porcelain skin.

There were only about ten minutes left, and despite the desire to lie on the bed and stare at the popcorn ceiling, shutting out the world (not to mention her neighbor that played classical music so loudly it was audible through the thickly insulated walls), she gathered her wits and ran to the bathroom.

Her reflection shot back in the mirror, eyes made bigger and brighter by a layer of eyeshadow and waves of blonde draping over her shoulders. Her hair always looked good. She couldn't mess it up if she tried. It was the one infallible part of her appearance.

The mirror still reflected her image, and she found her eyes staying up as she shimmied out of her clothes, cringing for a second when the band-aide on her palm rubbed over her jeans. Joe was awakening in her not only a desire for passion but a comfort in her own skin that grew stronger every time she stood in this spot.

She ran her finger over each scar and around her waist. Joe was attracted to every part of her, but she only seemed to wake under his touch, his warmth. She saw her beauty through his eyes; that was annoying but true. There was no denying their connection, but Lord have mercy. They had issues.

Leave it there, she'd thought at that moment, but she couldn't leave her thoughts in a good spot, just like she couldn't leave her hotel room this morning before requisitioning a vacuum cleaner and sewing kit for the broken stitching on the couch pillow. Housekeeping was convinced she'd gone mad, but no, that was just her. She dropped onto a pink velvet stool and wrapped her fingers together. She should've slipped the dress over her head and left. Why did she have to overthink and over-talk every aspect of her life? Her stomach felt heavy, streams of nausea running through it slowly.

Staying with Joe despite their clear differences—and his marriage— also left her having to acknowledge the physical future they had coming: sex. Thinking the word affected her body, not only with the underlying nerves of the nausea, but this anticipation that had her tingly in places she would never be able to say out loud. Based on the fire she felt every time they touched as much as fingers, it was fair to assume the sex would be amazing and totally worth waiting for, but that wasn't where the nausea came from.

For her, when they touched that way for the first time, the heat, the pleasure they'd both feel... Call her old fashioned, but she didn't want to picture the other women that had been there before her, like Nadine. Did he love her? Or them? How many were there, for that matter? Did he love her more? Did he say the same things, move the same way? Was he as turned on? Was she going to be enough for him? That thought wasn't necessarily related to sex, but he'd been all over the world, had a different life. Was she enough in a lifelong partner kind of way?

The nausea kicked into high gear, and she dropped from the stool onto the cold tile floor and lay on her back. Too bad the cream-colored ceiling couldn't be blasted away with some Harry Potter type magic and turned into the night sky. The light pulsated around the corners of her vision, tempting a headache to form. Couldn't she ever make it out of the bathroom these days without ending up here?

Suddenly, the floor vibrated beneath her. Clark was on his way to her room. It was time to leave. Savannah leapt into the air, sending the nausea lurching up to her teeth before smashing back in her stomach. Yanking the dress from the counter, she let it drop over her head and drape across her hips.

The front was modest, with no slit, and it came up to her collarbone. At her shoulders, the fabric thickened and fell in a pool around the small of her back. She bit her lip as she imagined the thin fabric under Joe's grip, him snatching it in handfuls and pulling her against him. A shiver raced up her spine.

Seriously? Joe was across the country, and they hadn't made up. For that matter, she hadn't made up her mind completely. It'd been all over the place, like some funhouse mirror maze. The end wasn't clear. Maybe it was good she hadn't met him until now. It'd always been her belief that she was a beacon of self-control and reasonable thinking. But, Lord, Joe was shaking her to the core.

Focus on the party. On the three-thousand -dollar dress you're wearing. And, for the love of God, try not to spill anything on it.

Her mom could definitely pick a dress, but it didn't feel right for a date with Holden. Either way, she was wearing it, so she strapped on her shoes and headed to the door, randomly looking sideways by her dresser and noticing something she hadn't seen before: a large package with a card. She opened it, immediately recognizing the stationary her mother special ordered from France.

Darling,

Enjoy the dress. I wanted to make it special, as I assume these wooded areas you'll be frequenting with Joe don't have much to speak of as far as dressy affairs are concerned. Not my cup of tea, but as long as you're happy, I am. I watched his Medal of Honor ceremony, and he seems like a good man. Promise me you'll come by the house for a decent meal once you return. Enclosed in the package are all the things I've been assured you'll need for your venture. Having never been to the woods myself, I reached out to an expert in the field. I love you. See you soon.

Mom

There was an overwhelming desire to rip into that carefully packed parcel and see what her mother found to be appropriate for her trip. Did Gucci even make hiking boots? But her phone buzzed incessantly, and Clark rapped on the door, in a rhythm that felt like "Row, Row, Row Your Boat." But it probably wasn't. This rectangular prism at her feet was as tempting as the apple in the Garden of Eden, but as hilarious as the reveal would be, maybe she should wait for Joe. They needed something to smile about, maybe even laugh at. Joe *was* a good man; they just needed more time to understand each other.

She opened the door, almost walking face first into Clark.

"We have to go. You look beautiful though. Joe's gonna be so ticked he missed this dress."

She smacked him lovingly with her clutch and looked him over as he did a little twirl.

"Seems your mom's skills are as good as you say." He smiled, and she admired the stunning black tux, only ill-fitting around where a gun was holstered at his waist.

They dashed out the door, careful to lock it on their way. Her phone vibrated madly, but not with texts from Joe. Holden was wondering what the hold-up was. He'd called five times and sent a text.

I was already in the car when you called. The back seat and trunk of the Maserati is full of last-minute auction items for the party. Clark will have to follow us there in your car.

She held the screen over so Clark could see it as they rode to the first floor, their dressy images reflected in the black glass walls. "I guess that'll be fine, unless there's a way to fit it and all of us in your car."

The elevator landed, and they stepped out into the lobby, the air conditioner pumping at its highest setting so wealthy residents wouldn't be momentarily inconvenienced with anything as burdensome as the air being seventy-two degrees instead of sixty-eight. Gene greeted the pair with a nod as they turned the corner, his black suit as crisp as if someone were invisibly ironing it out with every step he took. "Good afternoon, Ms. Carrington." He nodded toward the door. "Mr. Forsyth is waiting for you outside."

Holden could be seen leaning against his sports car through the front doors, black-tux-clad and blond hair gelled up on the side, fidgeting with a cuff link. The chandeliers burned brightly as she and Clark clicked along, but the sun beat through the windows so fiercely it washed out the delicate circles of light they usually cast over the floor.

As Clark took the handle, Holden looked up for the first time, pacing forward with a smile. "Hi. Savannah, you look beautiful. Clark, I'm so sorry. I didn't know you would be coming, so I'm all out of room in the Mas. I asked the valet to bring around Savannah's car for you though. Just so we're clear, I have hired a security detail, so Savannah will be incredibly safe."

Clark stifled a laugh and crossed his arms, looking into the backseat and the open trunk. Apparently, Holden was prepared for his packing skills to be double and triple checked. She squeezed her gold clutch as they eyed each other, a surprising amount of tension building. "That's fine, man. I'll follow behind you. But I'm not leaving Savannah's safety up to some dudes I've never met."

Clark really did need that drink.

The car spun around the side of the building and pulled up beside them. "That's understandable, after all Savannah's been through. So, in an effort of complete transparency, you should know we'll be making a quick stop at my family's warehouse first to pick up six gowns for the silent auction. It's my family's yearly contribution to this gala, which donates all funds received into services meant to rehabilitate addicts and fund programs to prevent drug use in the public-school system. It's a great cause. Anyway, after, we'll drive over to the club."

"Yeah, that's great." Clark took her hand and squeezed. "I'll be right behind you. See you at the party."

Savannah appreciated Clark's flexibility. Joe would've requested a real-time aerial view of the warehouse, and although she was being judgmental and was still upset with the constant level of scrutiny, there was no denying Joe's expertise was kind of hot. She nodded, and Holden held open the door for her, picking up the back of her dress as she sat down and pooling it in around her feet with care. Her fingers traced the beadwork of her clutch as she checked the clock on the dash. It was 2:00 p.m. She was suddenly very uncomfortable and was kind of wishing she had that aerial view after all.

He hadn't mentioned until now that they had to stop by the warehouse. It wouldn't normally be a big deal, but chances were, they'd drive right down the street where Joe killed those two men. Her heart pumped as she pictured the darkness, the screaming, the blood spattering on her blue dress before she ran.

Holden passed in front of the car and slid into the leather seat, sighing. "My apologies. I didn't mean to get Clark all worked up. I honestly don't mind if he comes, and I appreciate you accepting my invitation. You look a little flushed though. Is everything okay? I can turn the A.C. on."

He reached over and spun the dial before she responded then carefully wove through the downtown skyscrapers, the San Gabriel Mountains peeking out in the distance between the gaps in the buildings. Her arms broke out in goosebumps as they neared the Italian restaurant they'd eaten at, palm trees swaying on the foggy breeze, and she crossed them to keep in a bit of warmth. Even with the air conditioning, sweat built on Holden's temples. Was he nervous about driving through here too? She hadn't asked how he was doing now.

"I'm cool enough. Thank you."

He turned the dial back a few notches but didn't look her way as he pulled to a stop at a red light three blocks from the spot Joe shot those two men. Her shoes had crashed against that sidewalk to her right only a few days ago. They'd climbed into his car, this car, in a frenzy, Joe the main subject of conversation.

It flooded back in perfect clarity, drawing her into the past: the stained leather, Holden's knees and hands covered in blood, her throbbing head. She'd considered turning Joe in. Really considered it, per Holden's suggestion. *"I don't believe Joe will stop until you accept whatever it is he's trying to give you from a friend,"* he'd said.

Her stomach lurched. Her fingers shot to her temples as she thought back to five minutes before that moment, the darkness of the alley all around the five of them as the man pleaded under Joe's boot. The news had only referred to Joe as Yosef, and she hadn't called him that in front of Holden, had she? *Had she?* Her fingers pressed on the switch to her right and cracked the window. A breeze flooded over her cheeks as she rested her face on the glass. Of course, she had. That was ridiculous. She must've said something at dinner. She'd been so full and happy she'd yapped for a couple hours.

"Savannah?" She jerked her head to the side as he turned the radio on quietly to jazz music. "Are you sure you're okay?"

She shook away the negativity. Joe had really messed with her usual upbeatness. Was that a word? It was now. She swayed to Ella Fitzgerald's voice and responded, "Yes. I am. Thank you. And to respond to what you said earlier, thank you for inviting me to the party. I love that it's for a good cause, but I need to talk to you. I, um… Well, I want to be clear that Joe is the only man I have any interest in being with."

"Yeah, I gathered as much when he texted me this morning, asking for all the details of the party and assuring me that if I didn't keep you safe, he'd find me and… Well, there was a death threat."

Her stomach swirled. She'd spent the last twelve hours talking herself into being with him, and he did that? A heat wave soared through her body, clotting in her fingertips as it tried to force its way out. Joe hadn't uttered a single word to her but instead spent his time tracking down Holden's phone number—and probably his credit card statements too. Maybe she'd been right all along to keep her chastity belt latched uncomfortably tight. She never got hurt that way, and her life mantra was simple: Focus on everyone else's happiness, and you'll never have time to be upset. But as soon as she started looking for that rusty old key, things blew up in her face.

The breeze from the window and the air conditioning wasn't doing enough to cool her burning cheeks. She got herself into this situation by being selfish. She bit the inside of her cheek and tried not to make eye contact with Holden, because she'd cry; it was her m.o. Earlier, she'd decided not to leave on the trip with Joe today, and that was still a for-sure thing.

At least for right now, the idea of the two of them being together just wasn't going to happen. The feelings wouldn't disappear, and the guilt would eat at her soul every day over her promise not to leave, which would award her with the World's Most Selfish Human Award. She needed to get out of L.A. and recharge. Doing it without a glimpse into Joe's sad eyes would be completely necessary. Maybe Clark would be up for that tropical vacation he'd mentioned a little early? They'd have a window after the party and before Joe got to town. She looked in the side mirror as Clark followed along, one car length behind them, tapping on the steering wheel and singing.

She had her phone in hand, texting Clark. Things weren't supposed to be this way. *Joe apparently texted Holden, but I haven't heard anything from him. I need some space. I promise I will talk to him at some point, but I can't today. Would you go with me to a tropical destination for a few days? You can pick!*

Clark's response was instantaneous: *Doesn't sound like Joe. I'm texting him now. Give him a chance to set things straight.*

That was more than she should've expected as a response. His first allegiance was always going to be with Joe.

"Anything I can do?" It was Holden: sweet, infallibly polite Holden. "I didn't mean to upset you. You seem to appreciate honesty, and it was eating me up. Sorry I couldn't keep it to myself. You're free to read the message if you need to borrow my phone." He held it out in his palm but kept his eyes on the road.

"No. I don't need to see your phone. Thank you though. I'm just stunned. Please don't fear Joe. I can assure you he will keep his distance. But I should add that, no matter what happens between myself and Joe, you and I won't be together. I am sorry, and I do appreciate everything you did for my family over the last week. I wish I had a better way to say that, because you are incredible."

Holden still didn't look at her. In fact, he hadn't looked in her eyes since before they got in the car. He was still fidgeting with that cuff link and filling the car with a nervous vibe. "It's fine. I get it. I had to try because you're special. But I understand and accept your wishes. Today will be the last time you see me. That I can promise."

His eyes stayed glued to the road, and the air around them was suddenly whisked out the crack in the window. Holden needed her to back off, but the cuff link was giving her tunnel vision. She reached over to adjust it, and as her fingers grazed his wrist he leapt away, looking her dead in the eyes with pupils contracted to tiny dots. His head jerked straight to the road again, where he slammed the brakes for an unexpected red light, tires squealing and sifting a burnt rubber smell through that window crack. Multiple crashes sounded as everything from the back slammed into her seat and poured all over the floor.

His grip immediately released from the steering wheel, and he ran his hands over his face. She unsnapped her seatbelt and turned to put everything back in place. "Savannah, I'm sorry. Don't ruin your dress. Just leave it, it'll be fine. The light is green now, and the warehouse is up ahead."

"It's okay. Just let me help. This place is still hard for me to be around, too. We both watched those men die. I get it."

"I wish you did."

She patted his hand as they crept forward, but he cringed under her touch, so she retracted it quickly and leaned over the console. There was a small, framed painting, a gift card, and a rare book scattered on the black carpet, among other things. He'd already started ahead but slowed as they reached what she assumed was the warehouse, but she wasn't paying any attention. She reached low and put them in their bags as something else caught her eye under his seat. A button maybe? She hung over the console a little further and wrapped her pink fingernails around it as the car pulled up to a gate leading to an interior parking lot.

Holden retrieved a key card from his wallet and scanned it. "It should stay up long enough to let Clark in behind us so he can park too." The gate went up, and he laid it on his leg and pulled forward.

Savannah dropped back into the leather seat and opened her palm to a turquoise button—the same one that had been on Claire's shirt. Her arms and legs broke out into an immediate and all-over shake. She reached over for her phone to warn Clark, but her unsteady hand knocked her clutch to the floor as the key card caught her eye for the first time, with its sleek silver exterior…and green triangle.

CHAPTER TWENTY-EIGHT
Joe

The interviews were over. He'd wrapped them up in record time, answering every question with just the right amount of detail, never more. Getting back to Savannah was the number one priority. He hadn't slept, though three hours was an average night, so he could still function better than most. The dark circles under his eyes were always there. Closing his eyes meant he wasn't in control of what he felt or saw. His subconscious could take over and make the rules, and it had a dark sense of humor.

His mom was convinced Savannah would forgive him in moments, but she was an eternal optimist. Clark seemed to think it would take considerably more work to get back in her good graces and was annoyed he still hadn't texted Savannah. It was difficult to say the right thing, and if he couldn't see her in person, he'd have no way to know how she was reacting to his words. He could upset her more.

He'd written out three drafts of what he could memorize and recite to Savannah, before tossing them in the garbage. She wouldn't accept any of that. She wanted that gooey, raw emotion he kept locked in a safe in the back-left corner of his mind behind a row of Claymore mines. She was worth getting mentally blown up for, but he wasn't risking it if she was going to say no.

His last stop of the day had been to President Johnson's office, the Oval Office. It was still hard to believe he was welcome there, even if he did leave wishing he'd refused his mother's advice and handled things like a man. As if the President of the United States didn't have an entire country to keep afloat, he'd asked for the name of a divorce attorney that would be willing to move things along rapidly. It felt childish and unreasonable. But of course, the President had obliged, practically laughing at his uncomfortable stance as he reached up to slap him on the shoulder. "Joe, you're family now. Consider it done."

They'd been leaning against the resolute desk and rose, sharing a firm handshake before he went on his way. "Oh," Joe had added, stopping in the thick doorway and turning around, "tell Nathaniel if he ever needs to chat, he can shoot me a text."

President Johnson smiled, cheeks touching the rims of his black glasses and deep creases covering his forehead. "That's why I like you, Joe."

First Lieutenant Ted was back, waiting at attention outside the Oval Office. His eyes were fixed to a white vase with blue flowers on a pedestal but turned rapidly when he exited. They saluted each other and smiled. The secretary sat behind him, munching on yet another salad, bringing the total to five over the last few days. She wanted everyone to acknowledge her good choices, but it wasn't hard to notice her attempted stealth as she reached into her desk drawer for chocolate between bites.

Ted escorted him through the busy halls, and the not-so-busy halls, until they were nearing their exit. Waving him to a bathroom on the left he said, "The President said you might be more comfortable riding home in your own clothes. Said something about you looking stiff."

Joe laughed and tugged the red tie free from his neck before even getting through the door. He hated suits. They restricted your movements. His combat boots were laid under a wooden chair, with a tee shirt and jeans folded on top. He would've been just as content with fatigues like Ted had on, but this was a welcome change. President Johnson told him to keep the suit earlier in the day, so he changed and folded it over his arm before switching Allen's medal and his playing card over to the jeans and walking out again.

Ted laughed at his obvious posture change. "Seems the President was right."

The exit was a few feet ahead, and they passed easily through security. His feet adjusted to the change from the plush White House carpet to the rough pavement as Ted led him to a black SUV. Ted opened his car door and let him into the back beside his waiting parents. Ted, with a sidearm and Airborne whitewalls, shut the door behind Joe and climbed into the driver's seat, starting up the vehicle.

It was time to get on the road. Joe did a scan of the area as they passed through the White House gate. Everything looked secure, but with a thousand people wandering near the White House, it was hard to be absolute. He continued his observations as he buckled up, brushing his hand over his hip where a weapon should be. This was the longest he'd been without one since he was around six years old. His fingers twitched and he tapped his foot. His dad looked comfortable without anything, so why was he always so wound up?

With the interviews resolving quickly, President Johnson's staff arranged an earlier flight for him. It departed at 1300 hours, an hour and a half from now. With the time difference, he'd be able to pick up Savannah early from the party with Holden. It would start around 1400 L.A. time, which was right after he landed. Showing up early would be a gamble, but seeing her sooner rather than later was vital.

The SUV got on its way, his dad leaning out from the other side of his mom. "Did all the interviews go okay, son?"

"Yes, sir. I'm still not comfortable sharing my story with the world, but it's out there now either way. For some reason, everyone else is seeing success where I see failure, and part of that is me...comparing myself to you and grandpa. But I answered their questions."

His mother gasped and nudged his father to expedite a response that was already forming. "It's in our nature as humans, and men, to compare ourselves in different ways. Just don't lose sight of what's important. If you want to compare yourself to your grandpa and me, then do it like this: We three were willing to sacrifice our lives to protect our God and country."

His dad leaned back again. Joe's fingers ceased their twitching, and the car fell quiet except for the vibration of the road under the tires. It was good to be leaving D.C. and not only because Savannah was in L.A. This wasn't his scene. L.A. wasn't either. Too many people drowning in technology and ignorant to the real world that existed beyond the filters of social media.

Planes roared over the roof of the airport and into the sky. They were a few miles away. A semi had been trying to force its way into their lane for the last few minutes, starting a few cars back, but Ted slowed to let it in. Joe would've hit the gas and made it file in behind them, but Ted was nicer. It had four wide, metal bars sticking out the back, two on the top, two on the bottom. They were each loaded down with metal folding chairs, clanging around. The planes were still visible, but the roof of the airport disappeared.

Ted straightened and continued on. "Five more miles."

They nodded, and his mom began chatting about a fundraiser their church was starting, when his peripheral vision caught something unexpected. He jerked around and unbuckled, forcing his way to the front seat where he yanked the steering wheel from Ted's grasp and made a hard right as three folding chairs flew off the back of the top left bar and smashed against the side of the Tahoe, shattering the window where Joe had been sitting two seconds before. Glass rained over his parents, and his mom held his dad tightly. They were all breathing hard. Ted's usual meekness had dissolved into a string of whispered expletives. His mom was screaming. His heart pounded in his ears as wind pounded through the window at sixty miles per hour with a thunderous groan. If he hadn't acted, those chairs would've shot straight through the front window and killed them all on impact. But there wasn't time to rest, because the rest of the row was emptying, and the clamp that had once secured them dangled underneath the bar. Ted had control again, swerving cleanly and cussing as each chair screeched through the air.

While the men were looking at the chairs, his mom watched what was happening to the cars around them. "Look out!"

But it was too late. Joe was ripped from his perch on the console and thrown into darkness.

"Joe! Joe!"

His eyelids rose and fell. *Why is everything black? Are my eyes closed? I'm supposed to be on a plane, but I smell grass.*

His eyelids rose again and pulled shut quickly as the sun burned them. Someone stood over him, calling his name and removing the sun from its blinding position. He opened his eyes again and looked around, without moving. He was in the grass, sprawled out, with two medics attending to him. He hadn't noticed their touch before. Hadn't noticed the throbbing in his shoulder and head. Cars rumbled across the interstate overhead. Why was he by the street?

He lunged, but someone restrained his arms and legs. It was his dad. His mom stood nearby. With a dizzy head, he fell back into the grass and stopped fighting. Nothing made sense. What was going on? Why wouldn't the words form? He grabbed his head with his left hand, but a bandage was plastered across it.

Had he been in a wreck? Yes. He'd been on his way to the airport when the folding chairs whipped around like giant hail over the interstate. That's what it was. But he had to get out of this fog and understand his injuries. His lips parted as he moved his tongue around. It was dry, but his mom hunched over him with a bottle of water and held it out. He took a drink, the fuzziness still strong enough to be annoying.

"How long have I been out?" His palms pushed against the grass as the medics guided him into a seated position.

"Not long, sir," the young guy to his right stated calmly. He looked to be in his mid-twenties, pale blonde hair and tan skin. He was cleaning, repacking, and re-stitching his gunshot wound from the warehouse while the other medic attended to his head. Cars inched slowly down the highway, a few feet away. Despite the wreck, drivers still honked and forced their way into each gap of space, as the highway had been cut to one lane. His gaze widened. Ted was on the tailgate of a nearby ambulance. There were three others, four police cars, and a fire truck. Their SUV was in the process of being flipped back to all fours for towing. Another tow truck was already hauling a Jeep, and some police were managing the mess of a crushed sedan and speaking with the driver of the semi, who was doubled over in tears tugging on the straps of his overalls. It sparked a memory. That sedan had been hit with a chair or two before overcompensating and slamming into them. They'd flipped on their side while he was still out of his seat belt, and he'd slammed his head into the window.

"I remember everything now. It just took me a minute. Did everyone survive?"

"Yes. There are a few very serious injuries, since multiple cars were involved, but it seems everyone will make it out of this. However, we need to discuss your injuries. Appears there is no internal bleeding, but I'd like to be certain. You do have a concussion, which I assume you understand is still serious and shouldn't be ignored. You're a little bruised up all over. This gunshot wound on your shoulder opened up, and we've gotten it back to looking pretty decent. I've already talked to your parents, and to"—he cleared his throat as if surprised he'd gotten the chance to use the word—"the President. I know it's not necessary to report this wound, but I would feel better if you accompanied us to the hospital to do a more thorough evaluation. I understand you have other plans, but we could still get you on a flight sometime tonight."

His mom leaned to his ear, stroking his arm as she whispered, "Please, honey. We will let Savannah and Clark know what's going on. You won't be any good to them dead. I see the wheels spinning. You want to clear the air with Savannah and go to a doctor there. But if you have an unknown injury, flying isn't wise."

"Okay. But I don't want to worry them until I have answers and a new flight plan."

So, after forty minutes of driving to the hospital, three hours of uncomfortable tests, and nearly an hour of waiting to be discharged, Joe finally had his cell and was fetching a clean set of clothes from his bag— anything would feel better than a hospital gown. But he needed a minute before attempting his shirt and possibly messing up his stitches.

A bandage covered the ace of spades he'd tattooed on his arm three years ago. Something in the wreck sliced him pretty good, ripping the card in half. But there wasn't any internal bleeding. He powered up the phone and waited for a minute. Three texts from Clark came in, the last just a few minutes before.

On our way to the party. Following behind Savannah and Holden. Stopping by his warehouse first. She's all worked up because Holden told her you texted him.

Why haven't you said anything?

Shouldn't you have landed by now?

He rubbed the back of his neck and responded before starting to pull his gown off. Two nurses walked by his room, smiling and whispering, one touching her neck to indicate she was impressed by the glimpse of dog tags around his neck. He waved with a laugh and twisted the blinds closed as the women lingered near the nurses' station, flirting shamelessly.

If things didn't work out with Savannah, they'd always be here, easy to find—emphasis on the easy. He'd outgrown all that though. But putting the work into something meant opening up and risking heartache. It didn't take a genius to understand that's why things hadn't worked out with Nadine. She never heard him say I love you. It never felt right, which made him sound like a jerk.

Opening up to Savannah felt more natural. He legitimately wanted to, but Holden was cutting him off at the knees whenever he got the chance.

He'd never sent him a text, wouldn't have had time to, anyway. So, what game was he trying to play?

He responded and tossed the phone on the bed, delicately pulling his shirt on, when the EMT from earlier came in. "Hey, man. Saw your parents in the hall. Seems there's a flight in an hour with your name on it. But I found something in the SUV at the wreck site and wanted to bring it to you." He reached into his pocket and pulled out Allen's medal. "It got caught on something and this stitching here is loose, but I—"

Joe's eyes focused in, and he yanked away, waving the guy out and sitting in the chair by his hospital bed. He hadn't realized it was missing until now, but looking at it made him think of Allen and the mysterious video they still hadn't found. It was driving him nuts. He'd never handled loose ends well, and considering it dozens of times over the last few days hadn't brought him any closer to a resolution.

That EMT was right. Fingers running over the loose thread, he held it under the bedside lamp, the medal flickering as the white light reflected off its surface. A janitor wheeled by outside the room, barely visible between the cracked blinds, broom tapping against a plastic cart as the wheels spun just off balance. Giving Allen's medal to Savannah was still something he could do once he got back to L.A., but it'd be nice to fix the stitching first.

His mom carried a sewing kit in her oversized leather purse as long as he could remember. It—and she—had apparently saved the day at a church wedding when he was a toddler. No doubt she could fix it and would be thrilled to help.

"Mom," he yelled, swinging the door open and leaning out in her direction, "I need your sewing skills before I get discharged."

Her face lit up, even though she was already smiling, something about her expression changed. Letting go of his dad's hand, she rushed down the hall and into the room. "How can I help?" She was already holding the little clear box with the kit.

He placed the medal in her hand, and she took the seat he'd risen from just moments before, as it was nearest to the light. "Can you fix it?"

"Of course, honey, but are you wantin' it stitched back with cream thread like it is right here, or white like the rest of it?"

Joe's ears perked. Cream? Every Purple Heart was stitched with white thread. Always white. Allen's had been that way too every time he'd seen it. His knee cracked as he bent down to the floor for a closer look. His mom was right. Running his hand over the stubble on his chin, he thought, *Why would Allen stitch the medal with a different color thread?* He took the medal from his mom and breathed deeply before ripping the seam, tearing the fabric apart as a tiny flash-drive clattered to the floor. It had to be Allen's video. He must've left it in the medal, hoping Savannah would find it but no one else would.

Mom still sitting under the lamp, Joe leapt up, leaning out the door once more, but this time, his voice was higher and faster than normal. His dad was on his cell, sitting in a chair across the hall, presumably playing Solitaire.

"Dad, do you have that laptop you normally travel with?"

"Sure, I've got it in here somewhere." He dropped the cell into the outside compartment of his shoulder bag and unzipped the middle, pilfering through magazines and books before retrieving his computer. Stepping past Joe and into the room, he set it on the white-sheeted hospital bed and looked back at them. "What's going on?" His dad pointed at the flash-drive. "And what is that, son?"

"I think it's the video Allen took. He had it stitched up in the fabric of his Purple Heart. He went to a lot of trouble to hide it."

"Well, let's give it a look." Stanley MacArthur rubbed his back and leaned down, that same intense look transforming his eyes that always came over Joe's. Even though they weren't biologically related, certain traits were passed on from father to son. Joe pushed it in. Only one file popped onto the screen. He held his breath and double-clicked.

A video opened to a grainy view of a warehouse and Allen's quiet footsteps as he inched in closer to a first-floor window. He ducked into the shadows of the building every few steps because it was daytime, so the view wasn't steady. The phone that he must've taken it with pressed against the cracked-open windowpane, aiming first down and then up, before focusing on the center of a large room full of dresses and mannequins. No one was there.

In the bottom left corner of the image, a slim wallet rested on the windowsill, with a potted plant. A glass desk with metal legs sat on a red-woven rug with a modern-looking desk chair. A planner lay open on the desk, but without more advanced technology, it'd be impossible to read. And under the desk, sprawled across the rug, was a dead Middle Eastern man.

"What's that in the wallet?" his dad asked, leaning in, ignoring the dead body for a more important clue. Joe shifted his focus from the door adjacent to the desk and looked again. It was a key card, maybe for a business. Stamped in the corner was the same green triangle he'd seen on the business card of the man in the alley. That was something, and he could search L.A. for a business that used that as a logo, but it would take forever. He'd do it if he had to, but the video had another two minutes on it, so maybe there was an answer.

Thirty more seconds passed uneventfully before the doorknob turned and a blond-haired man treaded in carefully. Eyeing the dead body, he gasped and moved to the other side of the desk, hands wrapped around the back of his neck. Sweat pooled there, and through the middle-back of his tee shirt where it was now navy instead of royal blue.

No matter how Joe craned his neck, the guy's face wasn't visible (he wasn't stupid; the video was taken a certain way, but the impulse was there). Digging in the pocket of his blue jeans, the guy pulled out a cell, calling someone and tapping it on his hand when they didn't answer.

If he could just see that guy's face... Ugh. There were fifty seconds left.

His fingers dialed up Clark as he continued watching, but no answer. He called Savannah. No answer. His head pounded. Only forty-five seconds left as he texted them both without taking his eyes off the screen.

And the guy turned. Immaculately styled hair, sparkling white teeth, and a face more perfect than any guy should have.

It was Holden.

Fists clenched, Joe's nails dug into his palms, blood pricking against the surface of his skin. He was going to kill Holden. And then his heart skipped a beat. Clark and Savannah were with him ten minutes ago at his warehouse, presumably the same location as this video.

And with thirty seconds left, and the belief things couldn't get worse, his heart stopped altogether. The door opened again to a face that sucked him out of the hospital room, out of Washington D.C., and transported him back to the snowy peaks of the Afghani mountains. That was the man who ordered his whole team's death. That was the man whose drugs he'd burned and whose brother he'd killed. The man with a personal score to settle, who just happened to land in L.A. He wasn't dead after all. Even Hell must've turned him away. Azfaar Mudad was alive, and this time, Joe would have to cut his head off to make sure he wasn't coming back.

"Get the President on the phone *now!*" he screeched, pulling the screen closer to his face to hear the words passing between the two men. His dad left the room, dialing.

Holden spoke first, voice high, sweat rolling down his face alongside tears as he held his hands defensively in front of himself. "How did you get into America? Why are you here in person? Why did you kill your own man?"

Mudad smiled, straightening his long, white tunic and running a hand through his wooly beard. "I cut out the middleman. No reason to continue paying him for a job I can do myself now."

Holden shrunk, momentarily losing that image of a Ken Doll. "I need out. It's too stressful, the risk of being caught. The death. There's a dead man in my office! My family has an image to uphold! I only needed to make a little money, okay? Just a little bit to get us back in the black after my dad made some bad financial decisions. Please. It was only temporary to help my family. You're a business man. Please understand. I'm sorry. I can give back the cut you gave me and figure out another way. Whatever you want. I'll write you a check right now."

He took an ink pen from the desk with a shaky hand, but Mudad tripped him and smashed his face against the glass desktop, jerking the pen away and holding it against his carotid artery. "Your family problems mean nothing to me. You're done when I say you're done. A bit of pressure, and I can end your story now." He pushed until it drew blood and rose, strolling through the room, mannequins clattering to the ground as he brushed them with his finger. "I'm not done in Los Angeles. You've proven to be more creative than I could've imagined, trafficking my drugs in the beadwork and lining of these fancy dresses and testing new product on the scum that fill these filthy streets. But there is one priority in my life above financial stability for my people, and that is my brother. He sacrificed everything, time after time, for me as we grew up and was my greatest supporter. He was killed by an American soldier; one I believe to be hiding out somewhere on the West Coast, and I'm not leaving until I kill him. That's where you come in."

CHAPTER TWENTY-NINE
Savannah

"Could you turn a light on in here?" Savannah shuddered as Holden pulled into another warehouse three blocks from the first and cut the engine. He'd tossed her cell at his family's warehouse and driven her here at gunpoint.

He laughed, but it was hollow. "Is that really your most pressing concern right now? I've got a gun aimed at you!" Judging by his awkward grip, he hadn't ever held one, but he could still kill her with it. A gun was a gun, after all. But he was petrified, not angry. His other hand tapped the steering wheel rapidly. He was waiting for someone in the darkness of the abandoned warehouse. "Fine." He flipped on the headlights, cutting two bright lines through the space, only revealing a graffitied wall and hopeless emptiness.

She bit her lip and whispered, "Thanks for literally doing the bare minimum. Obviously, whatever we're here for is more pressing than my fear of the dark, and the fact that I haven't seen Clark since we pulled into the parking garage at your warehouse. Then there's my need to pee and the guilt in my stomach over not listening to Joe when he said you didn't have good intentions. I've been mad at him for like eighteen hours over you and he was right the whole time. Oh, and let's add this button I found in your car to the list." Savannah opened her palm and held it over the console. "I know it came from Claire's shirt. Did you kill her?"

Holden's face washed out. "No! Not me, anyway. Do you really think I'm a killer?"

She slapped her shaky hands on the console and screamed deeply, "You've got a gun in my face, so maybe now isn't the time to ask! Until ten minutes ago, I thought you were a nice guy who ran a fashion house. You're not exactly shining the best light on yourself!"

His head jerked around, still looking for the person she would presumably have much more to fear from than him. His pupils dilated to nothing as he pulled the gun back a quarter of an inch, far enough that her shallow breaths didn't fog up the end of the gun's barrel. "I *am* a nice guy. Or I was, anyway. It all started with my dad—not that you care! He doesn't know anything about running a business, and we were bleeding money left and right. Then he got cancer, and with those bills, we were getting by on fumes. I just wanted to help, just wanted to do something to get us back on our feet before I took over. So, I trafficked some drugs. It didn't seem like a big deal until I tried to get out. I'm sorry. I know it doesn't help, but he would've sent someone else if I didn't bring you here, *and* he would've killed me! I don't want to die! But big picture, he only wants Joe, and I think we can work with that. I begged him to show you mercy and keep you alive after he kills Joe. I'm trying!"

Savannah's chest grew with anger until she exploded across the console like a cat, screaming, batting the gun out of his hand and clawing at his neck and eyes. She'd never been mad enough to lose control, but it was gone, and her vision reddened. "You coward! Don't try to spin your own selfishness into something noble! You're willing to let other people die so you can live! And are you so daft that you haven't considered what these people will do to me even if I'm lucky enough to get out of this alive, after I've seen them murder Joe? You're not helping anyone, Holden! The only thing you've probably successfully accomplished is being at the top of your boss's hit list when he's done with us!" She fought across him as he cowered pathetically, unlocking his door and slithering over him as his face bled from the scratches.

He grabbed onto her the second her hands and knees connected with the concrete. Her clutch fell beside her and clattered all over the ground. It was time to run, but her back half was uprooted, knocking her face forward against the floor. Her teeth rattled. Holden had her by the ankles dragging her back into the car. Her fingers reached for anything to gain traction. All she found was a rusty nail. She wrapped her fingers around it, heart pounding. Blood trickled between her front teeth. She kicked, but the moment for escape was over.

Six sets of feet marched their way, crossing in front of the headlights. Her stomach emptied, and she felt all her organs, muscles, and bones evaporating with the loss of power. The man at the front was Middle Eastern, with skin darker than Joe's, though nothing was very clear in this space. He laughed deeply without opening his mouth. It was ominous and echoed off the walls like nails on a chalkboard, sending a chill up her spine.

"That's enough." He ripped her from the wet concrete by the hair. "Savannah, I've enjoyed learning about you from a distance, but now we meet. You're right about Holden, by the way. He's been practically useless: one failed attempt after the next." He waved three of the men toward Holden, who howled, pleading for his life. "Bring him with us."

Savannah wobbled on her high heels, eye-level with the man now, his brown eyes dull as he stared at her. "Where are you taking me?"

"To the basement." His venomous tone made his accent stronger. He tugged on her hair hard enough to pull a chunk of her perfect mane from her scalp. A tear rolled down her cheek, but screaming wasn't an option. She squeezed the nail harder.

A gun dug into the bare skin over her spine, pushing each vertebra apart, so following wasn't up for debate. Unlike Holden, these men intended to use their weapons. They were strapped with rifles, pistols, and all sorts of other items that had never shown up in her Williams Sonoma catalog. If Holden was right, these men, all white and black besides the one holding her, wanted Joe dead and had taken extravagant steps over the last week to make that happen. It wasn't coincidence. It went back to the kidnapping, to her dad hiding drugs, to the massacre at the soup kitchen, to the alley with Allen, and ultimately back to Afghanistan. What happened there that she was missing? Mudad was dead. How many other enemies did Joe have that he hadn't mentioned?

Each footstep rang out in a mental number (*sixty-nine, seventy, seventy-one*) as Joe came to mind, reminding her to breathe as they'd done together in the Conex. Her chest burned. She'd been holding her breath. Her lips parted and chilled as her breath passed through the cracks in her chattering teeth. The stale air sifted up her nose and back down again, this time slower. Joe would come. He would always come. He was probably back from D.C. now, tracking her whereabouts. He would come, and she would put aside the pettiness of their fight and jump into his arms as he whisked her away to a remote location. Yes, that sounded lovely. Better than Holden shrieking as their feet echoed across the concrete.

A dozen more guys, all armed, met them at the stairwell to the basement, and the man holding her growled. "Everything has been set in motion, just as we expected. Ready the traps and be on alert. No mistakes." They moved on around, and he turned to her, leering. "Come along, Savannah. I've prepared a seat of honor so you don't miss a moment of Yosef's death."

Her eyes blinked rapidly to keep out the whirlpool of thoughts drowning her with fear. If she could assemble the few puzzle pieces she had of Joe's past, maybe she could get some answers that would keep them both alive when he showed up, guns blazing. She needed the confidence his presence gave her, because it was hard to be brave alone. But if he came, there was a chance he'd get hurt...or killed. His strength and skills gave off this superhuman, many-names-for-one-man kind of image, but he was still human. And until he arrived, she was in the hands of Leader's boss, a man she hadn't believe existed, armed with only a three-inch nail. That said it all.

The last stair brought them face to face with a steel door. Light seeped through the crack at the bottom, making her heels sparkle. They were the only thing that sparkled here. Her teeth grated against each other, and she rocked back and forth. After crossing the threshold, there was no way to stop whatever they had in store. The man turned the knob and pushed her into a vast, dimly lit two-story room. The top floor was a metal grated walkway leading to rooms on each side, similar to a prison. The bottom held more rooms under each of the second-floor ones, secured with thick steel doors. At the very middle of the back of the room, maybe one hundred and ten yards away, was a second-floor door with a balcony made of the same metal grating. Based on the goosebumps, it was about fifty degrees in here, and the floor was coated in a good inch of water until it sloped up about half-way in and became dry. The water ran over her feet, soaking the hem of her gown so it plastered against her ankles. Incandescent bulbs hung from the ceiling by thin wires, swaying and blinking. One of the doors of the first-floor rooms stood open, two men monitoring something on computer screens, but the others remained closed.

And there was a chair, an iron chair with the silver coating rotting off. It sat directly in the middle of the room, bolted into the floor, giving the image that it grew from the lifeforce of the building, like a tumor.

Holden was still screaming, but it hadn't been recognized by her ears in some time because of the incessantness of it. What her ears did register was the moment when it stopped. He'd been pistol whipped and shoved into one of those rooms with the slam of a door. Now it was eerily quiet, except for the buzzing of lights and computers. Holden was no friend, but without him, she was alone with her nail until Joe came. And why wasn't he here yet? His flight should've landed a while ago. Maybe she could buy some time. She had to. Her body was rocking even harder, and thoughts were startlingly loud in her mind.

He's going to torture me, or...rape me. Or one of his men will. I can't live through it. I...can't. How do I fight back against an army? How do I gain leverage? I'm not Joe. All I can do is talk. Talk!

The words weren't coming.

Say something!

"Joe is going to be here any minute...and he's going to kill you."

He turned to her, face inches from hers, and ran his rough hand across the neckline of her dress. "Your confidence in him is charming but naïve. Joe, as you call him, will not be arriving for at least another hour and a half due to an accident in Washington. Oh, I know," he sneered, speaking with his lips against her ear, "I was hoping to kill him when it was actually a challenge, but with his injuries, it is sure to be less rewarding. I'm glad the wreck didn't kill him. I can still honor my brother. That cockroach has a way of escaping death. Either way, it gives us some time to get acquainted."

The realization slammed against her chest like a bus. "You're Mudad, aren't you? He told me you were dead."

"It was easier for him to believe after burning my livelihood and killing my only family. You believe Yosef to be an honorable man. He is not."

Her stomach lurched with the eggs she'd had for breakfast, but her hand was too slow to stop it. Vomit poured out of her mouth and all over his gray button-down as her head jerked to the side.

Mudad slapped her hard, her face throbbing. "Stupid girl! You're lucky to be a vital part of my plan." He dragged her through the chunks of vomit, heels sliding, toward one of those first-floor rooms as his men watched.

What happened in those rooms? Her stomach wasn't empty yet, but the fear had her head uncontrollably heavy to the point she could barely function. She fought back, wiggling and jerking, but his grip was tight. Her wrist throbbed. The nail drew blood on her palm. Joe was hurt and wouldn't be here for a while. Why hadn't she pushed her pride away earlier and told him she forgave him? All she could do now was hope the worst didn't happen while the devil had her in his clutches.

The room was about eight feet by eight feet. There were white walls, no window, and a light that burned too bright for the space when Mudad pulled the steel door closed and trapped them together. Her arms were tight at her sides. There was no bed, which suddenly brought a little feeling back to her extremities, until her eyes fixed on the desk full of explosives.

No, no, no!

Her body took over for her screaming mind, and she turned on a heel, wrapping her hand around the door handle as Mudad, the evil monster, flipped her around and thrust his hand under her chin. The vomit filled the space with a sharpness as he glared.

"Dear girl, don't outlive your usefulness. Your friend Clark is dangerously close. But killing American soldiers is something I like to take my time with. It's only rewarding when they cry for their mothers."

Her hand came up fast, nail jutting out between her fingers. She thrust it right into Mudad's eye, blood spewing onto her dress. He howled, something guttural and inhuman, knocking her into the steel door like a rag doll, taking away her consciousness before she could throw up.

CHAPTER THIRTY
Joe

Time was of the essence, though saying it out loud to an FBI SWAT team nine times hadn't been well received. But making friends wasn't a concern. They were waiting on confirmation from the heat sensor scopes that Holden's family warehouse was where Mudad was holding Savannah and, probably, Clark.

He tapped his finger over the Glock holstered at his hip. They were moving slow. He'd done the same job in Afghanistan with Taliban shooting at him from rooftops, and he'd done it faster. It was 4:42, which, if things went south around the time of Clark's message, meant Holden had most likely delivered Savannah to Mudad two and a half hours ago like the weak, little coward he was. What was she enduring at Mudad's hands?

He sighed loudly, which garnered a few annoyed looks. They weren't the only ones annoyed. He'd told their commander every minute detail over the phone as he sped to L.A. on an F-18 out of Andrews Air Force Base, per the President's request, reminding them to scout the area and report their findings without engaging. He was leading the team in, and that was for a couple reasons.

One: Mudad killed his team, and he needed revenge, needed the satisfaction that would come with ripping each of Mudad's teeth out with a pair of rusty pliers. He didn't express his desires out loud, because most people wouldn't understand, but it was true. Warriors thrived on a righteous hunt, a righteous kill. There was no manufactured drug that could bring the same sensation. The trouble was staying on the right side of things and not being drawn too deep into the darkness. The line was incredibly thin.

Two: He wasn't risking Savannah's life on some guy making a pivotal mistake. He needed control, and as big of a screw-up as he felt sometimes, he was also intelligent enough to accept that there were very few people as qualified to cause chaos as he. And now that he had an arsenal of weapons on his person, after his unarmed stint in D.C., he was ready for battle. No one had a better sense of Mudad's inner workings, was more prepared for any traps he'd lay out for them, and frankly, no one else had seen his face.

So, here they waited, in the blistering sun outside Holden's warehouse, like obvious idiots. Sean, the commander of the FBI SWAT team, stood beside him, waving over the men using the heat sensor scopes, with a burly arm and a stern look. He was about six foot seven, with a buzz cut and skin so dark it was hard to tell where his shirt ended and he began. He was geared up and ready for action, just like his men, just like Joe had been, but something had his teeth on edge.

Maybe it was the certainty these guys marched back with, the urgency in their voices to take out some bad guys. They'd registered six bodies moving through the one-story building. They'd traced Savannah's phone there, and it was the last-known location of Savannah and Clark. But how stupid would Holden have to be to bring her there? Better not to answer that question, as he was already planning to rip Holden limb from limb, but something was clearly not right.

Sean's eyes cut back as Joe wandered from the group, testing the limits he could stretch his arm. It was functioning at around sixty percent mobility. Nothing he couldn't handle, but his head really ached. Joe hung a thumb through the left side of his bulletproof vest and cupped the other hand over his eyes, taking note of each building around them.

Most were empty for the weekend, parking lots and garages barren, with the lights off. A couple blocks down the road, things turned from well-kept warehouses to abandoned ones, and it dead-ended after five of them, with a chain-link fence and railroad track running perpendicular to the street. It was already a quiet part of town, weekend or not, made even more so by the President and FBI's desire to keep this quiet. There hadn't been a news van in sight so far, which was a plus.

His eyes narrowed when he moved his hand away. They were in that in-between time of day when the sun was still up but the moon was out too. His foot tapped on the sidewalk beneath him. He was missing something, and that was unsettling.

"Joe." Sean waved him over, his strangely narrow eyebrows scrunched together and down. "Time to go in. My men are ready. Only six guys in there, so we can end this before happy hour."

Joe looked over the sun-drenched group of forty. They'd called everyone in for this and had LAPD's SWAT team on standby. Their mouths all set in straight lines, chests puffed out, locked and loaded. "No."

"Excuse me?" Sean was growing by the second, as if anger fueled his size, which was impressive, considering the number of men standing with him.

"You see it as any other mission, but for me it's personal. I want Mudad dead as much as he wants me dead, which is why I know this isn't his grand finale. Six guys? No. They are the diversion. He knew I wouldn't come alone and most likely assumed he'd take out some of your guys on the front end, so he'd have more time to toy with my life when we figure out where he is. That's what I'd do. I'm not risking the lives of your men on a game that ends unfruitfully. Tactically, it doesn't make sense. Let's figure out where he's operating and take him out there. Then you can blow this warehouse to Hell for all I care."

Sean was hard to read, rubbing his chin and audibly growling. "I know you got skills, man, but I also know you got a lot to lose if this goes south. How solid is your reasoning, before I send my men on a wild goose chase? I got the President watching. It may not be emotional for me, but we all got someone to answer to, and I can't drop the soap here."

Now he was rubbing his cheeks, dialed into Joe's unwavering stare. "I am ninety percent sure he is not in the Forsyth Fashions warehouse. If he's not, he'll be close, monitoring our moves, hoping I'll pick up on something and wander off on my own. I would guess he's holed up in one of those abandoned warehouses down the road. Close proximity, and he can booby trap it to high heaven without worrying about a nine-to-five crowd stumbling over something and getting splattered all over the walls."

Sean cracked his neck and sighed. "Fine. Okay. I'll go with you on this. Counts and Brown, your teams are staying put. Keep your eyes peeled for anything suspicious, and don't let anyone out of that building. All other teams are with us." He turned back to Joe. "You've got thirty-two men willing to go out on a limb for you. Don't screw me here, Joe."

He nodded, and the men assembled as his phone vibrated with a text message from a blocked number. "Get over here, Sean!" Joe growled, jerking Sean by the sleeve. He opened the text as they stood together, Sean blocking the sun behind him.

At six o'clock I will set off a series of explosions across Los Angeles. Don't bother the police with trying to find them. It would be useless. The only way to stop the explosions is to find Savannah and kill her first. If you kill the woman you love, I will cease my attack on the city and focus solely on ending your life.

Mudad

Sean was already on the phone, calling in backup from the LAPD. They needed more men if they were to tear through five abandoned warehouses to locate Mudad and end this. That's what Sean was doing, because he wasn't emotionally involved. Mudad wasn't a genius, just an evil man with a grudge, so there had to be a way to beat him, a way to save Savannah *and* the people of Los Angeles. His heart tightened, and fire raced through his chest. But what if there wasn't another way?

His face morphed into something ugly and hard. The right thing was always to sacrifice the one for the many, and if it was his life, he'd be jumping in front of a bus right now without a second thought. But it was Savannah's life and killing her would literally kill him. There was no doubt she'd make the same choice, but he couldn't take her life. He couldn't take her life. He couldn't. But he couldn't let hundreds of other people die either.

"Let's move." Joe took off, ignoring the churning in his stomach and giving everyone else the option to tag along as he headed down the street, taking note of every blade of grass, every broken window. His training beat his head with a hammer, causing a shooting pain through his temples as it chided, *Sometimes you have to sacrifice everything.*

Sean grabbed his shoulder, digging his fingers in to stop him. "We're gonna do everything in our power to save your girl. There's always a way. Don't lose sight of that."

He didn't react or respond; he just kept moving, with the FBI SWAT team all following in tactical formation. His head was on a swivel, looking in windows, between buildings, and on rooftops. They wanted to keep things quiet, but Mudad liked fanfare, so there was no telling what they were walking into. His grip was tight around the M4 as they proceeded, ready to shoot any scum sucker in the head with his red-dot scope and thirty-round magazine. His trusty Glock stayed at his hip. His heart pounded loudly but slowly, allowing that inner voice to squeeze in between beats.

Joe motioned to the others as they reached the first warehouse. They moved into position, and he turned to Sean, movement on the third warehouse rooftop catching the light. His eyes shot up, and so did Sean's. He leapt sideways, shielding the bodies of two men as Sean yelled, "Grenades!"

Mudad's soldier hadn't been brave enough to hang on to both grenades for a couple seconds before throwing them to be sure he blew everyone up, so the three seconds gave them a window. One grenade landed by Sean, and he acted quick and tossed it inside the abandoned warehouse to their right. Everyone plunged left as it erupted. The last hit the concrete and burst a second after, sending the five men furthest back flying up with crumbles of sidewalk and street.

Joe rose to his hands and knees, ears ringing, and looked around, spitting out dirt. That probably wasn't great for his concussion or the rest of his myriad of injuries. LAPD's SWAT team was pulling on the scene, which was fortuitous because the grenades must've been the signal to act. The two teams back at Holden's warehouse were moving in. He couldn't hear them, but one thing was for sure: No one was making it to happy hour.

The five injured men were being pulled away to the FBI's medics that had been waiting on the scene. Sean wobbled over, wiping his face. "Ready for round two?" he asked, cupping his mouth and yelling.

Joe slapped him on the arm. "My hearing is already coming back. Take it easy."

Sean smiled. "Let's get going."

If everyone wasn't focused and angry before, they were now. "Keep your eyes peeled for booby traps. He's old school. They won't be sophisticated, but they'll be deadly."

The men nodded, and they moved in on the third warehouse, Sean taking a team in the side entrance while Joe led the other half of the team in through the front door. And why not? There was no reason to sneak around. Mudad knew they were coming.

They stayed in contact through their earpieces. Both teams made it safely inside the pitch-black warehouse, lowering thermal night-vision goggles over their eyes before hard rock music blasted through a speaker system, rendering the earpieces useless. The walls and floor shook with the bass, and his head rattled. The only benefit was that it quieted the ruthless voice saying he might have to kill Savannah. Voice or not, his heart hadn't let him forget, as invisible daggers plunged into his chest every time her smile or laugh entered his thoughts.

The floor was littered with beams and empty paint cans as they turned left into a graffiti-covered hallway. He kept his breathing steady and watched for anything out of the ordinary. His feet skidded to a stop, signaling the men to halt behind him. A trip wire hung taut across the hall about an inch ahead. That was too close.

Peters, the man behind him and to the right, stepped off to the side so he didn't run into his back, and his foot came down over a beam on the floor with a snap. Suddenly, two bullets whizzed through Peters' foot and into the air from the beam, likely rigged with nails to set them off. Peters and another guy were down, but LAPD's SWAT team was bringing up the rear and pulled them out of the warehouse.

Joe wiped his forehead. There was no telling how many other traps were engineered in this place, and they didn't have any idea how many square feet the warehouse was or the general floorplan. The idea of running in here with no intel was sloppy. If it were different circumstances, he would plan until he was blue in the face, but it was 5:15—only forty-five minutes until Mudad blew up half of Los Angeles and killed Savannah.

That pain hit his heart again, harder with every strike, but they pressed forward. The green-hued hallway turned right. He got low and aimed around the corner, thermal imaging picking up the orange form of an enemy in a doorway thirty yards away. He shot twice, and the man dropped. He waited a beat, seeing if anyone else would emerge, but they didn't. So, he rounded the corner, with at least four of the team on his heels.

But they'd been waiting too and fired through the doorway, raining down lead. A bullet whizzed past his face, lodging in the wall behind him. At least five assailants bled out on the ground, bodies vibrating on the concrete from the music, giving the appearance of zombies about to come back to life. Bullets whizzed through the air in both directions, but because of the size of his team jammed in the hall, they were pinned there firing back and forth over the thirty-second battle.

He had three guys down. He turned his head and breathed in through the nose, out through the mouth. Mudad had someone popping up every few yards, like those Jack-in-the-box toys. He hated those. Of course, he also hated crowds, modern architecture with big windows, terrorists like Mudad, and making decisions that would rip the heart from your chest.

The men behind him were screaming and cursing. It wasn't audible, but their mouths made for pretty easy lip-reading. Now it was five twenty, and there was no telling how many more obstacles there were before they reached Savannah. If there was a way to save her *and* Los Angeles and he got there too late to figure it out, he'd die a failure at Mudad's hands. But the thought of stopping the explosions, saving Savannah, and killing Mudad was a dream he still entertained, no matter how futile.

The assailants were finally dead, so they plunged farther down the hall. He stepped over a body and was jerked back by the vest as another trip wire came into view. Who knew how the guy behind him had caught it, but man was he grateful. "Thanks!" he screamed, but it was drowned out in the noise.

They stepped over, and the others followed suit, looking high and low for any other surprises when the hall ended in a doorway. Mudad wasn't trying to pull anything over on them. This trap was out in the open, so they knew after they passed through there was no turning back. An electric panel was rigged to the doorway, connected to a large iron door that would likely slide shut behind them after their entry. He brought a couple of the other men close and retrieved a notepad from a pocket in his bulletproof vest.

After we go in, there's no coming out unless we win. If we don't try, we're dead anyway, or at least someone you care about is. There is no telling how many explosives are set around the city. Are you in or not?

The notepad was passed back to the last guy in their group of twenty-five, now that they'd gotten reinforcements from LAPD SWAT. The last guy looked it over and tossed it on the floor, flipping the bird to one of the few cameras mounted on the walls. All right. This was happening. But just in case Mudad planned to trap him in there to continue alone, he waved everyone else through the door first.

239

Twenty seconds later, he stepped through behind the last guy with a badge that read Holmes. One second after he crossed inside, the door slid shut with a slam, the music ceased, and the lights shone brightly. It was abrupt and uncomfortable, his ears ringing, but he locked in a new magazine and aimed between the open door and the closed door across the twenty-by-twenty room as everyone lifted their goggles, squinted, and spread to create a defensive perimeter.

He attempted to communicate over the earpiece, but they'd been disabled somehow and were only registering static. He tossed his on the floor when Sean stumbled through the room with two other men. Joe ran over, every footstep slapping against the concrete. They were all trapped until Mudad opened the third door. All that anger he'd sensed from the lip reading in the hall was coming out strong and loud as the door behind Sean slammed closed too.

"Don't ask me about everyone else. And don't ask me what he did to us. Let's kill that bastard and never think of this day again."

Joe slapped him on the back and assembled the team for what was sure to be the big finish. Savannah was close. His foot tapped as they waited in front of the door, but his upper half never strayed a fraction of an inch from the half-pulled trigger. He had to be ready, to take advantage of every moment he had left, which wasn't many. And if he already hadn't figured that out, Mudad had hung a giant clock on the wall to torment him, with each second clicking loudly by on a giant black hand.

At 5:45 the door creaked and swung open to what was once a staircase to the basement but was now a jagged first step followed by a dead drop. Sean had rope tied onto the back of his vest, which was a stroke of luck, so they knotted a swiss seat around him and began lowering everyone down to the basement door. He waited until everyone was together, which only took a minute, but it was a minute he would need, and his breathing wasn't as steady as he'd like. The training he'd had didn't matter anymore. He was just a man hoping to save the woman he loved…from himself.

A light shone under the door as Sean's team scanned the area, and he grabbed the knob. Sean leaned in. "I know you don't know me, but we trusted your lead before, and I need you to trust me now. These are the best men I've worked with. They will help you find a solution if you'll let them." And, with that, he pushed open the door, and they collectively lost their breath.

The room was half the length of a football field, two stories, with locked rooms lining the walls and two doors at the back. One was presumably an exit, and the other, a floor above, opened to a balcony. There were no obvious or hidden traps their force could identify. And it was empty, except for Savannah.

She sat in an iron chair bolted to the floor, a green gown flowing around her like a goddess and pooling onto the floor. Some kind of heartrate monitor was wrapped around her chest, with a cell phone attached to it. She was bound to the chair by her wrists and ankles, but she was alert and surprisingly calm as he rushed to her. "Joe," she whispered, "I know the choice Mudad gave you, and if I have to die so that thousands of people don't... Well, I can live with that." She forced something like a smile.

"That's not funny, and I'm not giving up. There is still time to find a—"

"Yosef. Cutting it close. *Tsk-tsk*. It's five fifty, which means you only have ten minutes to make a decision."

Mudad was on the balcony at the back of the room, with crisp, white linen pants and a matching shirt. His hair was slicked back and his beard groomed. He was forcing the image of purity, like a king high above his subjects.

But there was a bandage over his left eye that seemed fresh, and he was visibly cringing. You could even hear the pain in his voice. Something had gone wrong in his plan. One thing was still true though: He was angrier than ever, and his shirt didn't lie flat. Maybe covering a bulletproof vest? Or something more sinister.

The sight of him had Joe's mind bouncing across the globe, the grainy taste of sand between his teeth, but he held strong as the SWAT team spread out. "So, this is the grand finale planned for my demise? No traps, no bullets, no RPGs? Just you versus my whole team? What's to stop us from capturing you and breaking each of your bones to get the locations of the bombs and then shooting you in the head as we stroll out the back door with Savannah?"

Mudad's lip curled up. "Yosef, you speak as if I'm some sort of monster. I assure you, I'm not. You kill for your government, no questions asked, and pick up a paycheck when you're done. You, American soldiers, invaded my homeland and tore my life apart. The world doesn't belong to you, yet you continue to beat us down. I'm a survivor. A servant sent to right the stain of your existence on humanity. You should have been fighting *my* fight. You're not one of them. So, I gave you a choice, which is more than you gave my brother." He motioned to Savannah, and Joe's eyes followed, hungry for blood. "You no doubt noticed the monitor and phone on Savannah's chest. Let us call it a reverse dead-man's switch. She is remotely connected to the eight bombs I've planted in the city of Los Angeles. The bombs are on a timer now, showing only four minutes and twenty seconds until detonation. Kill her, and the timers will shut off, permanently disabling each bomb when her heart stops."

He disappeared through the door and appeared in the room with them fifteen seconds later, the door slamming closed behind him like those in the other room. Every SWAT guy had Mudad's head in their sights, fingers on the triggers as he approached, unbuttoning his shirt slowly for dramatic effect and to drive the minutes away until Joe had to make an instant decision. He wore a suicide vest, and they were all locked in.

Sweat built on Joe's forehead and creeped icy cold down his temples. It was enough to think about losing Savannah, to think about losing half of L.A., but now, to consider losing another team he was in charge of?

His hand squeezed Savannah's shoulder protectively, and she shuddered under his grasp, turning her head to watch the exchange. Tears dripped onto his hand. *My God, she's brave.*

"Please kill me, Joe," she whispered for only him to hear.

Mudad could see Joe's wheels spinning. He smiled. "And as for torturing me to get the location of the bombs, not necessary. Here is the first one, but I will not give up the others. So, you see, I am prepared to die for my cause and take you with me. Should these men have to die because you are too selfish to kill Savannah? You didn't spend any time considering whether or not to massacre my brother and leave him in that hole to rot. You have three minutes and fourteen seconds. Kill Savannah now, or kill all of us and a significant portion of L.A. You are—"

Bang!

A gun went off, and Mudad crumbled to the floor with a shot to the head. Blood spewed out of his right temple, and Joe spun around to find Sean with a smoking gun.

"I know you wanted to kill him, but he would never have given us the locations of the bombs and held no leverage for us to keep him alive. Now, let's try to disable this thing on Savannah. Time's running out."

Joe's instantaneous reaction had been fury, but Sean was right, and there was no time to argue. He used his knife to cut Savannah's restraints, and she collapsed onto the floor in his arms as the men discussed options and wove between them to try and make heads or tails of the device across her chest.

Her eyes overflowed, but her voice remained even. "There isn't another good option, Joe. Please. Hold me like this for another minute...and then do it quick."

He squeezed her tightly, and she turned her head to face him, brushing his cheek with her hand. And tears were wet on his cheeks, too. It was an unfamiliar sensation, but in this moment, it didn't feel weak.

Sean patted his back and approached quietly. "Savannah, I apologize, but there is no way to be gentle. We have two and a half minutes." Everyone crowded in and listened. "If we try and disable the monitor via the phone, there's a chance he'll have some sort of failsafe that will immediately cause the bombs to detonate. There is also a chance that if we try to cut a wire or dismantle the monitor, the bombs will detonate. Of course, this is all assuming that there are actually bombs out there. Also, what if we kill Savanah and it doesn't disarm the bombs? Maybe she was never remotely connected, and it was all a ruse to destroy Joe. The only way to be sure is to try our luck or kill Savannah. I'm sorry."

He scratched his chin, and everyone poised like birds on a wire, ready to take flight, because the decision was going to be fast, and there would be no going back. They would all either die or have someone to answer to on the outside for their decisions here. The room was cold, though it wasn't why he had goosebumps, why his chest burned with pain as he held Savannah in his arms for the last time.

The men were discussing, voting, all more level-headed than he could be at the moment. His mind swam, and his body was rooted to the spot, his back ramrod straight. Sean approached again. "We're going to try to disable the monitor. There are two wires, white and black. We will make a guess and hope for the best."

He reached out and grabbed Savannah's hand. But she pulled him in, grabbing the 9mm holstered at his thigh and holding it to her chest. "I can't let you risk anyone's life for mine. Please don't make me live with that decision." But as soon as she'd said it, she dropped the gun to the floor and gasped. "Earlier today there were men in that room on computers. What if there is an answer?" The phone on her chest continued the countdown as twenty men rushed the door. They were down to fifty-nine seconds.

"Joe. There may be an answer, and there may not. But I won't be able to live knowing my life was more important than so many others. The guilt will eat me alive. And I know this is an unfathomable request, but please don't let a stranger kill me. It has to be you, and you have to go on living."

He started to interrupt, but she placed a shaky finger over his lips as the door opened behind them. Her eyes were wet with tears, glistening blue and gentle. His were full too.

"I promised you I would never leave you, and I'm sorry that I might break that promise. But you always keep yours, so promise me you'll be happy one day. That you'll think of me and picture the life we could've had, with a smile and not tears. Promise me."

The air was gone from the room, the chair, Mudad's body. The timer was at twenty seconds, nineteen, eighteen...

"I love you, Savannah. And I will never stop dreaming of you when I smell roses and seeing your face when someone laughs with joy. Those are the moments I'll be happy."

"I love you too."

Seven seconds. It was only them as Joe held a gun to her chest with his right hand, a knife to the wires with his left, and choked out a sob. "I love you. I love you. I love you." He tightened his finger over the trigger.

Five seconds.

"JOE! CUT THE BLACK WIRE!"

CHAPTER THIRTY-ONE
Savannah

The sleeping bag was soft under her back despite the pebbles from the riverbank poking through. It was worth it, to be wrapped in Joe's arms. There was no more danger. No more. Clark might've been most excited about that since her parents sent him to the Maldives to heal. He'd already found a few women to act as "nurses." But this was what she needed, night two of their escape from reality.

The FBI hadn't even done a full debrief, just sent them on their way. Said they'd been through enough. That was an understatement, considering she still wasn't able to think of any of it without shaking uncontrollably. And on top of the FBI's generosity, her mother and father had done something very surprising; they met them at Savannah's apartment before their trip, with a new convertible for the drive and an intricately carved urn containing Allen's ashes.

"So you can spread them somewhere truly meaningful," her mother had said, then added, "Cole would be so proud of you, darling. One day, I know he'll tell you in person." Savannah had balled her eyes out, while Joe wrapped the urn in his arms so she could wrap her parents in hers. Then they'd left.

They weren't perfect parents, but she'd misjudged them or at least underestimated their love. She'd also misjudged Holden, who would be in prison for the foreseeable future. He deserved it, but do-gooder that she was, she still made it a point to approach him to say she forgave him before the feds hauled him away. It felt good, and minus the pictures that occasionally invaded her brain, she and Joe's drive out of L.A. was just as she'd imagined: her head on his arm, their breaths moving in unison.

Savannah sighed happily and buried her face in Joe's muscular chest, tracing a flag tattoo on his arm with her free hand. The stars glittered above them in a way they'd never done in Los Angeles, and the gurgling water flowing between the river rocks had nearly lulled her to sleep. Nearly. It was the stars that kept her eyes open, the way they twinkled and put on a show for the two of them.

"Savannah?"

"Yes?" Her voice was a whisper. She was so calm the words couldn't rise any louder.

"We've got a problem. We're—"

Her head shot off his chest, eyes wide.

He laughed and pulled her back down with a kiss to the head. "Bad wording. Sorry. I was just going to say we're out of marshmallows."

Savannah rolled to her back, laughing with Joe. *That* kind of problem, she could handle. But if anything serious came their way, she'd have her three-thousand-dollar, specially-designed Manolo Blahnik hiking boots from her mother to keep her going.

ABOUT RACHEL HOMARD

 Rachel's vivid imagination and creativity made her six years of teaching elementary school even more fun. But when she and her husband had their awesome son, she decided to stay home and save her hugs for him. Between playing trains and being chased by a three-year-old T-Rex and his furry, four-legged sidekick, Rachel picked up a pen and began writing stories like she did when she was younger. Even at four, when she couldn't write by herself, she recruited her mom to transcribe them for her.

Rachel pairs relatable characters to storylines of romance and suspense, and she loves adding in military characters. She has a great appreciation for all the brave men and women fighting for our country and wants to acknowledge them, like her father, a retired US Army Green Beret. *The Green Triangle* is Rachel's debut novel. The sequel will release Summer 2021.

Made in the USA
Monee, IL
26 July 2021

74297226R00152